Night Mage

Becky R. Jones

Copyright © 2021 Becky R. Jones

All rights reserved.

DEDICATION

To all my friends and family who encouraged me to keep writing and all the Dinerzens who provided all kinds of support. Most of all to Mike for everything.

CONTENTS

Acknowledgments i

Prologue 1

Chapter One 11

Chapter Two 18

Chapter Three 34

Chapter Four 53

Chapter Five 65

Chapter Six 81

Chapter Seven 97

Chapter Eight 110

Chapter Nine 122

Chapter Ten 133

Chapter Eleven 146

Chapter Twelve 161

Chapter Thirteen 175

Chapter Fourteen 187

Chapter Fifteen 198

Chapter Sixteen 211

Chapter Seventeen 222

Chapter Eighteen 236

Chapter Nineteen 245

Chapter Twenty 254

ACKNOWLEDGMENTS

Many thanks to all my beta readers for their thoughtful comments and typo-finding. Any remaining errors are all mine.

Prologue

THE COOL OF THE LATE WINTER NIGHT settled around him and the sound of crickets became more noticeable as the noises of the city slowly quieted. Declan shifted in his hiding place. He only had to wait another hour or so and then he would be alone in the historic prison. Briefly, he wondered where Simon was. His mentor had made it clear that while tonight was Declan's responsibility, he, Simon, would be watching to judge Declan's value as a pupil. Declan wasn't sure how Simon would be watching, but Simon was an exacting taskmaster and Declan was determined to prove himself worthy.

Using his mother's gift of Sight, Declan scanned the area near where he crouched, concealed behind a crumbling wall. He had walked into the prison trailing the last tour group. His ability to go invisible had its uses. Once he'd found a good hiding place, he'd dropped the invisibility. It took energy to maintain and he didn't want to use up his energy when he knew he had a possibly long night ahead of him.

As he waited, unsure of what he was facing, Declan thought back over the last semester. His sophomore year at Summerfield College had been interesting…if you defined "interesting" as "insanely crazy." He had changed majors to political science and gotten away from his original advisor (who'd turned out to be an actual witch. That explained a few things). His new advisor was Simon, Dr. LeGrande, who knew about Declan's strange combination of djinn power and the gift of Sight and was not at all bothered by it. In fact, Dr. LeGrande was a Fire mage and was extremely interested in learning more about Declan's powers – which were quite different than a mage's powers – and helping Declan do so as well. And his history prof, Dr. O'Brien, had turned out to be an Elemental mage. She was pretty cool too.

Staring out into the darkening prison corridor, Declan smiled shyly to himself. He didn't want to jinx anything, but he felt safe in thinking that he'd even managed to make some friends as well. The students he met during all that, Annmarie, Josh, and Geoff, had become the group he hung out with all the time now. They were mages too and weren't bothered by his powers. Other student mages who'd helped with the fight against the demon also said hi and sat next to him in classes now. It was an amazing feeling. For the first time since he'd arrived at Summerfield, he felt like he belonged.

And that demon fight! At the end of the fall semester he had helped Dr. O'Brien and the others defeat a demon in the middle of Philadelphia. That had been crazy! Not that he really wanted to go through that again, but just thinking about that battle gave him a shot of adrenaline.

A flicker at the edge of his vision brought him back to the present. Declan slowly turned his head. A pale, filmy wisp of something drifted out of one of the cell doors. It hesitated briefly and then floated down the corridor toward the center of the prison. Declan shivered and clasped his hands together to stop their shaking. The tour guide had said that some people believed Eastern State Penitentiary was haunted. *Well, they're right. I wonder how many ghosts there are in here?*

A small, almost unnoticeable, noise forced him to stop worrying about ghosts and concentrate on the real reason he was here. Simon had said this was a good way to get used to using his djinn powers and the Sight in combination. Ever since Simon, Dr. Wardmaster, and Dr. O'Brien had figured out last fall semester that he was at least part djinn, Declan had worked to understand and control his power. The fight with the demon on the winter solstice at Swann Fountain had frightened him, not because of the demon really, but because he had discovered that he had a great deal of power. The thought of what he could do, if he really got angry, scared him.

Simon had loaned him some books on djinn and their powers. Djinn had almost limitless powers and while he was only half-djinn, he still had far greater power than anybody he knew. He could make *things* happen to people simply by deciding to make them happen. That idea was beyond frightening. He knew that when he was stressed and angry, he tended to just lash out. What if he got really angry with one of his friends?

Working with Simon, and talking to Dr. O'Brien, had helped him learn to control his power and recognize his triggers. Declan shook his head remembering the day he had gone invisible in Dr. O'Brien's office when he'd heard a voice he truly dreaded, his now former advisor, Dr. Meredith Cruickshank. His reaction had shocked Dr. O'Brien, but she had covered for him and that had won her his complete trust.

The small noise repeated itself, once again pulling Declan out of his daydreaming. He carefully turned his head trying to locate the source or at least a direction. There. Down the corridor to the left. Away from the center of the prison. *Oh, good. I didn't really want to have to go into the middle of this place.*

As he peered toward the source of the sound, he could just make out something huge and very dark moving in the gloom of the abandoned prison corridor. It almost looked like smoke was drifting off it. *Are those wings?? Crap.* He noticed a couple more ghosts drifting down the corridor. When they encountered the darker shadow they floated over to the other side, avoiding it. This had to be why Simon put him here tonight.

Whatever that thing was, it had to be eliminated. It oozed evil. He wasn't sure why he was so certain it was evil, but his bones ached with the menace carried by that shadow. The fact that the ghosts didn't like it made Declan even more nervous. Simon said it was causing a lot of problems for the staff at the historic prison. They assumed it was the crumbling walls and structure, but Simon had thought it was more than that. Problem was Simon had not told Declan what he thought this thing was.

"Oh, no, my dear boy. I'm not giving that away! We need to test and stretch your powers as much as possible. Don't worry, I'll be watching and if it seems necessary, I will provide back up for you." The small, round man had made that pronouncement while bouncing on the balls of his feet as was his habit. The slight giggle at the end of his statement had not made Declan feel any more confident.

Declan squinted and saw the very large, very black, smoky-looking shadow flowing along the wall. *Yep. Wings. Shit. It can fly.* He had about an hour to deal with this before the people setting up a new interactive exhibit showed up. Simon had told him that this one was about the history of ghosts in the prison. He wondered what they would do if they knew the prison really was haunted. Declan reached for his power and made himself invisible. It took energy to maintain, but it was relatively easy to actually go invisible, especially now that he knew how to do it on purpose. He was unsure if the creature could see him anyway, but being invisible couldn't hurt. He moved out of his hiding place and silently followed the enormous shadow. He briefly considered just willing it to not exist, but he had a feeling that might backfire on him.

Declan stepped as quietly as he could and followed the huge, smoky shadow down the corridor. It wasn't a ghost...what was it? He didn't think it was a demon, but he didn't know what else it could be. Smokey with wings strongly suggested a demon. He racked his brain, going back over every conversation he'd had with Simon in the afternoon leading up to this. Since Simon had called tonight a "test" Declan assumed that that meant he should know what it was, and how to deal with it. He assumed that whatever this thing was, it could hurt him. *Okay. First thing...what the hell is it? Demon? Maybe...but that doesn't seem quite right. It doesn't look or feel like that demon at the fountain. Shit.*

He had to figure out what it was and then how to neutralize it. Even though he knew it wasn't human, he didn't like the idea of killing anything, so he worked his way around those thoughts. He was so caught up in his puzzle he barely stopped himself from walking right into the shadow. He shrank back against the wall, his heart pounding, and glanced around. The shadow had stopped at an intersection. To the right, a few hundred feet down the hall was the main door to the prison/museum and Declan could hear footsteps coming from that direction. That must be the security guard making one last pass before the art installation crew arrived.

As the guard entered the intersection where the shadow waited, Declan got a glance at the man's face. The guard's eyes went wide with horror as he walked into the shadow. Then the shadow reached out and touched him on the top of the head.

The guard toppled over, not moving.

Declan stifled a gasp. The man's eyes were still wide open in shock and horror and he wasn't breathing. *It just touched him! How can he be dead?! What the hell IS that thing?? And how do I kill it?*

The shadow moved down the corridor toward the main

entrance.

Shit! I can't let it get out into the city! Shitshitshit! He skirted around the body of the guard and ran as quietly as he could after the thing.

He must have kicked a rock or made some sort of noise because the shadow stopped suddenly and whirled around to face him. Or at least he guessed that was its face. Remembering the guard, Declan scrambled over to the wall, trying to get out of a direct line with the thing. The invisibility trick must be working because he could see the shadow's head swaying back and forth. Its giant wings beat slowly as it searched for Declan.

Declan frantically went over everything he and Simon had talked about that day. What the hell was that thing? He was pretty sure Simon had given him some hints. His mentor liked to present information in a puzzle format so that Declan would have to piece various bits of information together to figure out the answer. Simon said that simply memorizing information was not really learning. Right now though, Declan fervently wished he'd had a list of possible monsters and how to kill them memorized, then he could just pick one method and try it.

An almost off-hand comment made by Simon drifted through his mind. *"Well, my boy, that's about it. Oh, one last thing...I do believe that whatever is in the penitentiary is related to the creature that is your father."* Declan wished Simon wouldn't always describe Declan's father as "the creature that is your father." Yes, he was a djinn, but that djinn was still his father and it somehow felt wrong to call him a "creature."

But related to djinn? He furiously racked his brain again as the shadow slowly moved toward him, its head swaying back and forth seeming to sniff the air, seeking the source of the disturbance.

An ifrit! Was that it? He remembered that they were another type of djinn and they lived in ruins...the penitentiary certainly counted as a ruin even if they were trying to restore parts of it. Ifrits had almost limitless power too. Shit. Wait. They were djinns so, in theory at least, he could kill it with magic. Which was a good thing since he didn't have any physical weapons with him. *Maybe I should at least start carrying a pocket-knife. Or a flame thrower.*

He shifted his weight away from the wall and the ifrit's head immediately swung in his direction and it started towards him. Declan took a deep breath and waited until it could almost touch him. There was no sound in the prison. Even the crickets had stopped chirping. It reached for him with frightening speed and Declan threw himself to the floor to avoid that killing touch.

Sprawled on the floor half sitting against the wall, watching the ifrit come still closer, Declan dug deep into his magical energy and envisioned something like a lightning bolt. Scuttling to the side, he raised his arm and pointed at the ifrit's head. Because he couldn't do this silently, like the ifrit had done to the guard, he dropped his invisibility and released the magic and rage-filled lightning bolt from his fingertips.

"Die asshole! This is for that guard!" he shouted.

In a less than dramatic fashion the ifrit hissed, and as the magical lightning hit it, disappeared in a flame-tinged swirl of smoke and shadow.

After a heart-stopping moment, the sound of crickets returned with a startling suddenness.

Shit. Did I really just kill an ifrit? Declan drew a deep breath and willed his hands to stop shaking. He dragged himself upright, using the wall for support. Gingerly he extended his Sight and gazed at the spot where the ifrit had been. Nothing. Just a slight fuzz of magic where Declan had almost been its second victim. He slowly walked up and down the corridor using his Sight to look for any signs of the ifrit. He did see another ghost, but couldn't tell if it was the same one he'd seen before. He thought the ghost gave him a small salute before drifting off down the opposite corridor.

Declan did one more circuit around the corridor and then went back to the body of the security guard lying where the two corridors came together. He wanted to make sure the man wasn't left alone and that one of the installation crew would find him when they came in. He was shaking so badly he was afraid he would fall down.

He slid down the wall and sat on the floor next to the body and leaned back against the wall. *I'm really sorry, sir. I didn't know what it was, and I didn't know how to kill it before it got you.*

Declan took a deep breath and willed himself not to cry. Simon would certainly notice and give him a hard time about it.

Still silently apologizing to the guard, he saw a silvery substance rise from the body. The ghost of the guard materialized over the man's body. It looked around the corridor intersection and saw Declan. A questioning look appeared on its face.

"Ifrit, sort of a demon. I'm sorry. I killed it." Declan answered the unspoken question.

The ghost nodded.

Voices coming from the opposite corridor and lights being switched on overhead heralded the arrival of the art installation crew. The ghost glanced over its shoulder and then back at Declan.

He nodded. "I'll wait until they find you. Are you married? Kids?"

The ghost shook its head in the negative.

"Family?" The ghost nodded.

"I'll make sure somebody remembers to call them

tonight. I'm really sorry."

The ghost inclined its head in thanks and then, as if it knew where to go, drifted off in the direction of Declan's original hiding place closer to the center of the complex.

The voices drew nearer, and Declan drew on his remaining energy to become invisible. He pushed himself off the floor and stood up waiting for the crew members to come into the intersection of corridors. The corridor grew brighter as the new arrivals turned on the lights as they approached. The leaders in the group appeared in the intersection followed by about ten or twelve others.

"Oh, my God!" a woman in front half screamed.

"Fuck! What happened?" the man behind her leaned forward to get a better look at the body of the security guard. He stepped around her and moved over to the body. He bent down and put two fingers on the guard's neck. His face was somber when he stood up.

"There's no pulse. He's dead. Must have been a heart attack."

"Oh, hell. I'll call 9-1-1," said the woman, pulling out her phone.

"Thanks, Trudy. Can somebody else call Mack and let him know? I'm not sure how long the EMTs are gonna take. We might have to do the entire installation tomorrow." The man who had checked for a pulse sat down on the floor next to the guard's body just like Declan had done. "I'll stay here and wait for them. Trudy, go out front and wait for the ambulance. The rest of you do whatever you can do to get things started. We'll play it by ear."

"Tom, Mack says to do what we can and play it by ear," somebody called from the middle of the group.

Tom gave a tight grin. "On it."

Declan sidled to his right to put more room between himself and the man named Tom. He seemed like he would be the kind of person who would make sure all loose ends were tied up so Declan was confident that the guard's family would get notified. He also liked Tom for clearly staying so he could keep watch over the body. He gave a last glance down the corridor where the guard's ghost had drifted, but he didn't see anything.

Declan edged around the group of people bunched up in the intersection and headed for the exit. His arm brushed a woman's elbow as he wormed his way past and she looked around, startled. Declan kept moving in case she put a hand out to discover what had brushed against her. Reaching the exit, he willed himself back to visibility and stepped through the door onto the sidewalk. He saw the ambulance approaching and moved away from the entrance. He didn't want the EMTs asking him awkward questions.

Once outside the prison, he looked around for Simon. He jumped when he saw a good number of people walking up and down the street. *Duh. It's only about 7:30 at night. And it's Friday. Of course, there are people wandering around.* He'd become so wrapped up in dealing with the ifrit and the death of the security guard that he'd lost track of where he was. The rest of the world had kept on its usual path.

Thinking of the guard made him shudder. *I saw somebody die tonight. No, worse. I saw somebody killed tonight.* His hands started to shake, and he quickly laced his fingers together to hide the shaking. Where was Simon anyway? He stared up and down the sidewalk searching the passing faces for his mentor.

Chapter One

Dr. Zoe O'Brien glared hopelessly at the stack of essays sitting on her desk. There was no way around it, she was going to have to take them home with her tonight and finish grading them. She was already late getting them back to the students. *Dammit.*

She grabbed the offending papers and stuffed them into her bag. Many of her colleagues graded papers online, but that much reading on a computer screen gave Zoe a headache and she refused to admit she might need reading glasses. So, she did it the old-fashioned way and printed them out. Turning back to her desk, she shut down her computer, added her personal laptop to the essays in her bag, and grabbed her keys.

Zoe hesitated as she reached her door and sent out a tentative thread of Air to see if Meredith Cruickshank was in her office down the hall. She laughed at herself. Meredith was taking an "unscheduled" sabbatical this semester and she wasn't on campus on a regular basis. In the wake of the battle between the coven (of which Meredith had been a member), the demon, and mages, on the winter solstice in Logan Square, Meredith had been given the sabbatical leave for the spring semester, ostensibly to recover from a stress-induced breakdown. The coven had lost badly in the battle with the mages and their leader, the provost's former secretary, had managed to escape. The provost had suffered a serious mental breakdown and was now in a psychiatric facility. Worst of all, as far as Zoe was concerned, one of the coven members had been killed by the demon.

Zoe was perfectly happy to have a semester without Meredith around. Not only was Meredith just an all-round nasty, power-hungry sort of person, but she had involved students in the coven's activities against their will. One of Zoe's favorite students, Declan Jin, had been among the coven's intended victims. Those were unforgivable actions as far as Zoe was concerned.

Standing in her doorway, Zoe let the tendril of Air lapse and stepped into the hallway, closing and locking her door behind her. She always felt slightly guilty about snooping into Meredith's whereabouts, but she reminded herself this was self-preservation. Meredith wielded Zoe's lack of tenure like an offensive weapon, threatening Zoe's career every chance she got. Zoe had spent her first three years at Summerfield walking on eggshells around Meredith. The discovery that Zoe was a powerful Elemental mage had infuriated Meredith while giving Zoe a boost of self-confidence. Despite that, once back on campus and in the rhythms of the semester, Zoe had fallen right back into habits she'd had since before she discovered her mage powers last year. She suspected the harassment was Meredith's way of maintaining power, but Zoe wished those nasty whispers didn't make their way through faculty circles quite so easily.

Last semester, her means of avoidance had been to glance down the hall and then quickly tiptoe out her door and down the stairs. Most of the time this tactic had been successful, but there had been times when it seemed like Meredith had a preternatural ability to tell when Zoe was leaving her office. Hindsight is twenty-twenty they say, and Zoe knew now that

Meredith had probably had magical means of knowing when Zoe left her office so that she could intercept.

Zoe's discovery that she was an Elemental mage and had control over the four primary Elements – Air, Water, Fire, and Earth – had been mind-blowing to say the least. Magic existed and functioned. She'd had to wrap her head around that almost immediately and she was still trying to figure things out. Her best friend Mark Davis and his husband David Morgan had turned out to be Air and Earth mages and her department chair and mentor at Summerfield, Dr. George Wardmaster, was an Earth mage. Several other faculty members were also mages, including her now kinda-sorta boyfriend Kieran Ross who was a Water mage.

Since the battle with the demon on the winter solstice last year, Zoe had created time in her schedule to experiment and play with her powers. She was still in a bit of shock over the idea that not only did magic exist, and she had control of it, but that she had more power than any of the other mages she knew. If she thought about it too much, she freaked herself out very easily. This whole magic thing was wonderfully, amazingly cool, and simultaneously terribly frightening. It was what she imagined working in a high-wire act was like – exhilarating and deadly all at the same time.

Her cats had been working with her as well (another mind-boggling discovery…her cats could talk). As Watchers, along with the squirrels and crows, they had kept her up to date on all events magical and otherwise in her neighborhood. The events in the "otherwise" category usually involved issues of interest only to the cats. The fact that a family of possums had moved in under a neighbor's deck fell under that classification. She had strictly prohibited the cats, on pain of losing treats, from bothering the possums in any way.

Scolding herself for wasting time worrying about Meredith, Zoe walked quickly through the hallway and down the stairs.

Once home, she dropped the bag with the ungraded essays in a corner of her home office/guest bedroom and changed into cozy, comfortable sweatpants and a sweatshirt. She turned to go back downstairs, adroitly stepping around Moose and Flash as the cats attempted to wind themselves around her ankles. Although they could talk, and did a great deal of that, when it came to feeding time, they shamelessly employed the universal feline trick of wide-eyed looks, loud purring, and cute head-butts and ankle-rubbing.

She glared at the cats. "I'm working on it. If you guys keep this up, I am going to fall headfirst down the stairs, suffer a concussion, have to have Kieran take me to the ER and probably spend the night there. And then you won't get fed until *tomorrow* night."

"But we're hungry!" Moose had a trick of ending sentences with a small, pitiful meow that was seriously at odds with his big, grey, fluffy appearance.

"I am too, and if you actually let me get down the stairs, I can fix that. Sheesh!" Zoe grabbed the bannister, braced against the far wall and lifted herself over the cats and down two stairs. She rapidly descended the remaining stairs before the cats could trip her up again.

In the kitchen at the back of the first floor of her small house, she fed the cats and then searched the refrigerator for anything remotely edible that could pass as dinner. Not seeing anything, Zoe gave a sigh. She glanced over to where the cats were inhaling their food.

"I'll be back in a bit, guys. I'm going to run over to that new place and get a poké bowl for dinner."

Neither cat gave any indication they had heard her. Zoe sighed again, put on shoes, and walked to the front door grabbing her coat and keys on the way out.

Zoe walked along Fairmount Avenue planning out what

exactly she was going to include in her poke bowl. Salmon or tuna? Why not both? It was Friday night, Kieran was in town, but at a conference and he had a dinner thing tonight. She was going to indulge herself. *Oh, man. This is pathetic, Kieran's busy and I'm all excited about ordering a poké bowl.*

She shook herself out of her reverie and then shook her head again. There was an ambulance stopped in front of Eastern State Penitentiary. What happened there? And why was Declan Jin standing on the sidewalk in front of the penitentiary? He didn't live around here. She stopped in front of him, but he didn't seem to notice her. He was staring around at the people on the sidewalks as if he was looking for somebody.

"Hi, Declan," she greeted him. No response.

"Declan!" He jumped and jerked his head around to stare at her.

"Dr. O'Brien! What are you doing here?"

"I was just going to ask you that. I live a couple blocks away. What are you doing here?" She smiled as she asked the question. Declan was less jumpy than he had been last semester, but he was still prone to retreating into a shell.

"Um...I-I was w-working with S-Simon, um...Dr. LeGrande on something." Well, that answered one question. Simon had been working with Declan to help him figure out and get control over his powers. But the stuttering was a dead giveaway that he was extremely nervous.

Ever since she had discovered that the leader of the coven that raised the demon last year had tried to control Declan, a shy, awkward misfit at the time, Zoe had felt an obligation to keep a protective eye on him. What was going on here?

"Oh, okay. Are you okay?" He was still staring around at the people walking by.

"Umm...yeah. I-I'm f-fine. Just w-waiting for Dr. LeGrande to come back. H-he's my...um...r-ride back to…um…c-campus."

Zoe started to stare at the passersby as well. Declan's nerves were contagious. He was shaking so badly she half expected Simon to come running up the sidewalk pursued by some sort of monster.

Just as she was beginning to get seriously worried, she spotted Simon LeGrande bobbing along the sidewalk. He was a small, rather round little man who tended to bounce on the balls of his feet whether he was standing still or walking. He was bundled up against the chilly evening in a somewhat formal overcoat, scarf, and an Irish driving cap. *It's not that cold out…oh, well. Whatever keeps you comfortable, I guess.*

"Declan, my boy! Did you get it?" he called as he approached. "Oh! Dr. O'Brien! What a pleasant surprise to find you here! What brings you out on this chilly evening?" If he was surprised to see Zoe standing next to Declan, he didn't show it. He was chair of the political science department and she knew that Mark trusted him, so she did too, but she always felt that there was something just off about Simon. *It's probably just the old-world, archaic vibe he gives off. And that icky half-handshake thing.*

Zoe smiled at Simon. "Hello, Simon. How are you? I was just out grabbing some dinner when I ran into Declan. What are you two up to?" He probably wouldn't give her a straight answer, but it didn't hurt to try. Declan was just too nervous.

"Oh, you know. The politics of building prisons, where to put them, who runs them, that sort of thing. It's part of a research project I'm working on and I persuaded Declan to be my research assistant. So, he took the tour of the prison and interviewed the staff historian to get some background for himself. We're heading back to campus now." Simon bounced on his toes and cocked his head at Zoe.

"Sounds interesting. Well, I'll let you two get going. Declan I'll see you in class next week." Zoe smiled at Declan who gave her a small jerky nod and shy smile in return. Simon nodded at her and turned back up the street. Declan hurried after him.

As she continued on to get her poké bowl, Zoe thought of at least two more questions she probably should have asked Simon in order to reassure herself that his intentions toward Declan were not malicious. She couldn't quite put her finger on anything, but it seemed odd that Simon was avoiding questions about what, exactly, he and Declan were doing. Mark had mentioned that, when it came to his research, Simon sometimes forgot that his students were still undergraduates and needed to focus on more than just his projects. Zoe had the feeling that Simon was doing the same thing now with Declan. A student who was the child of a djinn and a mother gifted with Sight might be viewed as a living project by Simon. *Come on. Simon wouldn't harm Declan. That's silly.*

Putting paranoid thoughts out of her mind, she ordered her dinner and headed back home with it.

Chapter Two

Despite an abundance of committee meetings, the following week Zoe managed to find the time to worry about Declan and continue her education into her own powers. Mages were born into families of mages and grew up learning about their power. Zoe didn't have that advantage and so since discovering her powers last semester, she had been trying to figure things out on her own.

She knew that Elemental mages were rare, but she wasn't sure how rare. The others had all assured her that they didn't know any other Elemental mages. That meant that she was mostly on her own when it came to figuring out the extent of her powers.

George Wardmaster, the former chair of the history department and her mentor, had warned her after the battle with the demon last winter that she needed to learn control and finesse if she wanted to avoid draining her energy to the point of death. She had managed to, if not defeat the demon, at least send it back where it came from by the simple act of throwing unbridled, raw power at it from an internal well of rage and fear.

The thought that doing something like that could kill her

had broken through the smug feeling that killing the demon had inspired. She had a lot more to learn, especially about her parents, specifically her dad, and why her power hadn't manifested itself until now.

Zoe did congratulate herself on forcing a long-overdue conversation with her mother over the Christmas holidays. She often thought back over that afternoon, pulling it apart and reexamining her mother's story. Zoe had told her mother the story of the fight with the demon on the winter solstice. Her mother's reaction was not what she had expected. Zoe had finished the story and glanced at her mother's face. She was surprised at what she saw. Instead of anger and shock, or incredulity, her mother looked both proud and regretful. As Zoe was taking this in, her mother sighed heavily.

"I was afraid that this would happen. I mean, not the demon part, but your powers," Lydia O'Brien murmured. She gazed at her daughter. "I guess I better tell you what I know." Her tone had been resigned.

"Yeah, Mom. Please. I need to know. I was in a life and death situation because of this power!"

"I know, and I'm truly sorry. Please believe me. I was trying to protect you."

Zoe reached across the kitchen table and took her mother's hand. "I know, Mom. And I love you for it. But I'm a big girl now, and I need to be able to fully use my power. And use it correctly. George said I could have killed myself!"

Zoe didn't want to level a guilt trip at her mother, but in retelling the story of the semester and its culmination in the fight against the demon on the winter solstice, all the adrenaline had come back and her pulse was racing. She stared down at the table and took deep breaths to bring her heart back to a normal rate.

Lydia contemplated a spot on the wall behind Zoe's head. "You're right. And I am extremely proud of you and everything you have accomplished." Her eyes took on a faraway look and she dove into her story.

"I am a Fire mage, and your father is an Earth mage. We grew up in the same neighborhood. Mages tend to congregate together, and his parents and mine were no exception. Patrick and I spent a lot of time together. It seemed only natural to start dating once we reached high school. He was charming and handsome. I'd known him almost my whole life and I trusted him completely. We went to different colleges, but still saw each other on breaks and during the summers.

By the time we had both graduated from college, we had decided to get married. Our parents were a little hesitant, but there was no real reason to stop us. About two years later, you came along. Since we were both mages, we assumed that you would be too. You were about three years old when your father left. I'm still not sure what happened. He just said he couldn't stay with me, with us, any longer. He walked out and I didn't hear a thing until two years later." Lydia paused to get something to drink. As her mother dug through the refrigerator for a can of sparkling water, Zoe found herself focused on one small item. She knew that her father had left but assumed that the marriage had gone sour somehow. This felt worse.

Her mother sat back down, took a long drink of water, and resumed her story.

"Two years after he left, almost to the day, I got a phone call from your father. It couldn't have lasted more than five minutes. He just asked how I was doing, how you were doing, and if you'd shown any signs of power. I tried to get more information from him, but he wouldn't tell me anything. He did say he loved me and loved you, but by then, I didn't believe him. No word for two years and he expects me to believe that he loves me? No. I still don't believe him. You don't just walk out on your wife and child if you love them!" Lydia's voice went up and Zoe recognized the same hand-twisting habit she had.

"I'm sorry, Mom. But...what about Gran and Gramps? What about Dad's parents?" Zoe felt like she was intruding on her mother's renewed grief, but she had to know about her family. If she'd met her father's parents, she didn't remember it.

Lydia drew a shaky breath, wiped her eyes, and gave Zoe a watery smile. "Thanks, sweetie. Obviously, it still pisses me off."

"Really? I couldn't tell." Zoe returned the smile.

Lydia laughed. "Well, you did inherit your father's snarky sense of humor."

She glanced down at her still-twisting hands and pulled them apart, placing them palms down on the table. "Okay. So, that's about it. He checked in about every two to three years, but never sent you birthday or Christmas presents or obviously no graduation presents. Once you got to college, he quit checking in. I guess he figured you were no longer a child. I don't know."

Lydia took a deep breath "Your grandparents...yes, they're all mages, like I said. You come from a long line of mages of all Elements. But I don't think I ever heard that anybody else was an Elemental mage. I think you're the first...on both sides. After that first phone call, I stopped talking with Patrick's parents. I am sorry that I cut you off from your grandparents, but I got the feeling that they knew something and weren't telling me. I think they know where he is and why, but I never asked. They didn't really try to contact me again either. I was angry. Still am, if I'm honest," Lydia paused and took a sip of water.

"So, I'm not sure that I have any more or any different information for you. I know Fire, but I haven't used it in a long time. After your father left, I quit using it. I don't know that I made a conscious decision to not tell you about mages and power. I think that I was trying so hard to just move ahead and make a new life for us, without magic, that that came with the territory," Lydia shrugged.

"Mom…did you *stop* my powers? Is that why you freaked out when I told you what I was working on in grad school? And why you don't like me going to Ireland and the UK this summer?" Zoe was shocked to think that her mother might have deliberately blocked Zoe's access to her mage powers. Why would she do that? She knew the answer to her second question, but she had wanted to hear it directly from her mother. She didn't want to waste any more time guessing about motivations or reasons.

Lydia stared at Zoe. "No! I didn't block your power!" She paused. "At least I didn't do it on purpose. I just wanted you to have a normal life!"

Zoe stayed silent. Lydia glanced down at her hands and then up at Zoe. "I was afraid that you would figure things out if you started following fairy tales. But since you'd never shown any signs of power, I never thought you'd come into it now." Her mother took another deep breath. "But you probably figured out by now that I'm right about the fairy tales being real. I'm serious about that. You must be careful."

"I will, Mom. I promise." Zoe thought for a moment. "I promise if you promise me something…you'll start using your power again and quit hiding." She wasn't sure why this was important to her, but it was. She stared at her mother.

Lydia had looked away and then turned back and held her daughter's eyes. "I…don't know."

"Mom. Please."

"I will try. I can't promise you more than that. I will try."

Zoe shook her head and forced herself back to the present. Her mother's story had answered a lot of questions, but it did not help with figuring out how to use her mage powers, or how powerful she was.

Zoe shoved aside thoughts of mage power and student papers and grabbed her jacket and hat off the back of the door. She needed to clear her head. The day was sunny, if cold, and what little snow there was had been cleared from the walkways. A short walk to stretch her legs and give her brain a break from tortured undergraduate writing would be perfect right now. Exiting Cooper Hall, she gazed south towards the administration building, Shelby Hall. *You know what? I can make a full circle of the quad now. There's no more coven in Shelby creating weird, repellant clouds around the building.*

She turned back to the path and jumped at the sight of a squirrel sitting directly in front of her.

"Rowantree! Damn! You startled me!"

"My apologies, Zoe. I saw you from my tree when you came out of the building. I need a word with you," the squirrel responded.

Zoe's heartbeat quickened. The first time Rowantree had ever spoken to her (and talk about having a heart attack!) he had warned her about the coven that was forming and working in Shelby Hall. The coven that had ended up raising a demon in Logan Square in the middle of Philadelphia. Rowantree and the other squirrels were Watchers for the Summerfield campus. Their job was to watch for anything magical on campus that might harm those living and working in it. If he was worried about something, it was a magical problem, and likely not a small one.

"Uh-oh. I don't like the sound of that. What's going on?" Zoe managed to keep her voice steady.

"Perhaps we should keep walking since not everybody is aware of my ability to communicate with humans?" The squirrel put action to words and bounded over to the grass while Zoe continued walking down the path. She threw a quick glance around the quad just to make sure nobody was close enough to notice she was walking with a squirrel.

"So, what's going on?" Zoe asked again.

"I am not certain. It does not feel like last time when the cloud surrounded that building," he said waving a paw in the direction of Shelby Hall.

"So, is it stronger? Different? Is it around Shelby again?" Zoe liked Rowantree, but sometimes getting information out of him was like playing *Twenty Questions.*

The squirrel paused and cocked his head, thinking. "There does not appear to be one set location. It is diffuse and it travels around the campus. Watchers in areas nearby have said they felt something similar. But we feel it on campus almost every day. This disruption does not feel the same as the cloud created by the coven, but I do not like it. I apologize for my lack of detailed information, however I wanted you to be aware that there is something dark moving on this campus. I have told the young ones as well."

She knew that "young ones" referred to the students who had helped Zoe and the others defeat the demon and break up the coven last year. Rowantree's formal language always surprised her. You didn't really expect a squirrel to come up with involved, formally worded sentences. Of course, most people didn't expect a squirrel to talk.

"You don't think it's Declan, do you? The djinn?" she asked.

"No. The aura of the half-djinn is different and it is light. This is dark. I don't like it." Rowantree's voice went flat.

"Thank you, Rowantree. I will inform the others and ensure that everybody maintains a heightened level of awareness." *He's rubbing off on me. I'm sounding like a stuffy professor.*

Rowantree inclined his head and ran up the trunk of the nearest tree and Zoe continued across campus. Mulling over what she'd just been told, she changed her aimless walk into one with purpose and strode toward Davis Hall and Mark Davis's office. The building wasn't named for him or anybody he was related to, but their running joke was that he'd donated the building in order to secure his job.

Arriving at Mark's door she was relieved to find him in his office. She knocked on the doorframe, pulling his attention away from his own stack of grading. He smiled when he saw her standing in the doorway.

"Hey, Zo. What's up?"

"Hi. Well, I was out for a head-clearing walk when Rowantree interrupted it." She closed the door behind her and sat down in the chair beside his desk, pulling off her hat.

Mark's eyebrows shot up and his eyes widened a bit.

"Oh? Is there something going on again? I kinda hoped we were done with that, but I guess not."

"Yeah, I was sorta hoping for a quiet, normal semester too. But, no such luck," Zoe shrugged. "Rowantree said that there is something dark moving around campus. He can't quite pinpoint it, but he says it's not like the cloud the coven created around Shelby last semester. He also said he told the 'young ones,' meaning Josh, Annmarie, Geoff, and Declan. Oh, and he said it's not Declan."

"Damn," Mark swore softly. "Moving around. That doesn't sound good."

"I know. I don't like it. He asked me to tell you and the others, so that's why I just came over here. I'm going to go find George next and let him know. Kieran's in town, but at a conference, so I'll text him. And we need to let Jessica and Robyn know too," she said, listing some of the other faculty members who had helped to defeat the coven.

"Okay. I can go find Jessica and Robyn. I'll hunt down John Gardner as well." Mark stacked up the papers he'd been working on, pushed back his chair and stood up. "We should do it now rather than waiting."

Feeling like they were heading into battle, Zoe stood up sighing heavily.

"Good idea. I don't like any of this, but okay. I'll talk to you later." She opened his office door and started out.

Mark stopped. "Oh, I almost forgot. David's in the city for a meeting today and I know Kieran is at his conference…maybe we can all have dinner at the Faire Mount tonight?"

"Sure. I'll see if Kieran can make it." Since Zoe and Kieran had kinda sorta become a couple, something she really didn't want to jinx by assuming anything more permanent, they spent a good deal of time with Mark and David. All four were mages, and although Zoe, an Elemental mage, was the strongest, she was still a newbie at this mage thing. The others had taken turns helping her figure out how to use her newfound power.

"Great. We can compare notes at dinner." Mark pulled his briefcase out from under his desk and began loading it with papers and books.

Zoe left him to his packing and walked back down the stairs and out of Davis Hall. Outside, she found herself in the flow of students, faculty, and staff heading home at the end of the day. She retraced her steps toward Shelby Hall. Reaching the front door, she hesitated. Memories of the dark, nauseous cloud that hung over it when the coven was working to raise a demon, always made her pause before going into the building.

Taking a deep breath, she pulled open the front door and stepped inside. The front hall appeared as it always had – very formal, and slightly menacing. She glanced up at the chandelier that loomed over the entry way threatening to crash down on unsuspecting visitors. Stepping quickly, she passed underneath it and headed up the wide, curving staircase that led to the second floor and the offices of the higher-level administrators of Summerfield College.

The deep carpet muffled the sounds of her steps as she made her way about halfway down the hallway. An open door on the left indicated that at least George's administrative assistant was still in. Zoe smiled as she walked in the door.

"Hi Sarah!" she greeted the secretary.

"Hi Zoe! What brings you over here?" The two women hugged.

Sarah Riley had originally worked as a "Girl Friday" or gofer for the previous provost, Melanie Porter, and her secretary Susan Barker. It turned out Susan had been the leader of the coven. When Melanie and Susan had tried to force Sarah into becoming a corporeal home for the demon the coven was raising, Sarah had walked out and quit her job via email. In the post-battle changes to the administrative offices, George had asked Sarah to return to Summerfield as his administrative assistant and she had happily agreed. Although Sarah did not have any magical power herself, she had seen enough in action that she was extremely comfortable around mages and magic. In fact, she said that she felt safer working with George as she knew he could handle any weirdness that might come her way.

"So what's it like sitting at Susan Barker's old desk?" Zoe teased her friend.

"Well, Well, the first thing I did was completely disinfect it and then I had George check for any magical residue." Sarah laughed. "But what brings you over here?"

"Is George in? I have some information he needs," Zoe asked.

"Yeah, he's there and there's nobody with him. Is everything okay?" Sarah, understandably, looked a little nervous.

"I'm not sure, but it doesn't look good. You should come in and hear this too."

Sarah followed Zoe into George's office. He looked up

from his computer and smiled at the two women.

"I thought that was your voice, Zoe. What a pleasant surprise. What brings you over this way?" George Wardmaster looked like a cross between everybody's favorite grandfather and Santa Claus with green eyes. He was a powerful Earth mage and up until January, had been chair of the history department and Zoe's faculty mentor.

The previous provost, Melanie Porter, was on an "indefinite medical leave of absence" since contact with the demon had stripped her of her sanity. The president of Summerfield College, Morgan Ammon, had survived the battle, and the Board of Trustees decided that finding a new president as well as a new provost would be too much at once and could harm the reputation of the college – Zoe rolled her eyes every time she heard that one – so Morgan had remained president, but the faculty mages wanted a way to keep an eye on her.

George's solution had been to accept Morgan's "invitation" to become the interim provost. It was widely known among the faculty mages that George had informed Morgan that he would become the interim provost and that he was there to insure she did not make any attempts to take up magic again.

Zoe didn't know for sure, since she'd never met any of them, but she had a strong suspicion that there was at least one mage, if not more, sitting on the Board of Trustees. Morgan had very grudgingly agreed to the arrangement. Zoe shook her head. In the end it was still faculty politics.

She returned George's smile and accepted his invitation to take a seat in one of his comfortable guest chairs. Sarah remained standing in the doorway in case somebody came through the outer door of the office.

"Well...um...I ran into Rowantree earlier this afternoon and he asked me to pass on some information." Zoe stopped and pulled her hands apart before she could start knotting her fingers together. Repeating Rowantree's warning was increasing her nervousness about what might be happening on campus.

Sarah glanced into the front office and then back at Zoe.

"Rowantree. That's the squirrel?" she asked Zoe.

"Yeah," Zoe replied. "He's one of the Watchers for this campus."

Sarah gave a snort of laughter. "You'd think after everything I saw last year that talking squirrels would be mundane by now. But that one still freaks me out a little bit."

"Totally know what you mean." Zoe grinned at her friend.

George smiled at Zoe. "So, what exactly did Rowantree say?"

"Oh, sorry. He says there's something dark moving about campus. It doesn't feel like the cloud around Shelby last year, and he said it's diffuse and hard to pinpoint." She hesitated, recalling her conversation with the squirrel.

"He seemed more worried than he did last year when he first told me about the cloud around Shelby and the coven. I don't like it." Once again, she deliberately unlaced her fingers. She really needed to break this handwringing habit.

Voices in the hallway caused Sarah to look back out into the front office, but whoever it was continued on down the hall. She turned back to George and Zoe with a worried expression.

"George, don't forget that Holly Krueger has an appointment with you about that resolution the faculty senate passed. She'll be here in a few minutes."

"Okay. Zoe, we should finish up. I don't think it would be a good idea for you to be here when Holly gets here." George smiled at Zoe to take the sting out of his comment.

"Why? I don't know her. I mean, I know she's president of the faculty senate, but I don't think she knows who I am,"

Zoe responded.

"Well, let's just say she could give Meredith Cruickshank a run for her money in the areas of arrogance and condescension, and the proper place for you junior faculty types," came Sarah's sarcastic reply.

"Oh, geez. Really? I'm so tired of that crap." Zoe didn't care if she came off as disrespectful in front of the provost.

George grinned. "Well, as provost, I can't really say anything directly, but I can say that I have the utmost respect for Sarah's judgement."

Zoe and Sarah both laughed.

"Okay. Then I guess I'd better be going. If she's that bad, I don't think I really want her knowing who I am after all." Zoe stood up.

George smiled at Zoe. "Somehow, I thought that would be your response. It was good to see you, Zoe, even if it was because you're bringing worrisome news. Please drop by again soon. Sarah can keep track of my visitors and make sure we don't have any conflicts in scheduling. And, perhaps you can speak with some of the group from last year, including those students still on campus."

Zoe nodded. "Already on it. I have some of those students in class again. Maybe the faculty should arrange another happy hour."

"Good idea. Let me know what happens." George turned back to his computer and Zoe walked back out into the front office with Sarah.

"Okay, I guess I'd better get out of here," she said, giving Sarah a hug. "I'll let you know about the happy hour and you can join us."

"Sounds good." Sarah returned the hug and sat back down at her desk. "See you later!"

Zoe walked quickly out of Shelby. Emerging into the late winter afternoon – or as she preferred to think of it, early spring – she glanced around and spotted the senate president along with another faculty member, who Zoe thought was the faculty secretary, heading down the path towards the front door of Shelby. The two were deep in conversation and did not notice Zoe standing in front of the building. She moved rapidly away from the door and took the most direct route back to Cooper Hall and her office.

Once back in her office, Zoe collapsed into her chair. She felt like she'd just run across campus for some reason. *I think I'm stressing out.* She pulled her phone out of her coat pocket and texted Kieran about dinner with Mark and David.

Sounds great. Meet u there, came the immediate answer.

Zoe breathed easier after reading the text. As much as she downplayed the growing relationship between herself and Kieran, she always felt better when she knew she was going to see him.

She stared at the pile of essays sitting on her desk. Was it worth bringing them home? Probably not. She stacked them neatly to one side. That way she'd see them when she got in tomorrow. Justification complete, she packed up her laptop and, after checking to make sure that Meredith hadn't suddenly shown up (she hadn't), headed out to her car. Maybe she as being paranoid, but where Meredith was concerned, you couldn't be too careful.

After a surprisingly easy commute home, Zoe walked into her house and felt the stress dissolve. Insistent *thumps* against her legs announced that Moose and Flash were happy to have her home. For magical talking cats they sure spent a lot of time acting like ordinary cats. Zoe suspected it was for the treats.

"Hi guys," Zoe said, dropping her purse and bags. "Yes, I'll get you food, but I have news, too."

The cats paused in the head-butting and looked up at her.

"Did something happen?" Flash asked.

"Yes and no," Zoe responded, moving into the kitchen in search of the wine she'd promised herself and treats for the cats. "Rowantree says there's a dark magic moving around campus. He can't pinpoint it, but it's there. Oh, and Mark, David, Kieran and I are having dinner at the Faire Mount tonight which means I can't bring you with me."

She wandered back out to the living room, wine glass in hand, and dropped onto the sofa in front of her small fireplace. The cats jumped up beside her.

"Okay. After you feed us, leave the window open. We'll contact the others later." Moose started licking his tail. Zoe took a sip of wine and watched his meticulous cleaning routine.

"Okay. Let's get you guys some food, and then I'm changing into something comfortable."

Flash and Moose raced into the kitchen before Zoe even made it off the sofa. They reached the kitchen, turned around and started meowing pitifully.

Zoe laughed. "You guys are pathetic!"

When she arrived at the Faire Mount she found Kieran already there. He got up and gave her a hug and a quick kiss.

"Hi! I ditched the conference early. The panels were getting a bit incestuous. The audiences were all friends of the panelists," he smiled.

"A sure sign it's time to leave!" Zoe returned his smile, feeling a little giddy and definitely better than she had earlier.

Mark and David arrived a couple of minutes later. The four of them focused on the good food and beer and kept the conversation light. Finally as everybody was finishing up, Mark caught Zoe's eye and nodded. She swallowed the last bit of her cheeseburger and took a drink of her beer.

"Um…okay it looks like there's more excitement in the magical arena on campus." She looked around at the three men.

"I'd kinda hoped we'd get a quiet semester," Kieran sighed.

"Yeah, me too. No such luck, I guess." Mark rolled his eyes.

"Quiet is boring," David laughed. "What's going on, Zoe?"

"Oh, just more dark magic wandering around campus. The usual," Zoe said with exaggerated nonchalance. She told them about the visit and warning from Rowantree and Alder, and her conversation with George.

David looked slightly puzzled. "Did George say anything besides 'thanks for warning me?' That seems a little blasé for someone who was upset with himself for missing signs last semester."

"Oh, I think he's just got a lot on his plate right now. I'm sure he'll be there when we need him," Zoe defended her mentor. She pushed away the thought that he'd dropped her mage tutoring meetings with no signs of picking them back up again. *It doesn't matter. I can always ask David about Earth magic.*

"Zoe? Hey, earth to Zoe." Kieran's voice brought her out of her reverie.

"What?" she refocused on her friends.

"We were just saying that there doesn't seem to be much to do right now but keep our eyes open and be on the lookout for anyone acting strange," Mark said.

Kieran laughed. "We work on a college campus. People acting strange is the norm!"

"True, true. Okay…er…strange-er. Does that work?" Mark retorted.

Chapter Three

THE NEXT FEW DAYS passed uneventfully and Zoe, focused on locating the source of the dark magic roaming around campus, almost forgot about the somewhat strange encounter with Declan and Simon in front of Eastern State Penitentiary. That encounter was brought back to her one cold, gloomy afternoon at the end of the week.

She was staring at her computer looking for videos that she could show in class that would help illustrate a particularly tricky concept regarding the relationship between the British monarch and the Church before the changes brought about by Henry VIII.

A soft knock on the door brought her out of her trance-like gazing at links on historical sites. She quickly controlled her expression of surprise and smiled at Declan standing nervously in her doorway.

"Hi, Dr. O'Brien. Can I talk to you for a minute?" he asked softly. Out of habit, he glanced down the hall toward Meredith Cruickshank's office with a nervous twitch.

"Sure, come in. It's okay, Dr. Cruickshank is on sabbatical, remember? She's not here," Zoe reassured him. "What's up?"

Declan shuffled in and closed the door behind him. Now, Zoe's eyebrows did go up. This was not going to be a talk about class assignments or academic advising.

"Well, I-I wanted to talk to you after I saw you last weekend. Simon...Dr. LeGrande doesn't know...um...I didn't tell him I wanted to t-talk to you."

"Okay. If you like, I won't say anything to him. But, you know, you don't have to tell your advisor every time you talk to another faculty member." Why would he think he had to tell Simon he spoke to her? And, why was he obviously used to calling Simon by his first name? Simon didn't normally tolerate that level of informality from students.

Declan gave a jerky nod.

"Y-yeah. Okay. B-but..." he trailed off, staring at his hands as his fingers knotted themselves together.

Zoe supressed a sigh. Sometimes the excessive nervousness of this kid bordered on highly exasperating. But he had good reason to be nervous, so...

"It's no big deal. You should do whatever makes you comfortable. So, what's going on?" she poured all the reassurance she could find into her tone of voice. Her efforts were rewarded with a shy smile and a small nod.

"Well, Dr. LeGrande has been helping me figure out how my combined powers work, right? So...um...we were at the prison because there was something there that had been bothering the staff and Dr. LeGrande said it was a good opportunity for m-me to test out my p-powers. He...um...said he'd be there watching and would...um...help me if something started to...um...go wrong."

Zoe nodded. In experimenting with her own power, she found that knowledge came faster if she just tried to *do* something. So far, she hadn't burned the house down or caused an earthquake or tornado in her microscopic back yard. It helped that she knew mages who were willing to work with her in their individual Element. But since nobody knew any other Elemental mages she was mostly on her own when it came to figuring out how her power worked with a combination of Elements. And as far as she or any of the others knew, Declan was the only half-djinn with Sight on the North American continent. Experimenting was about the only way he was going to figure out how his power worked.

"Did something go wrong?" she asked.

"N-no. But...um...I saw somebody get killed. I killed the ifrit! B-but it killed the guard first. D-do you think I-I should...um...tell...um...the police?" Declan looked like the scared kid he really was. Zoe shivered internally at the thought of all that untapped and virtually unknown magical strength wandering around trapped inside a very skittish twenty-year old college student. She wracked her brain trying to remember what, exactly, an ifrit was. Oh! Right. Oh, shit.

"Those are a type of djinn, right? It killed the guard?" She was doing her best not to turn this into an interrogation. After all the kid had come to her with this problem. And how did you, could you, explain a magical killing to Philadelphia PD?

"Yeah. They're different than like...me. More like a demon." Declan looked miserable.

"Well, I don't think the police would believe you if you told them an ifrit was wandering around Eastern State Penitentiary. What did it do to the guard?"

"It...um...touched him on the head. At least t-that's what it looked l-like. Then...um...the guard just fell down. The art installation p-people thought he had a heart attack. And they called 9-1-1." Declan was still wringing his hands together signaling his high stress levels.

"Well, okay. If the art people and the paramedics thought it was a heart attack, then it was a heart attack. I don't think you'll make a difference if you tell them it was an ifrit." She was trying to maintain her reassuring tone and at the same time pulling news headlines out of memory to see if she'd heard anything about a security guard having a heart attack at the prison.

"I t-told his ghost that I would make sure they told his family. He said he didn't have any kids or anything. The guy who found him seemed like he would tell them, so I left. Was that okay? I was invisible." He rushed through the rest of his story.

"So, now the prison really is haunted?" Zoe tried to create a lighter tone.

"Oh, there are lots of ghosts in there. But I think they were scared of the ifrit. I don't know what they'll do now. I don't think they can leave anyway." Declan sounded very sure of himself. That was a first.

"Oh. Okay. Well, yes, I think you did the right thing and I think it's good that you were invisible. Did you tell Dr. LeGrande what happened?" What had Simon said, or maybe not said, that made Declan come to her? Simon was supposed to be in charge of both magical and academic education for Declan. She was just the secondary academic advisor.

"I-I told him about the…um…ifrit, but not…um…about the guard. Do you think I should?" The nerves were back.

"Only if you want to. As sad as it was, I don't think there's anything you can do about it, so if you don't want to tell him, then that's fine." Zoe sighed internally. *I should have at least gotten a certificate in counseling with all the life advice I'm giving out.*

Declan nodded and relief flooded his face. As he stood up to leave, Zoe thought of something.

"Declan, how did you kill the ifrit?"

"I blasted it with lightning. That's what I thought of first, so that's what I did. Simon said that was okay, but I need to be…um… 'a bit less flamboyant, my boy.'" He gave a very good imitation of Simon and grinned at her.

Zoe laughed. "Yeah, Dr. Wardmaster told me I needed to learn finesse. I'd almost forgotten about that. He didn't like how I killed that demon."

"You did great with that demon! Thanks, Dr. O'Brien. Okay. I'll see you later." Declan opened the door and started to walk into the hallway.

"Well, hello, Declan. What are *you* doing in this building? I thought you were a political science major now. They're over in Davis. Or did you forget that already?" Meredith's scathing, sarcastic tone carried the length of the hall. Zoe quickly got up and moved to the door, standing behind Declan, and looked down the hall in the direction of Meredith's office. Shit. What the hell was she doing here? She could feel Declan shaking.

"You know, you should really leave your door open when you have a male student in your office, Zoe." Meredith's voice dripped with false concern.

"Yes, thanks, Meredith. However, when it's a sensitive subject, I prefer the risk of shutting the door to allowing the entire hall to hear a student's concerns." Zoe smiled sweetly.

If Meredith wanted to go back to playing games, bring it on. Zoe was ready. With everything that had happened last semester, she was no longer overly concerned with getting tenure. With George as provost, any roadblocks created by personal vendettas would be removed. And more importantly, she knew that anything Meredith said would be disregarded.

"By the way, Meredith, what are you doing here? I thought you were on *sabbatical*?" Zoe emphasized the word and was rewarded with a flinch from Meredith.

"I had to get some books from my office. Being on sabbatical doesn't mean banned from campus, you know." Meredith sounded defensive.

Declan's head swiveled between the two women. As Meredith glared at Zoe, he ducked his head and scurried away toward the stairs. Zoe continued to smile at Meredith until she heard the main building door close. Then with a little flutter of her fingers at the fuming ex-wannabe witch, she stepped back into her office and firmly closed the door.

Once behind the relative safety of her closed door, Zoe immediately manipulated Air currents so that she could track Meredith's movements. She certainly didn't need magical help to hear Meredith stomp back to her office. Heels are always loud on linoleum floors. She continued to manipulate Air however, certain that Meredith would be telling somebody Zoe was entertaining male students in her office.

Sure enough, Zoe heard the phone being dialed. *Too bad we don't have the old rotary dials anymore. I could probably figure out the number from how long it took to come back around.*

She didn't need to figure out the number once she heard the voice that answered the phone. It still astounded her that she could make out a voice on the other end of the phone in an office down the hall. This mage thing was pretty cool.

"What is it, Meredith? I'm busy." Morgan Ammon, president of Summerfield College, sounded annoyed.

"I'm very sorry, but I thought you might be interested to know that I just interrupted Zoe O'Brien in her office with a male student...with the door closed. It was Declan Jin. I thought we could use that somehow." Meredith's tone was simultaneously subservient and gleeful. Zoe shuddered slightly. That was a chilling combination.

"That is useful. That can be put in her tenure file and used at review. Very well. Let Carolyn know. She'll take it from there." The click of Morgan hanging up the phone was followed by a muttered "bitch" from Meredith and the sound of her phone being returned to its cradle.

Zoe smiled a little at Meredith's pique, but quickly turned to the more pressing question of who was this Carolyn person and why did the president suggest that Meredith tell her about

Zoe? And to use Declan's visit against her? The conversation was disconcerting. Was this the dark presence that Rowantree had sensed moving about campus? Or was this just nasty faculty politics?

Zoe knew that in addition to George Wardmaster, the president blamed Zoe for the failure of the coven and the destruction of their demon last winter. With George acting as provost and in an office suite just next door to the president, Zoe had figured she didn't need to worry about anything coming from that direction. She hadn't counted on Meredith and the president teaming up again, never mind bringing in Carolyn, whoever she was.

She stood up quickly and grabbed her jacket. As nervous as she still was about tenure, Zoe had to admit that tenure problems were very minor compared to potential death and destruction from dark magic roaming around campus. Mark and the others needed to know about this potential new development.

She didn't want to do anything in her own office for fear that Meredith would find out. She quietly opened her door and glanced down the hall toward Meredith's office. The door was slightly ajar, but not enough that Meredith could see into the hall. Checking that she had her keys and phone, Zoe gently closed her own door, and walked quickly, but quietly, down the stairs and out the front door of the building.

Once outside, she took a deep breath of the cool air and gazed around the quad searching for Rowantree or Alder. No squirrels were in evidence, so she set off down the path towards Davis Hall and Mark's office.

Just outside of Davis Hall she ran into Robyn Harper and Jessica Sanders. Both women were in the English department and both were mages. Robyn was a Fire mage and Jessica was a Water mage. They had helped in the fight against the demon last year and the three had become friends.

"Hey, Zoe. What's up?" Robyn asked as they approached the entrance to the building.

"Oh, hey, you guys. Actually, do you have a few minutes? I'm on my way to talk to Mark, but you should hear this too," Zoe responded.

"Sure. We in for more 'interesting' events?" Jessica gave a wry smile and made air quotes with her fingers.

"Possibly. Maybe I'm just being paranoid, but I don't think so." Zoe returned the smile with a sideways one of her own.

"Oh, goody," Robyn sighed. The three women trooped into Davis Hall and up the stairs to Mark's office.

Mark looked up in surprise as Zoe led Jessica and Robyn into his office and closed the door.

"Okay. To what do I owe the honor of this visit?" He smiled at them.

"We're just along for the ride. This was her idea," Robyn said pointing at Zoe.

"Ah. Then I'm going to jump to the conclusion that this has something to do with Rowantree and his warnings?" Mark asked, also looking at Zoe.

"That's right. I told you about that last week. My mind is bogged down in grading." Zoe smiled ruefully.

"Oh, yeah. I remember now. Mark, you told me about it last week too. I'm with you, Zoe, my mind is clearly bogged down with grading and committees. Did something else happen since then?" Robyn sat down in one of Mark's guest chairs and crossed her legs.

"Well, I just had another interesting encounter with Meredith and ended up eavesdropping on a phone call she made." When it came to Meredith and her activities and attitude, Zoe had long ago quit caring if she violated etiquette by listening in on the wannabe-witch's phone calls.

"What's *she* doing on campus? I thought she was on

sabbatical?" Jessica asked.

"Well a forced sabbatical…bet she misses all the backstabbing." Mark chuckled.

"Oh, do tell!" Robyn grinned nastily. She had no liking for Meredith since the faculty mages had discovered that the coven was corrupting and using students in their quest to raise a demon. Robyn had been doubly incensed when she discovered one of *her* advisees was destined to be the earthly body of the demon after Sarah had left. Robyn tended to form strong bonds with her advisees and Zoe knew the English professor had not forgiven Meredith for that one.

"Well, there's a couple of things. First of all, Declan Jin came to my office to let me know that he killed an ifrit in Eastern State Penitentiary a few nights ago."

"What the hell was he doing in there at night?" Mark was angry. "That place is full of ghosts, and not all of them are harmless. You just don't go in there at night."

"Well, there was a security guard in there. Declan was there with Simon. Apparently, it was to test some of his magic." Zoe was taken aback by the vehemence in Mark's voice. How dangerous *was* the historical prison?

"One does not simply walk into ESP?" Jessica raised an eyebrow. "There's not a lot you can do about ghosts. How did he kill the ifrit anyway?"

"He said he blasted it with lightning. He also said it killed one of the security guards before he could get to it. The staff installing the new interactive art exhibit came in right after Declan killed the ifrit. They thought that the guard died of a heart attack. So, I told Declan to stick with that story. I don't think Philly PD is interested in hearing about ifrits in the city."

Mark was frowning. "I hope Simon didn't deliberately send Declan in there to deal with an ifrit."

"Um…I think he might have. I saw Declan and Simon right after that, actually. I happened to be walking over that way to pick up some dinner and ran into Declan outside the prison and then Simon bounced up just a couple of minutes later." Zoe told them about her conversation with Declan and his advisor. "I didn't hear anything else about it until today. Declan didn't tell Simon about the security guard for some reason. Understandably, he's freaking out about seeing the guard killed."

Mark nodded slowly. "I'm going to ask Simon about his work with Declan. I'm not really comfortable that he's taking him to Eastern State Pen to 'test' his power. Declan is an anomaly, but he's also a student. Simon sometimes gets a little too caught up in research and forgets that people are involved in some of these things."

"Okay, if you think you should. Just don't do anything that will get you in trouble with Simon. He's your chair, don't forget." Mark was also untenured, and that worry was always in the back of her mind and made her think twice, and give warnings to others, before she said or did a number of things on campus. The self-censorship really sucked, but she had to survive until tenure.

Jessica grinned at Zoe. "Don't worry, we'll give both of you glowing recommendations as excellent colleagues to work with who always have the best interests of the students and the college at heart."

"That's all absolutely true anyway," Robyn chimed in.

Zoe smiled at the two women. "Thanks! But there's something else you guys need to know about. Does anybody know someone on campus named Carolyn? Faculty or staff, not student." Tired of standing, she dropped into Mark's remaining guest chair. Jessica perched on the windowsill.

Robyn frowned. "Yeah, I do. There's a new teaching professor in psychology. She's not new to teaching, but she's new here. I've met her once, but that's it. Why?"

Zoe tried to call up a face. "Oh, her. Well, Meredith…"

Robyn snorted at the mention of Meredith.

Zoe continued, "...when Declan left my office Meredith was in the hallway. She got all snide about having a male student in my office with the door closed. I told her to get lost and she went back to her office. I admit, I listened in after she closed the door. She called the president to tell her about Declan in my office, and that it might quote be useful unquote. The president said Meredith should 'let Carolyn know' and that she, Carolyn, would take care of it. They're back together, Meredith and Morgan, and this Carolyn person is involved. And Rowantree said there's something dark moving around campus. I don't like the combo." Zoe sounded confused, lame, and paranoid to herself, but the expressions on the faces of her friends told her they shared her concerns.

"Oh, hell," Robyn sighed. "I was really hoping the president had learned her lessons last year. Damn she's stupid."

"And, power hungry. I think that's what's driving her." Mark scowled.

"Well, she's an administrator. What do you expect?" Jessica grimaced.

"Heh. Yeah, true. But what's the goal this time? There's no coven to raise a demon and one mage can't do something like that alone. We need to figure out what Carolyn's role in this is and why the president working with her." Mark turned to stare out the window.

Robyn was frowning in thought. "I didn't get a read on Carolyn, but then, both George and Simon are capable of hiding their power from other mages. She could be doing the same thing. I really need to figure that out for myself, too."

Mark turned back from his contemplation of the leafless tree outside his window. "There's nothing we can do now, except keep an eye on things and pay attention to what Carolyn is doing and who she's hanging out with. Damn I hate this feeling! I just want to punch something or somebody!"

Zoe had to agree with Mark. The idea of punching somebody sounded very therapeutic right now. But he was also right that there wasn't really anything they could do at the moment. She took a deep, calming breath. There was also grading that needed to be done before any more calamities claimed her attention. And, she had a committee meeting in few minutes. Zoe frowned and shoved herself up from the chair next to Mark's desk.

"I gotta go. I've got a meeting. Faculty Governance Committee." She grimaced again.

"Oh, crap. I'm on that committee now, too," Jessica said looking slightly panicked. "Gimme a minute to grab something to take notes on and I'll see you there."

Mark laughed. "Here you go." He reached across his desk, grabbed a pen and a pad of paper, and handed them to Jessica. "Have fun!"

Jessica gave him a relieved smile. "Thanks! Okay, Zo, let's go get this over with."

"While you guys are off having fun talking about bylaws or whatever, Mark and I will tackle the easy stuff like saving the world, or at least the college, from certain destruction. Again." Robyn grinned.

Jessica stuck her tongue out at Robyn as she and Zoe headed out the door, leaving Mark and Robyn discussing the dark presence and the renewed alliance between the president and Meredith Cruickshank.

"Honestly, I think I'd rather face that demon again, than go to this meeting. Tim warned me about this committee. Then he went and got a sabbatical, leaving me to take over his spot," Jessica groused.

"I'm with you! Do you know anything about Carolyn?" Zoe felt like she didn't have much time to figure out what the president and Meredith were up to. If it was anything like last year, the potential for disaster was huge and that just added to her stress.

"No, I don't. But I know I don't like that somebody who apparently just started here is already in with the president. That just doesn't smell right to me," Jessica responded.

They arrived at Harrison Hall and walked into the small meeting room just beyond the main entrance. Zoe gave a small sigh of relief when she realized they were not the last to arrive. While she had gained a great deal of confidence after last year, she still hated drawing any attention to herself in college-wide committee meetings. She and Jessica found seats at the end of the table closest to the door. While waiting for the stragglers to arrive, Zoe chatted with Andrew Smith from the chemistry department. Suddenly, his eyes widened at the entrance of one more person.

Zoe followed Andrew's gaze and found herself watching a red-haired woman wearing an expensive looking suit and high heels stride into the room. She moved up to the top end of the table and sat down next to Rob Burton, the chair of the economics department and of the Faculty Governance Committee.

"Great. We're all here now. I call the meeting to order," Rob said as the newcomer sat down and pulled out a laptop. "First off, I'd like to introduce Carolyn Detweiler from Psychology. She'll be representing the psychology department for the remainder of the semster."

He gestured to Carolyn who glanced up from her computer long enough to give a tight, almost obligatory, smile to the committee members gathered around the table. Rob looked like he expected her to say something, but she returned her attention to her laptop without speaking.

Rob coughed and looked down at his agenda. "Okay, we'll move on to our most pressing business. The president has asked this committee to look into tightening up the language in the faculty handbook and bylaws regarding sanctions for inappropriate faculty-student contact." He looked uncomfortable and glanced sideways at Carolyn who was still focused on her laptop.

Jennifer Bailey, a professor in the biology department raised her hand as she started speaking. "Excuse me Rob, but did the president tell you what she thinks is the problem with the language as it currently stands? We spent a lot of time crafting that language and it went through a vetting process that included *all* of the faculty at this college."

She sounded annoyed and Zoe didn't blame her. She knew that Jennifer had spent a lot of time on the language of the current bylaws. She was the first woman to be hired into the biology department at Summerfield and, from what Zoe had heard, had endured a lot of harassment and general old boys-type behavior over the years. Zoe had no doubt that language was as clear and strong as it could be.

Before Rob could respond, Carolyn looked up from her laptop. "Well, with all due respect, I do think that the language could be expanded in order to ensure that there are no further instances of inappropriate behavior between students and faculty." Her eyes flicked toward Zoe and there was a slight sneer in her tone as she gazed at Jennifer.

Zoe felt Jessica, sitting next to her, stiffen and raise her own hand. "I'm sorry, but as you say, with all due respect, you were not here when we dealt with all of this a few years ago, so I'd like to hear where you think the problems are. What 'further instances' are you talking about?" Her tone was mild, but the expression on her face was just this side of murderous. Zoe remembered that Jessica had worked with Jennifer on the changes and pushing them through the faculty. It had all happened during Zoe's first year at Summerfield, so she hadn't known any of the people involved then, but George had recommended that she read through the handbook and bylaws carefully to familiarize herself with the specific rules guiding faculty behavior.

Andrew Smith spoke up before Carolyn could respond to Jessica. "I agree with Jessica, Rob. I'd like to know what the president feels is problematic with the language." He glanced at Rob, emphasizing the word president and making it clear how he felt the hierarchy of the committee functioned.

An icy expression crossed Carolyn's face and Zoe regretted that she didn't have any popcorn handy. This meeting just got interesting. And she now knew without a doubt that Carolyn Detweiler was the Carolyn mentioned in the conversation between the president and Meredith. She put up a wall of mixed Air and Water around the committee members, excluding Carolyn. Zoe figured that since Carolyn was friends or at least allies with the president, the psychology professor knew Zoe was an Elemental mage, so there was really nothing to lose. Keeping Carolyn outside her impromptu wall meant that Zoe could keep herself and others out of harm's way while watching the fireworks and figuring out just what Carolyn was and how powerful she might be.

As the wall was completed, Carolyn's head snapped around and she glared at Zoe. Zoe recoiled slightly from the intensity of the woman's gaze, but she gave a tight smile and fluttered her fingers in a small wave. What the hell was going on? What was the president up to now? More importantly, what was Carolyn and why was she at Summerfield?

Jessica, the only other mage in the room, glanced sideways at Zoe and gave a thumbs-up gesture below the edge of the table. Zoe caught a thoughtful stare from Jennifer Bailey as well.

"...so, the president said she felt that the language needed to be changed to allow such incidents to be included." Rob was finishing his response to Andrew when Zoe returned her attention to the meeting.

Feeling slightly guilty, Zoe raised her hand. "I'm sorry, Rob. Could you repeat that last part? My mind wandered a bit, I apologize."

Rob smiled slightly. "I understand. Afternoon meetings have that effect. I was saying that the president felt that given some incidents that occurred last fall between students and faculty that the language needed to be updated. That was the word she used."

Zoe thought she had an idea of which "incidents" the president was referring to, but…"I see. Did she give you any idea of what these incidents involved?" She didn't expect an answer, but it might be good to get the idea out there.

Carolyn bared her teeth in what was meant to be a smile. But before she could respond, Rob answered Zoe.

"I was not given details based on the privacy issue, but you raise a good point. I'll ask for all information that does not reveal any private details." He made a note and ignoring Carolyn's glare, continued.

"I am going to suggest that this committee table this issue until we can get more information and background. I'm also going to look more closely at wording of existing bylaws. Does everyone agree?" he glanced around the table.

Carolyn drew a breath to speak but Jessica jumped in. "Thanks, Rob. I think that's a good idea. There is a governance process and the president cannot and should not simply ignore it." She eyed Carolyn as she spoke.

Rob nodded and still without looking at Carolyn, continued to the next item on the agenda. "Okay. So, moving along…"

"Well, I expect the president will be very disappointed with this committee's lack of action on this issue," Carolyn sneered, interrupting Rob.

Rob turned to look at her directly "*I* will inform the president directly of the decision of this committee. She may well be disappointed, but I'm certain she won't be surprised." He returned to the next agenda item. Carolyn scowled at him but didn't say anything more.

As the meeting broke up, Zoe used the cover of exchanging small talk with Andrew Smith and Jessica to linger until Carolyn had left the room. From the corner of her eye Zoe saw Carolyn direct a hate-filled glare towards the three of them as Carolyn walked out of the room. Andrew noticed as well.

"What is her problem? I think she hates everybody. Be careful around her." He sounded worried.

"Have you had to deal with her before?" Zoe asked him.

"Yeah, on another committee. For someone who just got here last fall, and in a non-tenure track position, she's pretty aggressive. I sometimes think she's out to get everybody who doesn't agree with her." Andrew lowered his voice even though the three of them were now alone in the room.

"We need to talk. Let's get out of here. We can go back to my office, it's closest. Andrew, I want to hear more about your encounters with her," Jessica said firmly.

"I've got a department meeting in half an hour, but I can talk for a bit," Andrew responded.

"I just have grading waiting for me, and my office hours don't start for an hour," Zoe said.

The three of them were silent on the walk back to Jessica's office. Zoe had never been in Jessica's office before and felt an immediate stab of jealousy when she walked in the door. The office was about half again as large as Zoe's and the furniture was definitely several steps up from the cast-offs that junior faculty typically found in their offices. Zoe was still grateful she wound up in Cooper with a window that opened, but damn this was a nice office with a great view of the center of campus. Jessica even had *two* windows.

Andrew voiced what she had been feeling. "Dang. Nice

office! What does it take to get one like this?"

Jessica looked around. "I just moved in here a couple of years ago. One of our older department members retired and I was lucky I was next on the list to upgrade. I've lusted after this space ever since I got to Summerfield," she laughed.

There was a small table opposite the desk with three chairs around it. Jessica sat down and Zoe and Andrew followed. Zoe shared a glance with Jessica who nodded.

Andrew caught the glance and a puzzled look crossed his face. Zoe took a breath and turned toward him.

"Andrew, please don't think I'm crazy, but...well...here goes...um...magic is real, and functions in the world." She stopped her hands from twisting and looked him in the eye.

Andrew smiled. "Oh, yeah. I know. My uncle, my aunt's husband, is a mage and my cousins are too. Our side of the family isn't, so my cousins can be kind of annoying sometimes. I take it you're a mage?"

Zoe hid her surprise. For some reason, she hadn't expected someone who was not a mage to know about magic. But then that didn't really make sense. She shook her head to clear her thoughts.

"Okay, well that makes things easier. Yes, I'm a mage, I'm an Elemental."

Andrews eyebrows went up and he looked over at Jessica.

"Me, too. I'm a Water mage." she smiled.

"Since you're familiar with mages, this will be a lot easier," Zoe went on. "I'll get right to the main thing. I created a wall of Air and Water around the committee and excluded Carolyn at the beginning of the meeting, and she felt it. I haven't gotten close enough to her to know for sure, but I'm thinking she's a mage. Obviously, I don't know what Element. I also don't like that she appears to be best friends with the president, especially after what happened last semester."

Andrew's eyebrows rose again. "I heard about some of

that from my uncle. He heard the name of the college and let me know. Was Carolyn involved in raising the demon? I mean, she was here last semester."

"Word travels fast," Jessica noted. "No, she wasn't involved. At least, not that we know of. She wasn't at the fountain when we fought the demon. I'm pretty sure I'd've remembered that red hair."

Andrew nodded. "Okay. Yeah. Well, you asked me if I'd ever had to deal with her before. We were both on one of those task forces put together at the beginning of the fall semester to start figuring out a process for the process for dealing with accreditation review. Totally exciting committee." He grimaced. "But she went all in, proposing all kinds of overly complex and really unnecessary ways of measuring teaching impact, learning goals, that sort of thing. For somebody with no tenure and no prospects of it, she's sure acting like a full professor holding an endowed chair."

Zoe stared at him. "Why would she care about that?"

"I think she knew it would bring her to the attention of the provost and the president. And, it did," Andrew answered.

"Yeah, no kidding. Now we just have to figure out why," Jessica sighed. "Here we go again."

Chapter Four

Zoe spent the next couple of days mulling over Carolyn's comments and actions during the committee meeting. One early morning found her curled up on the sofa, sipping coffee and gazing out her front window. What the hell was going on? This semester had started quietly enough. That was clearly not going to continue. A few conversations with Mark and the others about Carolyn's end goal had come up empty. An hour of fruitless worry later, Zoe reluctantly concluded that she had run out of excuses for avoiding grading those draft research papers. She wandered back upstairs to get dressed and go into campus to face down the dreaded papers.

Sitting in her office, deep into the long-avoided grading, Zoe's concentration was broken by a knock on her door. She looked up to see Declan hovering in her doorway.

"Hi, Dr. O'Brien. I-I know it's not your office hours, b-but...um...can I talk to you for a minute?"

"Sure, Declan. Come on in." Zoe kept her tone calm. If Declan was stuttering, he was nervous. She hoped it was normal schoolwork problems and not magical issues, but the odds of that were low.

Declan cast a nervous eye down the hall toward

Meredith's office. "Is-is Dr. Cruikshank in today?"

"No, she's not. And, I'm really sorry I didn't check to see if she was here last time. I'm hoping she's finally realized that sabbatical means you don't need to come to campus every day. Come in and have a seat." Zoe was in complete agreement with the relieved expression that crossed Declan's face. Life was a lot less stressful when Meredith was not on campus.

Declan gave a shy smile, closed the office door after himself, and moved to the nearest of Zoe's guest chairs.

Zoe returned his smile. "How are things going?"

"They're good. Mostly. I like working with Dr. LeGrande. He pushes me, but it ends up being a good thing."

"That's good. It's always good to stretch yourself and get out of your comfort zone. But I'm guessing that's not why you dropped by." Zoe had discovered that direct questions and statements were the best way to get Declan to talk.

"No, you're right. I m-mean, I like talking to you…um…but I think something's going on." he dropped his eyes, and Zoe figured he was twisting his hands together. It was a nervous habit they shared.

"What do you mean? Has something happened?" Was this connected to Carolyn? And what was she up to?

"Well, yes. Um…not to me specifically, I don't think…but I was there…actually all of us were…um…" Declan was clearly nervous and that was making Zoe nervous again. She made a small rolling gesture with her hand to encourage him to keep going.

"Well…um…I was hanging out with…um…Josh and the others. It was after dinner last night. We were heading back to the dorms from the dining hall. And…um…like you know where those trees are, like along the path? Um…well, we were like…sort of in the middle of that line of trees when there was like a snapping, cracking sound and a giant branch landed on the path right by us. Josh and I were in front and Annmarie and Geoff were walking behind us. The branch fell between them and us and…um…scared the heck out of all of us." He finally looked up Zoe.

"Holy shit! Sorry…" She tried not to swear in front of students. Declan gave a small smile and waved a hand to show he wasn't bothered.

"Was there anybody else around? Did you tell anybody? Do you think it was supposed to hit you guys?" Zoe's questions poured out.

As if finally trusting that she was taking him seriously, Declan gazed directly at Zoe. "No, there was nobody around, and no we haven't told anybody else yet. Since I only have one class today, we decided that I would come talk to you. And…um…yeah, we think it was supposed to hit at least some of us. Geoff and Annmarie had slowed down a bit because Geoff was showing Annmarie something on his phone. If they hadn't slowed down, the branch would have landed right on them."

Professor and student stared at each other working through the implications of Declan's story.

A loud tapping on the window caused them both to jump. Zoe spun around in her chair to see Rowantree and Alder sitting on the small ledge outside the window. Declan's eyes went wide, but he didn't say anything.

Zoe went to the window and opened it, letting in a blast of cold air. She lifted the screen and the squirrels jumped from the window sill onto her desk. Zoe quickly closed the window to keep the warmth in. Declan stared wide-eyed at the squirrels sitting upright on her desk.

"Declan, this is Rowantree and Alder. They are part of the group of Watchers on campus. Rowantree, Alder, this is Declan Jin, one of my students," Zoe made introductions.

"Ah, you are the half-djinn. It is very nice to finally meet you," Rowantree inclined his head politely. Alder nodded at

Declan.

"Um...very n-nice to m-meet you, too," Declan muttered, still staring. Zoe recognized the small movements in his arms as a sign that he was twisting his hands again.

"I don't know if I ever told you, Declan, but Rowantree and Alder were the ones who first told me about the cloud around Shelby last semester and the coven that Susan Barker started. That's what they do. They're Watchers. Has Dr. LeGrande told you about them?" Hopefully, Simon had given the kid some basic information.

"Y-yeah, he did, I guess. I just never really thought about it." Declan seemed to relax a little bit.

"As I said, it's very good to finally meet you. And I'm glad you're here with Dr. O'Brien. You can pass on my information to the other young ones." Rowantree was a diplomat. Small, fuzzy, and cute, but a diplomat nonetheless.

The squirrel turned to Zoe. "Last week I told you about the wrongness we felt moving about campus. It is still here, and it appears to be concentrated in Harris Hall, although it also shifts around campus. I am not sure where in the building exactly, but I am positive it is tied to that building." Rowantree cocked his head at Zoe.

Alder nodded. "I have felt it most strongly there too. I have also felt it in the Big Building, the one you call Shelby Hall. It is not as strong there as it is in Harrison Hall, but it is stronger there than other places on campus. It appears to be anchored in both locations." He bobbed his head again and clasped his paws in front of him.

"Yeah, I think it's Carolyn Detweiler. She's in the psychology department and they're in Harrison Hall. I had an encounter with her a couple of days ago in a meeting." Zoe told the squirrels about Carolyn's reaction to Zoe's wall in the committee meeting.

Rowantree cocked his head and stared at her. "Yes, that

does seem most likely. Her actions indicate one who is trying to cause problems in both the magical and non-magical worlds."

Zoe nodded. "Yeah, she's certainly playing faculty politics. She's totally in with the president. I just wish we could figure out why. Well, why beyond faculty power." A sudden thought occurred to her. "Did you feel any magic working last night around...seven?" she glanced over at Declan. He nodded.

Rowantree and Alder shared a look. "Yes, we did and it had the feel of the dark magic, but we could not locate the source. What happened?" Rowantree asked.

Zoe nodded to Declan. He took a deep breath and told the squirrels the story he had just relayed to her.

When he finished, Rowantree cocked his head at Declan. "Young one, please think back to the moment before the branch fell. Did you feel anything odd or off?"

Declan stared at Rowantree. He closed his eyes for a moment. When he opened them his face took on a thoughtful expression.

"I think I had a small...um...premonition? Um...like, something odd was about to happen, but it was really small, so I didn't really pay any attention to it. Do you think I felt the magic or um...intention to use magic to break the branch?" Zoe had to remind herself that Declan was high strung, not unintelligent. He'd picked up on the reason behind Rowantree's question before she had.

"We understand that you are also the child of one gifted with the Sight. That means that you are likely able to feel magic as it's working if not right before. This gives you an advantage over others," Alder spoke up and directed a grave look to Declan.

Declan swallowed hard. "Yes, sir. I will pay attention more." Alder nodded once.

Rowantree turned back to Zoe. "Unlike last semester, we are able to move freely about campus. This magic is not painful as was the cloud over Shelby Hall, but it is dark. We would advise the mages to remain alert. I believe the tree branch was just the beginning." The squirrel's voice took on a note of gravity. Zoe was reminded once again that while he might sound like Alvin the chipmunk, Rowantree was anything but flighty.

Zoe nodded her understanding along with Declan, and Rowantree and Alder moved toward the window. She stepped over and opened it for them. Another nod, and the two squirrels jumped on to the ledge and scampered down the roof. She closed the window and turned back to Declan.

"Well, that was interesting, and adds to our confusion," Zoe commented sitting down.

"Um…yeah…um…like what did they mean by dark magic, Dr. O'Brien?" Declan's voice was hesitant.

"I believe that whatever the squirrels are feeling here on campus, and it's highly likely it's Professor Detweiler, is evil, or at least has bad intentions," Zoe replied. "Declan, what exactly did you feel right before the branch fell?" She worked to put the pieces together in her mind.

"Um…well, it felt like…um…a small push or surge…you know how sometimes you can tell that somebody is watching you? Like that, I guess," he sounded puzzled.

"So, you know what you have to keep an eye out for, so to speak. And maybe not walk directly under any more trees…" Zoe trailed off as a memory surfaced. Somebody in the coven last semester had managed to dislodge bricks from the façade of Davis Hall intending to have them fall on her head. "Don't hang around under any brick overhangs or balconies or anything like that either," she added.

Declan looked alarmed and nodded. "Okay. Do you think the branch was meant to hit me or just any of us?"

"I'm not sure. There seem to be a few things starting to move around. And, the president knows that Josh, Annmarie and Geoff are mages and probably thinks you are one too. I just don't like it." Zoe shook her head.

"Should I tell Dr. LeGrande?" Declan hesitated.

"If you feel like it, sure. But everybody will need to be told anyway. Is there some reason why you wouldn't?" Zoe tried to hide her surprise at the question.

"No…it's just…um…well, like…um…I guess…um…I just don't like to tell him everything…like, what happens between me and my friends doesn't affect my magic." Declan's words were rushed.

Zoe raised an eyebrow. "Okay, I see. It's no big deal. And, you're right, you get to have a private life. But I'm going to have to tell the faculty mages about the tree branch and what the squirrels just told you and me. That way the big bits are covered and you don't have to feel any pressure to tell Dr. LeGrande about your conversations with your friends. This is affecting all of us, after all."

Declan smiled shyly. "I know. I'll figure it out. Thanks, Dr. O'Brien. I gotta go. I'll tell the others to be careful and tell them about what the squirrels said." He stood up and opened the door. Stepping through, he glanced back at her.

"No, leave it open, thanks," she answered the unspoken question. "I'll talk to you later. And text me if anything comes up."

Declan disappeared down the hall and Zoe heaved a sigh. It was looking more and more like this semester was going to be as exciting as last semester. Yay.

She pushed the stack of research paper drafts aside and pulled a pad of paper towards her. This time, though, she was going to do her damnedest to keep track of things so that she didn't feel like she was running around like a headless chicken. *Do they really run around headless? That's a disturbing image.*

Putting pen to paper, she wrote down everything she could remember from the committee meeting along with what Declan had told her about the tree branch, and what Rowantree and Alder had said. If she thought of this as a research project that needed to be mapped out, it helped to organize information and see if any patterns appeared.

* * *

The next morning Zoe sat in yet another committee meeting nursing a large cup of coffee, this time discussing upgrading the technology in the classrooms. One of the negatives of teaching in a small college was having to sit on a number of committees. But one of the benefits of a small college was that there was almost always somebody else you not only knew, but liked, on any given committee with you. In this case, she was grateful that Mark was on the same committee representing the political science department – very grateful because Carolyn Detweiler appeared to be on this committee as well. How and why somebody listed as an assistant professor of teaching was on so many committees were two more items Zoe added to her growing list of questions about Carolyn.

Not long into the meeting, Zoe was writing notes when she felt something push against the light wall of Air she had erected around herself as soon as she saw Carolyn in the meeting room. Without looking up from her notes, she sent out a thin tendril of Air towards Carolyn who sat across the table and a few seats to Zoe's left. Sure enough, the sensation of something off, something not quite right, came back. Zoe nudged Mark with her foot. He had also raised a shield when he saw Carolyn. He nodded and Zoe felt and saw him sending out a small thread of Air of his own.

Zoe finished writing her notes and glanced over at Carolyn. The glare she received in return would have melted glaciers if there were any nearby. Zoe had just verified her own feelings about Carolyn and found the source of Rowantree's campus-roving evil.

As they left the meeting, by unspoken agreement Zoe and Mark walked quickly back to Zoe's office as it was the closest. Once in her office with the door closed, they turned to stare at each other.

"Well, I think a number of questions just got answered," Mark spoke quietly.

"Yeah, but a lot more questions just appeared as well. Now we just need to figure out what exactly she's after and why," Zoe responded. "And, why she's such good buddies with the president. That's what I really don't like," she added.

"Have there been any other attacks or attempted attacks on students or faculty?" Mark asked.

"I only know of the one against Declan and the others. Have you heard anything else?" Not that she wanted there to be more attacks, but Zoe had been feeling twitchy the last couple of days.

"No. But I'm going to ask around. Something may have happened that got dismissed because it seemed like it was a genuine accident. Until we figure this out, I'm going to assume that there's no such thing as an accident. Be careful when you're walking around campus or dealing with electronics, or even driving. I'm not sure why Carolyn wants us out of the way, but I'm getting the feeling that there are very few limits to *what* she'll do to achieve that." Mark's tone was grim.

Zoe swallowed and nodded. She still hadn't gotten used to this idea that magical fights could get deadly. *You fought an actual demon last year and a woman lost her life and another one lost her mind. Start dealing.*

"I'll try to get a hold of George. Or at least talk to Sarah this weekend so she can tell him. He's been hard to find lately. I think he's getting buried in administrative provost-type stuff," she sighed.

"Good idea. We need him to be paying attention. Between him and Simon, they have the most knowledge and more experience than the rest of us," Mark agreed.

"Should we see if we can get the others, maybe including the students, to get together for a happy hour or something like that at the Faire Mount?" Zoe's neighborhood pub had become a meeting place of sorts for the mages in the run up to the fight against the demon. She was happy the pub seemed to be the unofficial headquarters of what she had come to call the Faculty Mage Committee. The Faire Mount was only a few blocks from her house which meant she didn't have to worry about drinking and driving, or worse, hunting for parking when she got home in the evening.

"Another good idea. You are just brimming with good ideas today." Mark laughed. "I'll find out what David's schedule looks like and I'll talk to Robyn and Jessica," he added.

Zoe smiled. "Why, thank you! Josh, Annmarie, and Declan are in my class tomorrow, so I'll let them know and I'll text Sarah and tell Kieran when I see him tonight. Will you tell Simon?"

"Oh, yeah. We have a department meeting tomorrow, so I'll talk to him then." Mark stood up. "Okay. I've gotta get some more grading done and then I'm going home. I'll see you tomorrow."

THUD. CRAAAACK.

The sudden sounds came from outside. Zoe jumped up and looked out the window. Mark joined her. Nothing seemed out of place on the quad below, but...

"I can feel something, can you?" Zoe asked.

"Yes. I don't like it. Let's go," Mark's voice was tight.

Zoe grabbed her keys and phone and the two of them ran downstairs and out of the building. Mark paused and Zoe could see him sending out a burst of Air seeking the source of the sounds. She needed to get better at that sort of thing.

"Over there! The parking lot behind Shelby." He started running toward the administration building. Zoe had to sprint to keep up.

Another loud *crack* reached them as they rounded the building. Standing a couple hundred yards into the parking lot were Simon LeGrande and Declan Jin. Facing them, her back to the path Mark and Zoe were on, was Carolyn Detweiler. Simon looked exhausted and angry, while Declan appeared badly frightened. There was a thin wall of Fire in front of Simon and Declan.

Zoe immediately threw a wall made from all four Elements in front of Simon and Declan. Carolyn spun around and Mark threw a stream of Air, like water from a fire hose straight at her.

Simon made a frantic gesture to Zoe and yelled "Balefire! She uses balefire!"

"Oh, shit!" Mark exclaimed. "Zoe, make it so Simon can get to her and put a wall between her and us!"

Puzzled and frantic, Zoe did as Mark ordered. Fire streamed out of Carolyn's hands toward Mark and Zoe. The flames had a strange black ring around the edges.

"Use the other three Elements together! Like a blanket! No Fire! It's balefire, you can't put it out with just water!" Mark exclaimed.

Not really certain what he meant, Zoe nevertheless did as he asked. She gathered Air, Water, and Earth rapidly creating a shield between Carolyn and herself and Mark. At the same time, Simon threw Fire at Carolyn from behind, but it seemed to bounce or slide off her and die. Watching that failure, Zoe curved her wall so it encircled Carolyn. Carolyn was now enclosed in a three-Element cylinder.

The black-tinged balefire hit the inside of Zoe's cylinder and lashed back towards Carolyn. She screamed in fury and made a slashing motion with one hand. The fire disappeared. Before she could do anything more, Declan pointed his right hand at her and made a strange throwing gesture with his left. Carolyn vanished.

Panting from the exertion of running and the energy expended fighting Carolyn, Zoe could only stare at Declan as he and Simon slowly walked toward her and Mark.

"It's okay, D-Dr. O'Brien." Declan was still shaking. "I-I just sent her b-back to her office."

"Simon, what happened?" Mark's voice was tight and low.

Simon looked up at Mark and mustered some of his usual bouncy nature. "My dear boy, we were caught off-guard. She attacked us." His head drooped, and he leaned against the nearest car.

"We're going back to my office," Mark announced, putting a hand under Simon's arm and helping him stand up straight. Simon took a deep breath and straightened out his jacket before nodding and slowly starting in the direction of Davis Hall.

Chapter Five

ONCE BACK IN MARK'S OFFICE, Zoe pulled bottles of water from his small refrigerator and handed them out. Simon collapsed into the nearest guest chair and drank half of the bottle before setting it on Mark's desk and lowering his head into his hands.

"Simon," Mark's voice was gentle. "What happened? Are you hurt?" He turned to Declan. "How do you feel?"

"I-I'm okay," Declan stuttered a bit, but Zoe noted that while his hands were shaking, it was very slight compared to what she'd seen before when he was nervous.

Simon drew a deep shuddering breath.

"Well, my boy, I have learned a harsh lesson for myself today, but no, I am not hurt. Simply exhausted." He sounded subdued and stared down at his feet in their shiny wingtip shoes.

"I-I should go. I promised Annmarie and Josh I would meet them to study for an exam," Declan said softly.

"Please stay a moment. I owe you an apology as well, young man," Simon's voice dropped. "I assumed that I was the strongest mage on campus and best equipped to teach you. I have spent decades studying everything I could find regarding mages, Elements, and of course, Fire. Today I was badly beaten." He glanced up at Zoe and Mark. "If you two had not come along when you did, I am afraid that young Declan and I would not have survived that woman's attack. For that I am grateful. Declan, I apologize for putting you in that situation." Simon dropped his head back into his hands.

"Simon…"

"Dr. LeGrande…"

Mark and Declan spoke at the same time. Mark gestured for Declan to go ahead.

"Dr. LeGrande, y-you didn't p-put me in any 'situation'. We were p-practicing and experimenting with my p-power when she showed up. You didn't know she would sh-show up…a-and attack us." Declan stared unseeing at his twisting hands.

"Simon, don't beat yourself up. Zoe and I only confirmed today, about an hour ago, that Carolyn Detweiler is definitely the source of the dark magic Rowantree and the others have felt stalking around campus." Mark's eyes held sympathy but also something close to an "I told you so" look. Zoe wondered if Simon's know-it-all attitude as a mage was reflected in his attitude as department chair. "She seems to be ramping her activities up quickly. And now we know she uses balefire. We just need to figure out what she's doing here and what she wants," Mark sighed.

Simon finally raised his head. "Well, my boy, the use of balefire does indeed confirm the hypothesis of her as the source of the dark magic. She is a Night Mage, a trafficker in the darker side of Elemental magic," he said with a shadow of his old tone creeping in.

"Why did she show up, Simon?" Zoe asked.

"I believe it is because she knows I am a Fire mage and that I have done a great deal of research into the uses and abuses of Fire," Simon paused, and a red flush suffused his face.

Zoe exchanged a glance with Mark, who shrugged. He didn't know why Simon was blushing either.

Simon took a deep breath. "I may have been, ah, shall we say, less than cautious, when discussing that research with Carolyn at one point in the fall semester."

Mark grimaced. "You were bragging, weren't you?"

Simon looked indignant and then sighed again. "Yes. Direct as always, Mark. I was showing off. She must have felt she could and should remove me from her equation."

"But how did she know where to find you today?" Zoe asked.

Simon shook his head. "I am not certain. Young Declan and I were just about finished with our practice session when she announced her presence by throwing a fireball at our heads."

It was Zoe's turn to shake her head. "Hopefully she's as tired as we are."

Simon nodded. "I believe using balefire and having to stop it were fairly big drains on her energy."

Zoe sensed a growing discomfort in Declan. "Guys, Declan needs to go meet the others so he can let them know what happened, as well as study for his exam."

"Yes, of course," Mark answered. "Thanks for dealing with Professor Detweiler, Declan, but be very careful. Please keep a shield around yourself all the time. I don't think she's going to hesitate to take you out if or when she sees you again. I'm not comfortable with you going around by yourself right now."

"I will, Dr. Davis. I'll be okay. Luckily, I don't have her for class." Declan's voice was soft. "And, thank you, Dr. LeGrande. If it's okay with you, I'd like to keep working with you to figure out my power." He barely raised his eyes to glance at Simon.

"My dear boy, of course. I'm honored. Thank you for your

trust," Simon responded with more spirit than he'd shown a moment earlier.

Zoe followed Declan as he slipped out of the office. "Declan, wait a sec," she called softly.

He turned around. "I really am okay, Dr. O'Brien."

She frowned. "Okay, I'll take your word for it. But I need to know what you did to Professor Detweiler…besides send her back to her office."

"That's it. I just sent her back. Dr. LeGrande and I have been practicing with my power to see what exactly I can do. One thing I figured out really fast is that I can move things or put them any place I want." Declan sounded more confident than Zoe had ever heard him.

She cocked her head and smiled at him. "You've come a long way since last fall. I've very happy to see that."

Declan blushed. "T-thank you, Dr. O'Brien." Zoe winced internally. She didn't want him to revert to his old constantly nervous self.

She smiled. "But what I meant was, is she just sitting in her office now?"

"Oh. Y-yes. Um…I didn't want to do anything else. I-I'm…um…still trying to figure out how strong I am. D-Dr. LeGrande says I need to be careful." Declan stared at his feet.

"Declan. It's okay. You did the right thing. And, we're all glad you did. Just keep an eye out for her and be careful if you see her. Tell the others as well." She smiled again. "I'll see you in class tomorrow."

"Okay. Thanks." Declan turned and headed down the hall.

Zoe went back into Mark's office.

"Aside from obviously thinking he's indestructible, Declan says he really did just send Carolyn back to her office. So, we can assume that we now have an extremely surprised, and very angry, Carolyn sitting in her office. Hopefully, she doesn't come marching back over here," Zoe reported.

Simon looked up at her. "She uses balefire. That is a serious problem. On the other hand, because she used it just now, I believe she will need time to recover. We, and Declan, should be safe for the time being." He dropped his head back down into his hands.

Zoe glanced at Mark. "What exactly is balefire? I saw that your Fire, Simon, looked like it slid right off her. How did that happen?"

Mark ran a hand through his hair. "Balefire is a type of fire that always burns and cannot be put out. You saw that black around the edges of the flames? That's how you know it's balefire. It can be blocked with a combination of Elements, like what you did with your wall, but as you probably noticed that takes a lot of energy…what did you do, anyway?"

"When you yelled, I made a wall with Earth, Air, and Water. Then I made it into a sort of cylinder around her. I didn't expect her balefire to bounce back at her. I was just hoping I could stop it from reaching us or Declan and Simon," Zoe answered.

"Well, my dear lady, you have indeed saved the day, so to speak." Simon was slowly regaining his usual bouncy attitude, albeit with a little less cockiness.

Zoe nodded her thanks. "But you still haven't really answered my question. Can any Fire mage use balefire? How does she use it?"

Simon shook his head. "No. As you know, this power we have is simply a tool. It is neither good nor bad. However, when one uses power to hurt others simply for the sake of hurting them, or to gain personal power at the expense of others…that way is, as they say, the road to hell. Carolyn has likely used her power to advance her career which would bring her closer to the path leading to access to balefire. It also attracts the attention of creatures that are best avoided…like the demon we encountered last semester. Balefire exacts a deep cost, at the level of one's soul, every time it is used. She went too far either purposefully or was lured. Either way, she has trapped herself and will be unable to return. It's like being addicted to heroin. You need more and more. It's never enough. Until it kills you." Simon's voice was at once sorrowful and hard.

Zoe sat down hard on the windowsill. Oh, shit. "Why is she here? What is she doing? What or who is on our campus that she wants? I mean, magically? Are we the X in 'X marks the spot'?"

Mark was scrubbing his face with his hands. "I don't know. I don't know what, if anything, is here. Do you?" he looked at Simon.

Simon stared at his hands. "I regret to say that I have not spent as much time learning about my surroundings – aside from the power locus in the fountain in the city – as perhaps I should have. I do not know of anything here on campus or close by. George would know better than I anyway, as he is an Earth mage and an historian."

Mark glanced at Zoe. "George. What's he doing anyway? I mean, I know that the provost job is busy, but you would have thought he'd at least check in every now and then to see if anything was going on. I mean, after last semester…" his voice trailed off.

Zoe shrugged. "I don't know. I can drop by his office tomorrow and see if I can talk to him. If I can't, I can at least see what Sarah knows."

Simon lifted his head and turned to Zoe. "Yes. Please do so. I believe that George will react better to you than he would to me. I must admit, we have a bit of a history between us that might cause him to be, shall we say, less than immediately receptive to any concerns I might bring up."

Zoe raised an eyebrow, but nodded. "Then I'll make sure

I stop by tomorrow at some point. He needs to know about what happened today. I'll let you guys know what he says."

The next day, Zoe detoured through Shelby Hall on her way back from her afternoon class.

"Hi, Zoe! I haven't seen you in a while. How are you doing?" Sarah greeted her.

"Hi, Sarah. I know. We need to get together for a beer soon! If you're around this weekend, let's figure something out. Um, I actually came by to see if George is around and available? There's a couple things going on that he needs to know about." Zoe felt a little guilty about not seeing Sarah more frequently. They didn't live that far away from each other after all.

"That would be great! I am around. I'll text you and we can figure something out." Sarah paused to glance at the calendar on her computer. "George is...um...where...oh, yeah. Meeting until five this afternoon, and then a senior admin staff meeting with the president until six. He's been swamped lately."

Sarah's office phone rang, and she glanced at the caller ID.

"Damn. I need to take this, I've been waiting for an answer all day." She looked up at Zoe apologetically.

"Oh, okay. Well, I'll send him an email or text him. All right. Text me this weekend. Let's make sure we really do see each other!" Zoe gave Sarah a quick hug and left the office. Hopefully, she would see Sarah this weekend, since it now appeared that getting to George would require interrogating Sarah outside of the office. What was going on with him anyway? Had he really gotten so caught up in the administrative side of the provost position that he was completely ignoring all things magical? She shook her head.

Back in her own office, Zoe pulled out her notes from the committee meeting where she had first encountered Carolyn.

She read them over and decided she could quit beating herself up about missing anything. Yes, Carolyn was nasty and yes, she had apparently felt Zoe's shields but there had not been any indication that she would attack people so directly. Zoe pulled out a pen and added today's exciting developments to her notes. She also made a note to herself to speak with Moose and Flash when she got home that night. The cats had contacts within the network of Watchers and hopefully should be able to get more information.

She stared unseeing at her notes, trying to put the puzzle pieces together. Rubbing her hands across her face in frustration, she glanced at the clock. Oh, crap. There was still a large pile of grading sitting on her desk just taunting her. *Hell. I need to do that before I go home. Then I can get the cats to help with the magical problems.* Sighing, she put the notes in her bag, carefully tucking them into a zippered pocket. She found a red pen and pulled the stack of grading towards her.

Two hours of sustained concentration and intellectual pain later, she finished the last draft paper in the stack. She could go home with a clear conscience. Zoe packed up her laptop, grabbed some assorted research items, stuffed those into her bag, and headed out of the office. As she stepped out of the door of Cooper Hall, a crow cawed. Movement on one of the trees closest to the door caught her eye. Alder paused on the trunk of the tree, stared directly at her, and then ran down the tree and over to a corner of the quad that was sheltered by more trees. Zoe glanced around the area and then moved over to the same corner.

"What's going on?" she quietly asked Alder as she moved under the trees.

The crow flew into the tree and perched on the lowest branch. He turned his head to eye Zoe and dipped his head once in a nod of greeting. Zoe recognized Darkwing, the crow whose mate had died from the noxious cloud created by the coven in Shelby Hall. She politely returned the nod.

"We," Alder began, waving a paw to indicate Darkwing and himself, "have been tracking the one called Carolyn Detweiler. She is the source of the dark magic we have felt stalking the campus…"

"You must stop her quickly," Darkwing interjected.

Alder shot a sideways glare at the crow, but simply continued. "The crow is correct. She must be stopped. She will most likely attempt to destroy all who stand against her."

Zoe's mouth fell open. "Destroy?! Why?? What is she after? What the hell does she want? We figured she was the dark magic, but what is she doing?"

Darkwing bobbed his head, a somewhat incongruous movement for an intimidating bird. "Power. What else is there?"

"Okay, but power from where? Us? I still don't get it." Zoe's stomach knotted up and her hands started to shake. How did you fight someone when don't know their goal?

"She is drawing power from here." Alder waved a paw to include the entire Summerfield campus. "There is a source somewhere. We have felt vague hints. We do not believe she has fully tapped into this power source, but Rowantree believes that is only a matter of time."

Zoe stared at the squirrel. "So, there's an unknown power source somewhere on campus, the crazy psych prof is accessing it somehow, but not fully, and we need to stop her. Oh, and she's attacking mages, including students, so we need to watch out for that as well." She took a deep breath to damp down the panic that was threatening to overwhelm her.

"What do you mean attacking you?" Darkwing tilted his head and fixed her with one beady eye.

"I told you about the students who had a tree branch dropped on them, right? Well, on top of that, Declan, the half-djinn, and Simon were attacked in the parking lot this morning. Mark and I heard it and felt it…didn't you?" If the squirrels could feel the dark magic, they should have felt the attack, shouldn't they? Zoe felt a headache starting to form. She quickly filled Alder and Darkwing in on the attack by Carolyn. The squirrel and the crow listened intently.

"We, Mark and I, had just figured out for sure that she was the source of the dark magic, but that attack showed that she uses balefire. Which according to everybody is very, very bad." Zoe rubbed her hand across her face and finished her story. She really needed to go home, sit on the sofa, and have a glass of wine.

Alder cocked his head. "No, we did not feel that. I do not know why. Balefire. I do not like that. I will speak with Rowantree about all of this." He glanced over at Darkwing. "Will you please bring this information to your murder?" Darkwing bobbed his head in the affirmative, jumped off the branch, and flew away.

Alder turned from watching the crow. "Please be careful, Zoe. Rowantree and I believe that you are the main target for this Night Mage." He turned and ran up the tree with no further explanation.

Zoe dropped her head into her hands and tried to collect her thoughts. She could barely remember what a normal semester felt like anymore. This was getting crazy. *Er. It's getting crazy-er.*

She slowly continued out to her car. Driving home she let her mind go blank and focused only on driving. She really didn't need to add a car crash to the mountain of problems piling up.

After circling her block three times, she finally found a parking spot around the corner from her house. Gathering up her bags, she trudged up the sidewalk.

"Hi, Zoe!" The voice came from behind her. Zoe turned

around to see her neighbor and Fire mage, Kim Smith, coming up the sidewalk.

"Hi, Kim. How are you doing?" Kim and a few other neighbors had helped Zoe and the faculty mages fight the demon on the winter solstice.

"I'm good. How about you? You look kinda tired," Kim said sympathetically.

"I'm okay, I guess. It's been a long week." Zoe made an immediate decision. "Do you have a few minutes? I'd like to run some stuff by you and see what you think." She gestured to her house in a vague invitation.

"Sure. Let me just drop my stuff at my place. I'll be over in a few." Kim's eyes were full of questions, but she didn't voice any of them.

"Great. I have wine." Zoe smiled and started up the steps to her front porch.

"Wine and interesting questions...works for me!" Kim laughed and headed up the street to her own house.

When Kim returned to Zoe's house a few minutes later, Zoe handed her a glass of wine and curled up in the armchair. Kim settled herself on the sofa. Flash and Moose wandered into the living room tails high. Flash jumped up on the arm of Zoe's chair and Moose plopped himself next to Kim. She rewarded the big grey cat with scratches behind his ears for his efforts.

"So, what's going on? More demon raising on campus?" Kim laughed.

"No, not this time. I almost wish it was," Zoe sighed. "It seems to be a combination of revenge, faculty politics, and magical power grabs." She sipped her wine. Flash and Moose sat up and stared at Zoe.

"Well, that sounds like fun. Gimme the run down," Kim grinned.

Zoe launched into the details of the last couple of weeks,

trying to keep everything in some sort of chronological order.

"So now George seems to be too busy to deal with things, Carolyn, the Night Mage, is running around attacking students and faculty, Simon is feeling guilty, and Declan and the students seem to feel that they're immune, or at least very well-protected. And I feel like I have a constant headache." Zoe ended her tale with another sigh.

"Well, going in reverse order, college students always think they're immune to everything. That's just them. I don't know Simon well so I can't say whether his guilt is deserved or not, but I'm going to go with deserved until and unless he shows otherwise. I'm more worried that this Carolyn person is attacking people in broad daylight and that George is too caught up in the usual academic politics. Why do you think this is revenge combined with academic politics?" Kim got everything out in her usual high-speed manner.

"Well, I wasn't aware of it last semester, but Carolyn was doing her absolute best to get the attention of the president…and now she's succeeded. Meredith Cruickshank, who was in the coven, is technically on sabbatical, but she keeps showing up on campus when she doesn't really need to be. And, now that George is provost, I think the president is trying to keep him distracted and out of her hair while she does whatever it is that she's doing. Or that Carolyn is doing." Zoe sighed again. "I was really hoping for a calmer semester."

Kim barked out a laugh. "There's no such thing as calm when you're dealing with mages. Especially power-hungry mages. Which, I'll tell you, since you're new to this whole thing, is not uncommon. When someone does get power hungry, they can cause a hell of a lot of trouble! And, I'm very worried that she's using balefire. That's bad, very bad."

"No kidding! What exactly is balefire? Simon said the ability to use it came from, using her power to purposely harm and doing it often? What exactly was he getting at?" Zoe hoped

Kim could give her some insights. She didn't really feel like pressing Simon any further.

Kim leveled a steady gaze at Zoe. "Well, yeah. Power is a tool, but there are aspects to each Element that can only be accessed with evil intent. Not trying to take out somebody who's trying to harm you or somebody else, and not even destroying something or somebody. But using that power for the *sole purpose* of causing harm. That intention attracts, shall we say, beings that are better left alone. Like your demon. So, in a simplistic way, I guess you could say, using the power of your Element simply because you like messing with people is what starts it. Do that often enough and you start to move further down that road all the while justifying your increasingly nasty actions to yourself. In the end, you have sold your soul for access to power."

Kim paused and looked out the front window before turning back to Zoe. "You're in a somewhat more precarious position since you are an Elemental mage. That opens you up to temptation more. I think that's why, at the fountain that night, George mentioned you needing to learn finesse. He doesn't want you falling into that trap."

Zoe swallowed. George himself had not mentioned the finesse idea again, at least not to Zoe's face, when he started tutoring her in using her power and she had pushed the idea away in favor of focusing on strengthening her power. The way Kim was looking at her now, she knew she needed to pay attention and actually learn finesse, better control, and her limits. Flash climbed onto her lap and Moose jumped off the sofa and leapt into Zoe's lap as well. She absent-mindedly petted both cats while her brain tried to wrap itself around the idea that not only could she be killed, Kim and Simon seemed to think that she had a soul that could be in danger. Her soul. She hadn't really given much thought to souls before.

Kim was still gazing at her. Zoe swallowed again. "I didn't

know that. How do I, can I, protect my, um, soul?"

"Learn your limits and stop yourself before you go beyond them and drain your power. Don't give in to the temptation of using your power to hurt somebody, or 'teach them a lesson'. Remember, power is a tool, *you're* the one who decides how to use it," Kim answered.

She went on. "Learning finesse, to use your term, means you will have better control, you won't let your emotions get the better of you. Remember at the fountain when you started hacking at the demon? Your rage almost got the better of you and you were ready to destroy everything in your path in the name of punishing the ones who hurt you. And, you have every Element at your call. You could be very destructive if you wanted to."

Zoe's stomach dropped and her heart sped up. "I never thought of that," she said in a low voice. "You're right. I need to grow up and figure out how to control this power."

Kim nodded. "Going into a blind rage can leave you doing things that you can't take back. Like hurting people just because you can. That's how you start down the path of harming yourself, your soul. That's why George was concerned about finesse. Like I said, it's a matter of control."

Zoe's stared at her lap where her hands twisted around themselves.

Kim reached over and gave her shoulder a squeeze. "You'll be fine. I know you haven't had much time to figure everything out, but you have a lot of friends who, I know, will help you."

Zoe looked up at her gratefully. "I've never heard of balefire before today…um…can I ask you…um…will you help me figure all this out? At least the Fire part?" She made a vague gesture meant to encompass everything that had happened in the last several months.

"Of course! But what happened with your tutoring with

George?" Kim smiled.

"Well, I think he's too caught up in the actual job description of the provost. I haven't really talked to him in a few weeks." Zoe felt guilty ratting out George, but she really needed some help. She glanced down at the cats who stared back unblinking.

Zoe looked back up at Kim. "So, thanks. Mark, David, and Kieran have been helping me with their Elements, but Simon is the only Fire mage and he's been…well…busy too…I guess…and um…well, I don't really like the idea of spending a lot of time with him, he's not in my department…" she trailed off.

Simon wasn't a bad person, but the academic hierarchy was asserting itself again and she simply didn't feel comfortable asking the chair of another department for help with a magical power. It just felt weird.

Kim nodded. "I get it. I'm more than happy to teach you. Most mages learn from their parents or other family members. But since you just now came into your power, you don't have that advantage."

"Thanks, Kim. I really appreciate it. You've made me feel much better." Zoe smiled at her neighbor.

"Great! Tell you what. Let's go grab a burger and beer at the Faire Mount and get you out of your own head."

"That's a great idea," Zoe said. Claws dug into her leg. "Ow! What?"

"You're not going anywhere until we get some food. We're starving!" Moose ended his complaint with a very pathetic mewl.

"Okay! Okay! I wasn't going to abandon you guys, you know," Zoe reassured the cats, although she was pretty certain they could have gotten their own food.

Kim snorted. "Moose, for a well-fed cat, you do a good imitation of starving!" She looked at Zoe. "Lemme just go grab my wallet. I'll be back in a minute."

Flash jumped down from the sofa, tail high.

"Well, if you only *fed* us, we wouldn't need to remind you that we *are* starving," he stated, marching with great dignity into the kitchen. Moose didn't respond, just leapt down and stalked after Flash.

Kim laughed and headed out the door.

Chapter Six

Sitting on her front steps waiting for Kim to return, Zoe sent a short text to Kieran to let him know their plans. His response was almost instant.

I was about to text you. I'm at Faire Mount. Escaped conference. See you soon.

"Oh, cool. I didn't realize he'd gotten away," Zoe muttered to herself, doing a little internal happy dance at the thought of seeing Kieran.

"You look happy. Get some good news while I was gone?" Kim walked up to Zoe's steps.

"Yes, as a matter of fact. Kieran just texted to tell me he's at the Faire Mount now. So, he'll join us for that burger and beer…if that's okay with you?" Zoe felt a little guilty expanding the group without telling Kim.

"That's great. I haven't seen him since the Great Demon Battle of Philadelphia." Kim laughed, her tone capitalizing the words.

"Are you guys seeing each other now?" She cast a sideways glance at Zoe as they strolled up the sidewalk.

"Yeah, sort of…I guess. For a couple of months now. How did you know?" Zoe felt her cheeks going red.

"You got a sort of giddy look when you told me he was at the pub. I took a guess." Kim smiled. "You work together, does that make it difficult?"

"Well, we're in different departments so that's a good thing. But, yeah, we're not exactly advertising it. It's not like we shouldn't be seeing each other...I don't know...I guess I just don't feel like letting everybody at school know. Mark knows, but he's not saying anything." Zoe was a little surprised at how much she was telling Kim, but it felt good to have somebody who *didn't* work at Summerfield to talk to.

"I get that. From what I can tell, things can get a little, well...incestuous on a small campus. I mean you guys spend a lot of time there, you do a lot of extra stuff. Your social circle gets kind of constrained." Kim's tone was thoughtful.

"Yeah, it does. I think at a bigger school it would be different, but at Summerfield we're all kinda stuck with each other," Zoe replied.

"And then your infighting spills over into the real world and the rest of us have to deal with your demons!" Kim laughed.

"On behalf of Summerfield College, I apologize for allowing our demons to run wild in the city. I can assure you it won't happen again." Zoe adopted a haughty tone and then burst out laughing with Kim.

When the two women entered the pub, they found Kieran sitting at a table in the bar area with a beer in front of him. He waved at Zoe as she and Kim moved over to the table.

"Hi Zoe, hi Kim." He smiled and gave Zoe's hand a squeeze. "Thanks for letting me barge in on your dinner."

"It's fine. Both of you can help me sort out some things." Zoe returned his smile.

"I'm happy to do that, but let's get you guys a beer and some food first. I know I'm starving after sitting through three panels today. But the conference is done now, so I'm drinking," Kieran answered.

"I like the way you roll," Kim said eyeing the menu the waiter put in front of her. "Ooh! A new IPA. I'll try that, and the pub burger, please."

"So, any more excitement on campus?" Kieran asked after the waiter had left with their orders.

"Excitement. I guess you could call it that…" Zoe said slowly. "I don't even know where to start. It's been a long day."

Kieran's face took on a worried expression. "Are you okay?"

"I'm fine. I'm just trying to process everything." Zoe paused while the waiter delivered their beers. She took a long drink before answering Kieran.

"Well, we discovered that Carolyn Detweiler, you know, the teaching prof in Psychology? Well, Simon says she's a Night Mage. She attacked him and Declan in the parking lot behind Shelby this morning. With balefire."

"Holy shit! A Night Mage? That's not good…and she using balefire out in public?!" Kieran exclaimed.

"You're not kidding. Zoe told me all this right before we came over here and I've been trying to wrack my brains to think of any other stories of Night Mages. I mean, I've known people who've gone bad, but this is an entirely deeper level of bad. It's evil," Kim commented.

A random thought struck Zoe. "Carolyn's a Night Mage and can use balefire. But what if she weren't a Fire mage to begin with? What if she were, I dunno, an Earth mage? Would she still use balefire? Or something else? Weaponized ornamental cabbages?" She giggled at an image of David lobbing his beloved plants at somebody he didn't like.

"Ha! Weaponized cabbages! Good one!" Kim laughed. "Well, balefire is unique to Fire mages. And, I think most Night Mages start out as ordinary Fire mages. I guess because Fire is seen as more destructive, and so more tempting to use it to destroy or hurt people," she mused.

"I'd probably use something like heavy water. But that kills slowly and it's not as spectacular as balefire," Kieran said slowly. "I've never really given it a lot of thought."

Zoe stared at him. "Simon said Carolyn's...gone down a path that will be difficult to reverse...is how he put it," she said in a small voice. She was still trying to grasp that idea on top of the visions of balefire that kept running through her head.

Kieran put his hand on Zoe's. "I'm not serious about the heavy water." He smiled gently. "But Carolyn *has* gone down a bad path." His voice was firm. "You don't get the ability to use balefire without paying an extremely high price. And to get there, you have been using your power to deliberately hurt people, just for fun and to give yourself more power in the non-magical world."

Zoe swallowed hard. Kieran confirmed what Simon had said. She had harbored a faint hope that Simon had been exaggerating and that Carolyn's powers were just average for a Fire mage. Kieran did not exaggerate like that. This was taking things into a realm she didn't really want to think about. Things were going beyond fairy tales coming to life. She didn't like this development but there wasn't anything she could do about it.

Kieran glanced over at Zoe and noticed the expression on her face. "Yeah, souls are tangible and definitely need to be taken care of and paid attention to. People forget that, given how secular everything is these days, but using magic teaches you that lesson." There was understanding in his eyes as he watched Zoe.

Kim put her hand on Zoe's wrist. "I know it's a lot to take in. But you can come talk to me about any of it."

"Me, too," Kieran added.

Zoe looked at the both of them. "Thanks, you guys. I'll be okay. I just need to think about everything. But you need to know the details of what happened today," She smiled at Kieran.

He took a long pull off his beer. "Fire away. I'm ready."

Fortunately for Zoe, the waiter appeared with their food right then, so she busied herself with the wonderfully good bacon cheeseburger for a couple of minutes before diving into the entire story in all its gory detail with only occasional pauses to take a bite of food or a sip of beer. Kieran and Kim listened closely and didn't interrupt. Once she'd finished, Zoe concentrated on eating her cheeseburger while the other two considered what she'd just told them.

"Do you think Simon and Declan were in real danger?" Kieran finally asked.

"I think so. I've never seen Simon so…well, quiet. He even apologized to Declan for putting him in danger. Oh, and he said that he was wrong about him, Simon, being the strongest mage on campus and the best suited to helping Declan. I mean, that's a hell of an admission coming from him, don't you think?" Zoe glanced at Kieran over the top of a French fry.

"Yeah, that's a good point," Kieran frowned.

"Did Simon tell you how they wound up in a position where they were attacked?" Kim asked.

"Declan mentioned that they were working in the parking lot when Carolyn appeared and started attacking them. I'm still not sure what happened before Mark and I got there. She must have surprised them, or Simon didn't have a shield up…or both. By the time we got there Simon and Declan were looking exhausted and it seemed like they were getting pushed back. When I made the wall, Simon threw Fire at her, but it fell off like water. It was weird. But that gave Declan enough time to send her back to her office," Zoe answered.

"Declan's the kid who's half-djinn, right?" Kim took a drink of beer, a thoughtful expression on her face.

"Yeah. And his mother has the Sight. He's got some

interesting magical combinations, I guess," Kieran told her.

"No kidding! I didn't know there were djinns on this continent, and I've never directly known a human who hooked up with one." Kim gave a short laugh.

Kieran looked at Zoe. "What do you think's gonna happen next? I mean, you know Carolyn won't let this slide. She's already tried to go after the students who helped us out last semester. It seems like she's going after everybody who was there…" he trailed off.

"What? You just thought of something. What is it?" Kim caught the look on Kieran's face before Zoe did.

"I'm…not sure," Kieran answered slowly. "The first day of the conference, so a couple of days ago, I was getting some coffee and the big urn they had it in tipped over when I pushed on the lever thingy. I managed to jump out of the way and only got coffee on my shoes. The hotel waiter who was there freaked out. He thought it must have been too close to the edge of the table and overbalanced. But, if I try to remember it, I see it sitting where you would normally expect it to sit on the table." He paused and stared at Kim and Zoe.

Zoe's mouth fell open. "Do you think that was on purpose?"

"From what you've just told me about her, I think it might have been a way to see how far away she could be and still control things," Kim answered her.

Kieran grimaced. "There was also something weird at home the other night. My downstairs neighbor said that she almost fell down the basement stairs when one of them gave way right as she stepped on it. It's a strong and well-built staircase. That shouldn't have happened. Crap. I need to ward the house. I just warded my apartment. I didn't think anybody would come after my neighbors." He sounded worried. Zoe knew Kieran lived in a converted row house. It had been turned into three apartments, one on each floor. Kieran lived on the third floor.

"Do you really think that the step breaking wasn't just an accident?" Zoe desperately didn't want to think about Carolyn coming after people at their homes.

"No. That staircase is strong. There's no wear, and nothing loose on it." Kieran was adamant. "There's no way it just fell apart." He picked at his fries and took another sip of his beer.

Kim polished off the last bite of her cheeseburger and wiped her hands with her napkin. "Zoe, don't forget that the coven tried to blow up our whole block last year. Worrying about innocent bystanders is not how people like that roll." She paused and looked at Kieran. "Kieran, I have something of an idea. Feel free to veto it, but this may help for at least the short term."

Zoe and Kieran looked at her curiously. "What is it?" Kieran asked.

"We're trying to avoid getting innocent bystanders caught up in a magical battle, right? Well, I have a small mother-in-law apartment in the basement of my place. It has its own entrance that opens on to the street and access to the back yard. What if you move in there? The place is already warded, you can add your own wards to the basement and you won't have to worry about innocent neighbors getting caught up in this Carolyn person's revenge attacks." She glanced at their faces. "I said you could veto it."

"Actually...that's not a bad idea...I like the idea of not worrying about the neighbors and basically consolidating our forces. You live just down from Zoe, right?" Kieran sounded thoughtful.

"Yeah, I'm four houses down. Um...yeah, the more I think about it, the more I like the idea, too," Zoe answered. Plus, it had the added bonus of Kieran living only four houses away instead of several long blocks away.

"I'm thinking the sooner you move, the better. At least for your neighbors. When's your lease up?" Kim gazed at Kieran over her beer.

"Luckily, I have a month-to-month now, so all I have to do is give thirty days' notice. I'm just worried about what else can happen in thirty days," he replied. "But I can ward my whole building…it's really just a row house, so that's not so bad."

Zoe glanced over at Kieran. "What if you just moved anyway? Like give notice, but move immediately?"

Before Kieran could say anything, Kim jumped in. "I think that's a good idea. I'm not making any money off the apartment right now anyway, so another month won't make a difference for me. Move now and start paying rent after the thirty days. That way you won't have to pay two rents." She smiled at both of them.

Kieran nodded. "Okay. If you're okay with that, I'll do it that way. Thanks, Kim. I do feel better. I like my neighbors, and I don't want them to get caught up in whatever crap is going down right now."

Kim grinned. "Besides, now you're closer to Zoe."

Kieran's eyebrows went up. "Well, yeah. Um…did you tell her we're together?" he turned to Zoe.

"No, actually. She guessed. She's pretty good at reading people." Zoe smiled. She didn't really care who outside of Summerfield knew she and Kieran were dating. She figured it wouldn't be too long before everybody inside of Summerfield knew anyway.

"Okay, new living arrangements are decided. What do we do about Carolyn and her balefire?" Kieran smoothly changed the subject.

The three of them discussed possible tactics and ways to gather information over a second round of beers. After about an hour they really hadn't made any progress except to agree to keep each other informed and Kim said she would contact Rob Andrews, an Earth mage, and Joe Chapman, an Air mage, who lived one block north of Zoe and also had helped fight the demon, and get their help.

They left the pub and continued the discussion for about a block before Kieran turned to go to his apartment.

"Okay, thanks for the offer of a place, Kim. I'll let you know when I'm ready to move." Kieran gave Zoe a quick kiss before turning up the street.

"I think you guys make a good couple." Kim smiled at Zoe as the two women continued walking.

"We've only been really dating for a couple of months. I'm not sure I'd call us a couple yet," Zoe protested.

"Still...you look happy," Kim replied.

"Yeah, I am." Zoe smiled.

"Well, having you both living on the block, means I can hit you up for some help with organizing this year's block party," Kim said with a smile.

"But, I don't know anybody!" Zoe protested. "I'm still new!"

"Oh, no, you don't get out of it that easily. You've been on the block for a couple years now, time to become a full-time resident of the best block in Philly!" Kim laughed.

BOOM! BOOM!

"Shit! What the hell was that?!" Zoe yelled, turning around. She could hear people yelling from the direction they just came.

"Crap! Kieran!" Kim stared at Zoe before spinning and running back the way they came.

"Oh my God!" Zoe ran the three long blocks back up to the intersection, her stomach churning.

Turning the corner where they had left Kieran, Zoe saw flames raging out of one of the row houses about two blocks up. She frantically pulled her phone out of her bag before she heard sirens approaching. Kim was well in front of her, racing up the street.

Zoe put all her energy into running, trying not to think about what she might find when they got closer to the house. She was certain it was Kieran's house. *Please God, let there be nobody home and we find Kieran standing on the street. Please.*

Gasping for air, Zoe almost ran into Kim when the other woman stopped. A police car that must have been in the neighborhood was blocking anybody from getting any closer to the house and Zoe heard more sirens approaching. She anxiously scanned the gathering crowd, breathing a sigh of relief when she spotted Kieran standing in front of the house. Three other people, two women and a man, stood with him. One of the women was clutching a frantically squirming cat while the man held a medium sized dog. Flames were shooting out the third floor windows where Zoe knew Kieran's living room was located.

Zoe tapped Kim on the shoulder and pointed. "Thank God. There he is, over there with the people holding the animals. I'm going to try to get over there." She shifted to start working her way through the growing crowd.

"Wait a sec." Kim grabbed her arm. "Take another look around and see if you see this Carolyn person here. I don't know what she looks like, but I'm guessing she's not that far away, if not right here so she can check her handiwork."

"You think she's here? That she did this?!" Zoe's voice turned into a squeak.

"Yes. I think she wants to make sure she was successful," Kim sounded grim.

Zoe glanced over at the other woman and then carefully scanned the crowd. It was hard to see anything past the flames, and the firetrucks obscured a great deal of the area. Wait. What was that? In the crowd on the other side of the house, it looked like there was somebody standing just away from everybody else and staying close to the shadow of the other houses, out of the circle of light from the street light.

Zoe grabbed Kim's arm and nodded her head in that direction. "See the red-headed woman standing in the shadow over there?"

"I see her. You sure?"

"Yes. Mostly. Maybe. But, I'm getting a strong feeling of...I don't know...malevolence? That sounds very dramatic, but that's the best word I can think of. I'm pretty sure it's her...that red hair," Zoe muttered.

"Okay. You go find Kieran. I think he's going to be moving in sooner rather than later, now. I'll keep an eye on our friend over there." Kim moved slightly to her right to get a better line of sight on Carolyn.

Zoe nodded and moved to go around the crowd and get closer to Kieran. She wormed her way through the people and got as close as she could without interfering with the firefighters.

"Kieran!" she yelled to be heard over the noise of the fire, and truck engines.

He turned around and she waved frantically, "Kieran! Over here!"

Kieran waved back and turned briefly to speak to his neighbors before heading over to Zoe.

Not caring who might see her, Zoe hugged him hard. "Oh my God! Are you okay? Are your neighbors okay? I mean, what the hell?" She knew she was babbling, but she couldn't stop herself.

Kieran returned her hug and kissed her on the forehead. "I'm fine and they're fine. Alex and Caitlin managed to get their dog and cat out, so we know we only have property damage. Of course, I think it's total property damage," he said gazing at what used to be his home. The firefighters had managed to control the fire before it spread to the neighboring homes, but Kieran's building was severely damaged. Zoe was reminded once again of the hazards of living in a row house...attached houses meant when one home caught fire, there was an extremely high chance others would go up as well.

Zoe pulled back and looked up at Kieran. "Kim and I spotted Carolyn over on the other side of the crowd," she told him, very carefully not looking in that direction.

"Why am I not surprised? Where is she?" he said, turning back to Zoe and not glancing around.

Zoe carefully glanced back at the spot where she'd last seen Carolyn. "She's gone now. She was over there, sort of off to the side and away from everybody else," she said softly.

Kim made a show of wandering over to them. "I think she's left. I'm betting she saw Kieran so she knows she didn't get him, but I'm guessing she thinks she at least sent a message. And obviously, she has zero scruples since your neighbors were home and she blew up the house anyway." She kept her voice low and glanced around the scene.

A police officer and another man wearing a white firefighter's helmet walked over to them.

"Excuse me sir, but I've been told you're the other resident of this building?" the police officer addressed Kieran.

"Yes, I am. I'm Kieran Ross. I live...er...lived on the third floor," Kieran answered.

The second man spoke. "Mr. Ross, I'm Nick Gutiérrez, the fire chief. Sir, I'm afraid the building is a not habitable...especially the third floor. We're opening an investigation into the cause of the fire, but you can come back tomorrow afternoon to see if there is anything salvageable. I'll give you a call when that's possible. I'm very sorry. Do you have some place to stay tonight? And, may I have your number so the fire inspector can contact you?"

Kieran looked over at Kim and Zoe. "Um...yeah, I think I can find a place to stay," he hesitated.

Kim nodded. "Yes. The basement apartment is clean and it has some furniture. I'll give you some sheets and towels."

Zoe hugged him. "You can stay at my place, too."

Kieran gave them both a relieved nod and turned back to the police officer and fire chief. He pulled a couple of business cards from his wallet and handed them to the two officials.

"My cell and my email are on there. My cell is the easiest way to contact me."

Chief Gutiérrez tucked the card into his shirt pocket. "Thank you very much. Just one more question. Do you have any idea how this fire might have started? It appears to have started in your apartment."

"No, I don't. We were out at dinner until just now," he answered indicating Zoe and Kim. Kieran looked puzzled. "Do you think a gas line exploded or something?"

"That's my likely guess, but we'll know more once my inspector finishes her report," Chief Gutiérrez responded. He shook Kieran's hand. "I'll contact you if I have any more questions." The chief walked back to his SUV.

"Thank you for your time, sir. I'm very sorry about this," the police officer said in parting.

"Thank you." Kieran sounded a bit lost as the reality of what had happened started to settle in.

"Are you okay?" Zoe asked as the two officials walked back to their respective vehicles. She wrapped one arm around his waist.

"I'm not sure. I'm having a hard time remembering exactly what I had right now, so I don't really know what I'm going to be most upset about." Kieran had a dazed air about him.

"Let's get you back to Zoe's house. I'll fix up the basement and then text you and you guys can come over and Kieran can get settled in." Kim took charge of the situation.

"Good idea. I have some beer in the fridge. We'll have one and then figure out what happens next," Zoe said.

"Okay. That sounds good." Kieran shook his head, trying to clear it. The three of them started down the street. Kieran reached for Zoe's hand.

Moose and Flash greeted them at the door of Zoe's house, pacing and clearly agitated.

"There was a huge wave of dark magic about an hour ago. Where have you been?" Flash yowled when they walked in.

"We know. Carolyn blew up Kieran's house," Zoe told them.

Both cats stopped in their tracks. "She blew up your house?" Moose looked up at Kieran.

"Yeah, we're pretty sure it was her," Kieran answered.

"Move, guys. We need beer and then we're going to figure out what's next. Don't worry, you'll be included in the discussions." Zoe pushed the cats gently to the side so she and Kieran could actually enter the house.

Once inside, she pointed Kieran toward the couch while she went into the kitchen to get the promised beers.

When she returned to the living room, she found Moose and Flash on the sofa head-butting Kieran who was absently petting them while staring into the fireplace.

"Hey. You okay, really?" she asked gently.

"Yeah, I guess. Just trying to wrap my head around everything." Kieran looked up and smiled at her.

Zoe shoved Flash aside and sat down next to Kieran. "Here." She handed him the beer. "I'm going to shift the focus and say, this means war. The fire is bad enough, but what if Carolyn had killed somebody? She obviously doesn't give a crap about who she hurts when she's trying to get to any of us. I mean, she was really trying to kill Simon and Declan the other day!" Zoe's nerves were getting the best of her, but she was extremely angry as well.

"I'm with you. This is war." Kieran put his arm around Zoe and kissed her. "Thanks for the support," he added, clinking his beer bottle against hers.

"Gack. I totally reek of smoke. I'm going to jump in the shower," Zoe stated, sniffing at her t-shirt.

Kieran sniffed at his jacket. "Blech. You're right."

"I have a couple of extra-large t-shirts if you want to take a shower too, and change clothes. I think there are also some of your clothes here," Zoe said.

Showered and in clean clothes they sat on the couch drinking beer and petting the cats. A short while later, a knock at the door announced the return of Kim. Zoe let her in and got another beer for her.

"I had to take a quick shower as soon as I got home. I smelled like a fire pit," Kim commented when she walked in.

"Us, too," Zoe told her.

"Okay," Kim started, sitting in the armchair and tossing a set of keys to Kieran. "I've managed to put together some semblance of a living space for you. I found an unopened toothbrush and some other travel toiletries, got towels, and made the bed. Later, we can look at some spare chairs and a table I have, and you can decide if you want them or not." She took a sip of her beer.

"Thanks, I really appreciate it, Kim. You've taken a lot of stress off of me," Kieran said.

"You still have your overnight bag." Zoe pointed to the bag sitting at his feet. "And, you have those jeans and a couple other t-shirts here."

"So, my wardrobe isn't a total loss," Kieran managed a grin.

"I just said there were clothes here. Your wardrobe is an entirely different matter," Zoe shot back.

Kim laughed. "But why do you have an overnight bag?"

"Oh, I had a really early panel this morning, so I stayed at the hotel last night. Makes it a lot easier…that seems like a long time ago now," Kieran answered.

"That makes sense. Do you have to teach tomorrow or the next day?" Kim asked.

"Yeah, day after tomorrow, but I might just cancel classes. I have a feeling this is going to be a mess to deal with." Kieran grimaced. "I don't like it since I've been at the conference for three days, but I don't think I'm going to be able to teach."

"I'm sure the department will understand. And, it's not as if the students will care," Zoe reminded him. "Put up a couple of videos and assignments for the videos and you're covered for at least one day."

"Good point," Kieran said. "I have a couple I was going to show in class this week anyway. I'll use those."

Kim looked at them both. "We need to talk about Carolyn. You just told me about her tonight, and now she's already blown up Kieran's building. Could she know that you guys are seeing each other? We have to assume that she knows pretty much everything else. You said she's got an in with the president, that means she has access to the information she needs. And that Meredith person is tracking everything Zoe does and likely feeding Carolyn information. She's moving fast."

Chapter Seven

Zoe thought back to the few in-person encounters she'd had with Carolyn. There'd been the committee meeting, and then the fight in the parking lot. Two extremes for sure, although Zoe figured the committee meeting could also be classified as a fight, if of a slightly different nature.

"She's power hungry. Both for academic power and magical power. But I think for her they're connected. Rowantree said there's something on campus that she's drawing from. But he doesn't know what it might be yet." She looked at the cats who were draped across Kieran's lap. "Do you guys have any idea about a power source existing on campus?"

Moose looked up from his intensive tail grooming routine. "Not that I know of, but we can ask around. Maybe the Air mage and the Earth mage can help." He went back to his tail.

Before Zoe could respond, Flash stepped into her lap. "Ask the Earth mage, the one that's partner to the Air mage, to go through some of the books he's collected. There might be something in there." He turned around and flopped down in a furry puddle.

Zoe raised her eyebrows and glanced at Kieran and Kim as she stroked Flash. "I guess we talk to Mark and David."

"Yep. Well, at least we have a place to start…along with avoiding Carolyn as much as possible," Kieran sighed.

Kim frowned. "I get the academic and magical power thing, but why is she at Summerfield and why is she trying to take you all out *before* she gets that power?"

Kieran stared at her. "I hadn't thought of it that way," he said. "I guess I just assumed power because that's what everybody in academia does…goes after power before they have any so that they can keep it and get more."

"Yeah. We're so wrapped up in the faculty politics stuff, that I think we're missing the magic end of things. She does seem to be going about it backwards," Zoe added.

"That's what's been bugging me. The squirrels think that there's a power source somewhere on campus that she's after. You do have a lot of mages on campus, maybe she wanted to take out some of the opposition?" Kim mused.

"Take out potential opposition, find and control this mysterious power source, and then what? Take over the world?" Kieran asked.

"Well, yeah. Or at least take over Philadelphia? Or let more demons in?" Zoe thought the "take over the world" reason sounded plausible. Carolyn seemed to have the ego for it.

Kieran and Kim appeared to be ready to spend the rest of the night discussing possible reasons for Carolyn's escalation of her activities. Zoe just felt the beginnings of a stress headache.

She glanced at the two of them. "We're not going to solve this tonight. Let's go over to Kim's house and check out the apartment. We'll figure out what to do tomorrow. We can talk to Mark and David and see what they have. I have to go to campus tomorrow anyway, so I'll find Mark." Zoe wanted to move instead of sitting around dwelling on things. If she focused on something else, she could let all the information settle into her brain and maybe make sense of it later. And stop the incoming headache. The adrenaline rush from the fire was wearing off and she knew she was going to want to collapse into bed sooner rather than later.

"Good idea. I'll show you the basics and you can let me know if there's anything else you need tonight," Kim agreed.

Grabbing her coat and keys, Zoe looked at the cats. "Do you guys want to come with us?"

"Yes. We can find some of the squirrels and talk with them." Moose ambled toward the door.

The three mages, trailed by the two cats, walked up the street to Kim's house. Zoe found she really liked the idea of Kieran living only a few steps away. She wasn't ready to have him move in with her right now, but this worked. She reminded herself that while he was probably okay with the new arrangement, it wasn't supposed to have happened like this. *He's just lost everything in a fire. Stop it.*

Standing in front of the street-level basement door, Kim gestured to Kieran. "The brass-colored key is for this door."

He pulled out the ring with three keys on it that she'd given him earlier and put the indicated key into the lock.

The cats pushed past the humans and, in the manner of all cats through time, strolled through the door like they owned the place. Walking into the small apartment, Zoe was surprised at how pleasant it was. While it was definitely small, it didn't feel cramped. The main area was open with a small kitchen along one wall. A short hallway led to the rear of the house with a bedroom, bathroom, and a small closet with a stacked washer and dryer. The end of the hall had a door into the back yard. Kim pointed everything out and opened the back door to show them the small patio just outside.

"This is your area, so feel free to use it." She smiled at

Kieran.

"Thanks, Kim. I'm still in shock I think, but I really do appreciate all of this," Kieran sounded bemused.

"Not a problem. The key with the sort of fatter shaft is the key to the back door and the last one is for the gate lock on the side that leads to the back yard. Other tenants I've had have used either the street door or the gate for an entrance." Kim paused. "But, given what's happened, maybe you should use the side and back. I think leaving by the side-gate is a little less obvious since it's between the houses and set back from the sidewalk. No point in making it easy for anybody to track you." She gave Kieran a thoughtful look.

Kieran shook his head. "As much as I hate the idea, you're probably right. Is it okay with you if I add my own wards to the apartment?"

"Of course. Just layer them on top of the ones I have on the whole house. I'm going to strengthen everything anyway," Kim nodded.

"Okay." Kieran was still gazing around with a slightly off-balance expression on his face.

Kim watched him for a minute. "Okay. I'll let you get settled and talk to you both in the morning." She gave Zoe a hug and walked to the back door. "Don't forget to lock up behind me," she called out. The door closed softly behind her.

Zoe turned to Kieran. "How are you doing?"

He reached out and pulled her into a hug. "I think I'm shellshocked right now. I'm very grateful to Kim, and we just talked about me moving here...but I didn't expect it to happen like this...I mean..." he trailed off.

"I know. You told me last semester that you'd seen some doozies of fights between mages...how does this rank?" She looked up at him.

He gave a short barking laugh. "Above anything I've seen so far!"

"I'm really sorry…" Zoe was about to say more, but an insistent head-butting against her calves reminded her they were not alone.

"What?" She looked down at Moose who was doing the head-butting while Flash explored every inch of the small living room.

"We're hungry. We need to go back to our den," Moose whined.

"Oh, for…" Zoe glanced at Kieran. "Will you be okay? Do you want to stay at my place tonight?"

He smiled. "I think I'll stay here to get used to it. I'll be fine…I'm just going to crash. But…um…can I come over for breakfast tomorrow? I don't think there's even any coffee here." He put on a hopeful expression.

Zoe laughed. "Of course! I can't let you face whatever tomorrow might throw at us without coffee! I'll text you when I'm awake and making the coffee."

"Thanks. I'm really glad you're here," he said softly, giving her a lingering kiss.

"Me, too." Zoe returned the kiss.

"What are you doing? We're hungry!" The plaintive meows came from the short hallway leading to the back door.

Zoe rolled her eyes. "Well, I guess that's my signal to leave."

Kieran frowned. "Are you going to be okay walking home by yourself? I mean, Carolyn did just burn my house down."

"I'll be fine. It's only four houses, and besides, I don't think these guys," she gestured at the cats, "will let anything get between them and their food. But I'll make sure I have a strong shield around us anyway," Zoe reassured him.

"Okay. Let's go out the back door like Kim suggested. That way I can make sure the gate is locked as well." Kieran pulled the small key ring out of his pocket. "This one, right?"

Once outside the gate and hearing the lock click home

behind her, Zoe paused and glanced up and down the street before she moved out into the open. Just like last semester when she was avoiding Meredith Cruickshank, she felt like she was living in a bad spy movie.

Moose and Flash did not do their usual wandering back and forth, but rather stayed on either side of Zoe as they walked back up the sidewalk. She noticed a small shape sitting on the front wall of the house just before hers. The squirrel raised a paw and nodded at her as she passed but didn't say anything. She felt better knowing there were a lot of friendly eyes and ears out and about. Once back in her own kitchen, she took care of the most important task and fed the cats. Feline death by starvation averted, she then reinforced her shields around the house, and finally collapsed into bed.

Waking up the next morning she opened her eyes to find orange fur filling her vision.

"Hey. Move." She shoved Flash off her neck. "What time is it anyway?" She rolled over to squint at the clock.

"The sun is up, and we're hungry," Flash announced, recovering his dignity at the foot of the bed.

"It's only six-thirty. It's not late and I don't have to teach today, and I don't have any meetings…I don't think. I'm pretty sure I can go in whenever," she retorted.

She shuffled downstairs and started the coffee, remembering to text Kieran while she was doing that. He replied saying he'd be over in about an hour. Good. That would give her time for a quick shower and to put on something resembling real clothing.

A little over an hour later, dressed in jeans and a comfortable sweater, coffee in hand, and bacon cooking in the oven, Zoe was sitting in the living room with her laptop, reading through news sites for any information about the fire when Kieran knocked.

"Good morning!" He looked and sounded a lot better as

he gave her a hug and a kiss. "Do I smell bacon?"

"Yep. And the coffee is ready." Zoe led the way into the kitchen and poured him a cup.

"Thanks, I really need this. I got a call from the fire chief just before I came over. The house is actually stable so I can go over later and see if anything is salvageable. I'm not sure what, but maybe something survived?"

"You never know," Zoe said gently. "Do you want me to come with you?"

"Do you mind? That would be great," Kieran sounded relieved. It was clear that he was still trying to process everything.

After a big breakfast (Zoe was proud of her ability to put a good breakfast on the table), Kieran and Zoe walked the several blocks to what used to be his house. The cats opted to stay behind this time.

As they neared the house, Zoe thought that it didn't look as bad as she had expected based on what she remembered from last night. Right before they got to the house a squirrel scrambled down one of the trees lining the street. Zoe reached for Kieran's hand and slowed down as they approached the tree. Her experience with Rowantree on campus had honed her ability to talk with squirrels without anybody else seeing her. Kieran glanced at her with a raised eyebrow. She tipped her head in the direction of the tree. Stealing a sideways look at the tree, Kieran nodded and slowed his steps.

"You probably are aware of this, but the one who did this is a Night Mage," the squirrel said. "She was here last night but has not been back since. You should be able to find signs of her in what is left of your home. We are sorry this happened. We did not detect her immediately last night."

"That's okay. I suspect she's good at hiding," Kieran responded.

"What do you mean, signs?" Zoe was puzzled. It wasn't

possible to tell Carolyn's Fire from a fire started by a for-real gas explosion, was it?

The squirrel cocked his head. "Your magesight will tell you what you need to know," he answered somewhat cryptically.

Zoe sighed. Fine. "What is your name?" she asked.

"I am called Redbrush." The squirrel managed to give a half-bow while clinging to the tree trunk.

"Thank you for the information, Redbrush," Zoe replied politely. "It is greatly appreciated."

The squirrel nodded, turned and scampered back up the tree.

"What do you think of that? And what does he mean 'use my magesight'?" Zoe asked testily. "I'm tired of all this mysterious clue shit."

Kieran grinned. "It's not really all that mysterious. Just use your magesight when you look at the damage."

His tone turned grim. "I also think we got confirmation that she's powerful. I mean really powerful. We need to be extremely careful and ramp up our response."

"I agree. I am definitely going to push George to pay attention. He needs to get his head out of the sand or administration crap. Same thing. He's hiding in that," Zoe muttered.

Kieran gave her a small smile and they walked up to the police officer standing in front of the house. Zoe gave a small start when she recognized Officer Tony DiNello. He had been the officer who had the bad luck to deal with the immediate aftermath of the fight with the demon at Swann Fountain.

"Good morning. I'm Kieran Ross, I lived on the third floor. Chief Gutiérrez told me I would be allowed in to see what I could salvage from my apartment," Kieran greeted Officer DiNello.

Tony DiNello turned around. His eyes narrowed as he

looked at Zoe and Kieran.

"I know you guys...where do I know you from?" he muttered.

"Um..." Zoe started.

"Wait, don't tell me. The weird thing that happened at Swann Fountain right before Christmas. You guys told me it was a fireworks thing by a...coven or something." He stared between the two of them.

"You're both here again for this," Officer DiNello waved a hand at the house. "That can't be good. Do I want to know what really happened here? I was told it was a gas leak."

"Um...yeah, that's what the chief told us too." Kieran gazed at the police officer.

"Fine. Go on. But one favor...if you find anything that you think is important...about the fire I mean, will you let me know? I have an idea of what I saw last year, and I need to know if something is happening again." Tony didn't look happy and Zoe felt bad for him. Should they tell him what was going on? Maybe later. She didn't think he really wanted to know everything right now.

Kieran nodded. "Of course. Thank you." He moved into the house and Zoe followed. The smell of smoke and damp hit like a sledgehammer when they walked into the building.

"It doesn't look too bad down here, does it?" Zoe asked tentatively.

"No, but I think she must have thrown fire directly into my apartment, so I'm thinking it's going to be worse up there. But it just occurred to me...she didn't use balefire. The fire department wouldn't have been able to put it out if it was balefire." Kieran was going into researcher mode. Zoe did the same thing when confronted with any kind of puzzle.

"Well, that would have been difficult to explain," she commented.

They carefully made their way up the stairs. The smell of

damp smoke got stronger as they went up the stairs. Kieran went first, shoving grit to the side as he climbed. Zoe was beginning to wish she'd brought a bandanna or something to cover her nose with. She settled for pulling her sweater over her nose and mouth. That helped a little.

The door to Kieran's apartment was broken open after the fire department had busted in to tackle the fire. He cautiously pushed the door all the way open.

The door opened into the center of a small hallway. The bedroom was toward the back of the house with the main living area, including the kitchen, toward the front. Most of the damage appeared to be at the front of the house bolstering Kieran's theory that Carolyn had launched fire through his front windows. There didn't really look like there was anything worth saving in the front, but Zoe headed there anyway while Kieran slowly moved toward the back and his bedroom.

Zoe stood and surveyed the almost total damage in the front room that Kieran had used as living room and an office. What the fire hadn't destroyed, the water had. The smell of smoke was overwhelming and she tried not to breathe too deeply. Remembering what Redbrush had told them, she switched over to her magesight and looked closely at the room. Well, damn. There was a faint sickly green haze hovering over the burnt areas a few feet inside the windows. Was that where the fireballs had landed? Zoe thought she should be able to tell exactly *who* had created those fireballs, but nobody had really given her an explanation of how that worked yet. Still, there was clearly magic involved in the fire.

Staring around the room with her normal vision, Zoe saw something gleaming silver underneath the shell of a chair. Stepping carefully, she made her way across the room. She poked a cautious finger at what looked like a picture frame and pulled it out. Turning the frame over she started with surprise. The picture and the frame were miraculously undamaged, and it was of her standing in the park. She remembered when Kieran had taken the picture. It had been one of the first sunny days this year and they had gone for a walk by the river. Her heart did a little flip and she smiled.

Holding the picture, she continued her scanning of the destroyed office. Most of the furniture was ruined, but there was a bookcase that looked like it might be okay. The books were a loss, but hopefully those could be replaced. It would take both of them to get the bookcase out if Kieran wanted it. She picked her way back to the middle of the apartment to find Kieran.

He was standing in the small kitchen area with a dazed look on his face. Zoe glanced around. There didn't seem to be anything left standing in the kitchen. The destruction was almost as bad as the front room.

"Do you think she did the same thing here? Tossed in a fireball and had it land in the kitchen?" she asked quietly. "I can see the same greenish haze here that I saw in the front room." Zoe glanced at him out of the corner of her eye.

Kieran shook his head, coming out of his daze. "Greenish haze? Oh, magic residue? Yeah, that's what I'm guessing. But why the kitchen?"

"Maybe she thought you would be in here eating dinner or something. I mean…if you hadn't been out with me and Kim…" she couldn't finish the thought. Instead, she handed him the picture.

"I found this in the office. And there's a bookcase in there that looks okay."

Kieran smiled at the picture. "Cool. This is a good picture of you. Let's go see if there's anything left in the bedroom. Maybe some of my clothes at least."

The bedroom had suffered very little fire damage, but the water damage was extensive. The closet doors were closed and there was no indication that the fire had gotten that far.

After about an hour they had managed to dig out most of his clothing and shoes and the knickknacks he had in the bedroom, and a chair. Flames had scorched a corner of the bed and Kieran decided against trying to salvage the water-logged mattress. The bookcase and the picture were the only other things that were in good enough shape to be saved. The clothes went into the plastic trash bags Zoe had remembered to bring and they brought the bookcase and chair out to the curb last.

Officer DiNello looked at the pitifully small pile of a few trash bags, a chair, and the bookcase.

"Is that it? I'm sorry, man," he sounded sincere.

"Yeah, well, what are you going to do? Thanks," Kieran replied in a quiet voice.

Kieran went to retrieve his car from up the street. Fortunately, it was undamaged.

As Kieran walked up the street Officer DiNello turned to Zoe. "Was this a magical attack?"

Zoe blinked. "Um…"

"My sister-in-law is a Water mage. She doesn't use it a lot, but I've seen it in action once or twice. I know that you guys are supposed to keep it quiet, but well…family." He looked apologetic.

"Uh, yeah. Um, yeah, it was a magical attack. Um…there's some stuff going on at school…" Zoe had no idea how much she could or should tell the police officer. After all, he was the police and if the police got involved…

"I'm not going to tell anybody, but I wanted some confirmation for myself," DiNello responded. "It helps if I have to explain something in a report. Do I want to know what you mean by 'stuff at school'?"

"No, probably not. But I will definitely let you know if anything escapes into the city," Zoe promised.

Officer DiNello nodded, pulled out a business card and handed it to her. "Thank you."

Kieran double-parked and they managed to get the bookcase in the back, shoved in the trash bags and chair, and drove the short distance back to his now new apartment in Kim's basement. Once there, Zoe tossed the clothes into the washer and turned to Kieran.

"We should go to the grocery store and then see if we can start replacing some of your stuff," she suggested.

"Good idea," Kieran agreed.

Chapter Eight

Wrapping her hands around her mug of coffee, Zoe stared out her office window. She decided she liked early morning on campus. It was quiet, the calm before the storm of students heading to classes. The landscaping guys were usually the only other people out and about. She enjoyed the feeling of the campus waking up. Sipping coffee and watching the trickle of students grow to a steady stream, Zoe sent up a small prayer of gratitude for this job and this career in this place. She reluctantly turned away from the window and back to the class prep that was her reason for being on campus this early.

Zoe finished prepping her lectures for the next week faster than expected and moved on to preparing the rest of the month. She felt a bit smug about getting ahead of things. At least *something* was going well. A sharp rapping sound broke her concentration. Turning around she saw Darkwing perched on the ledge outside her window. She opened the window and lifted the screen so the crow could enter her office. As usual though, he refused and cocked his head at her.

"The Night Mage is working with someone. It is not the woman who is the leader of the school. It is the one who led the coven." His voice was raspy and low.

Zoe's heart jumped leapt into her throat. "What? What do you mean the one who led the coven? Susan Barker? But she ran off!"

"She has returned. Several members of my murder saw her on campus yesterday. The squirrels have more information and said they will contact you later." He fixed her with one beady black eye, ruffled his feathers and flew off.

"Well, okay then," Zoe muttered to herself as she closed the window. "What am I supposed to do now? Just wait for Rowantree or Alder to show up?"

She turned back to her prep, but a fruitless twenty minutes later was forced to admit she was just too agitated by the news of Susan Barker's return to concentrate. Susan had been the leader of the coven that had raised the demon at the end of last semester. Her job as the provost's secretary put her in contact with all the senior administrative types and she recruited or tricked almost every woman working in Shelby Hall, including the president and then-provost, into becoming a member of the coven. After the demon had been sent back to wherever it had come from, Susan had run off and disappeared. Zoe assumed she had gone into hiding, but obviously she was back and still searching for a power source.

Agitated, Zoe shoved what she needed for her two back-to-back classes into her bag, grabbed her keys and coat, and half ran out of the building. Mark and the others needed to hear this new information and she sure as hell wasn't going to do that over the phone.

Walking quickly across campus she scanned the quad for any signs of squirrels. Darkwing had said they had more information, and she was anxious to hear it. *Let's get all the bad news over with as quickly as possible.*

Grateful that her classes were in Davis Hall, where Mark's office was located, Zoe took the stairs two at a time. Arriving at Mark's door out of breath, she was relieved to find him in the office.

He only had to glance at her face to see how agitated she was.

"What happened? What's the matter?" he asked sharply.

Zoe stepped into the office, closing the door behind her. She sat down on the chair alongside Mark's desk.

"Darkwing just showed up at my window. He says Susan Barker is back on campus, *and* she's working with Carolyn!" she blurted out.

"What the hell? When? How long as she been here?" Mark's mouth dropped open.

"I don't know. He said that the squirrels have more information and that they would tell me. I tried waiting in my office, but I couldn't take it. I have class in a few minutes, which is going to be interesting, but I had to tell somebody," Zoe gasped it all out in one breath.

"Okay. Breathe. Don't panic." Mark took a deep breath himself. "You go to class, and I'll start letting people know. I have a meeting in a few minutes as well, and Robyn and Kieran are on that committee, so I'll tell them. I'll text you if I see Rowantree or one of the others, okay?" He stood up and reached for his coat.

"Okay. Yeah. I'm okay. Declan and Geoff are in this class and Annmarie and Josh are in my next one. I'll tell them." Zoe felt better knowing that at least one other person knew what was going on right now. She needed to make sure as many people as possible knew that Susan Barker was back on campus, or nearby. That woman was dangerous, and Zoe was convinced she had no inhibitions about injuring or even killing somebody.

"Rowantree said that Carolyn is tapping into a power source. We need to figure out what power source. Why is she working with Susan? I don't like it at all," Mark scowled.

"I don't either. Okay. I'm going to go teach…and try not

to freak out in class. You go to your meeting and we'll keep each other posted." Zoe managed a small smile.

"It'll be okay. We took care of the demon, we'll handle this." Mark gave her a quick hug and followed her out of his office.

When Zoe walked into the classroom on the first floor, she immediately focused on Geoff and Declan. Geoff was a Fire mage and friends with Josh. He had helped with fighting the demon and the coven last semester.

"Hi, everyone," Zoe greeted the students already in the room. She walked to the desk and podium at the front of the room and put down her bag. As she logged into the computer, she glanced up and gestured to Declan and Geoff. "Oh, hey, guys, I need to ask you something."

Both students got up and moved to the front of the room.

"What's up, Dr. O'Brien?" Geoff asked.

"Susan Barker has been seen on campus. Darkwing showed up at my office earlier to tell me," Zoe kept her voice low.

"Shit."

"Hell."

The simultaneous expletives jumped out from both boys. Zoe made a small calming motion with her hand. Geoff in particular had reason to be angry – he'd been one of the students Susan had tried to control last semester.

"I know. It's bad. You guys need to keep a sharp eye out and make sure that every other student mage knows. After what Carolyn did..." she trailed off as the students looked worriedly at her. "Just pay attention, let everybody know, and travel in groups, even in the daytime," she continued. In a slightly louder tone she said, "Okay, thanks. I'll let you guys know."

Declan and Geoff made their way back to their seats and Zoe started class.

* * *

Having successfully made it through both classes without freaking out and remembering to tell Josh and Annmarie about the latest developments, Zoe checked her phone for messages once again. She had checked multiple times in the fifteen minutes between classes with nothing to show for it. Now, finally, there was a message from Mark.

Saw R. Got more info. Need to find George.

"Well that's cryptic enough," Zoe grumbled to herself.

"What's cryptic? Teaching?" The snide voice startled Zoe. Carolyn was standing in front of her with a dark look in her eyes.

"Message from my mom," Zoe lied smoothly, sliding her phone into her coat pocket. She surprised herself with her calm reaction.

"You know how it is. Later!" Zoe moved around Carolyn and bolted out of Davis Hall before the other woman could react. She didn't really care what Carolyn thought of her mad dash out of the building. She simply wanted to remove herself from target range. The crowds of students moving through the hallway should be enough to stop Carolyn from doing anything radical. At least for the time being.

Once outside Zoe slowed her pace to a rapid walk and headed directly for Shelby Hall. It didn't matter what George was doing right now. He needed to know what was going on and pay some damn attention. How did he let himself get so caught up in administrative stuff?

Zoe approached the front of Shelby Hall and cast a quick look around the quad. There were enough people moving around that it was difficult to tell if anybody was watching her, but she didn't think Carolyn had followed her outside. Besides, she reminded herself, there were several reasons she could be going into Shelby. She shook her head. Paranoia was becoming a part of her routine.

Once inside the door, she pushed away her fears of Carolyn and her general dislike of the entry hall of Shelby. The looming chandelier gave it a slightly dark feeling. That, combined with her memories of the horrible, depressing, life-draining feeling that the coven had created in the building, made her reluctant to enter it for any reason. She squared her shoulders, reminded herself she was annoyed with George, and marched up the broad, curving staircase.

The deep carpeting in the upstairs hall muffled her footsteps. She could see that the door to George's office suite was open. So at least Sarah was there. That was better than nothing.

She poked her head around the door to find Sarah just hanging up the phone. The door to George's office was closed.

"Hi, Zoe! How are you?" Sarah looked up.

"Hi Sarah. I'm good. Um…is George in? It's really important." Zoe tried to keep the panic out of her voice, but Sarah narrowed her eyes.

"That doesn't sound good. Yeah, he's here. Let me check…and pull him away from whatever he's doing because I really don't like the look on your face." Sarah got up, tapped on the door to George's office, and opened it without waiting for a response.

"Sorry to interrupt, but Zoe's here and she says it's really important. I don't like the look on her face. It has magic problems written all over it," she announced.

"Oh. Well. Okay. Yes." George sounded distracted, but Sarah waved Zoe in. Zoe sat down in one of the guest chairs in front of George's desk while Sarah took up her usual spot, leaning in the door frame.

"Hi, Zoe. It's good to see you. What's up?" George's green eyes crinkled with his smile.

Zoe returned the smile. She missed having George as her mentor. "Well…um…Darkwing stopped by my office this morning, right before I had class. He had bad news…the crows have seen Susan Barker on campus." She stopped, chewing on her lower lip.

George sat up straight and Sarah went rigid.

"That bitch is back on campus?" Sarah's voice was low and tight.

"Yes, that's what the crows say. And she's working with Carolyn," Zoe answered. Sarah had worked for Susan and had been hand-picked by Susan to be the human vessel for the demon. Sarah, understandably, had seriously objected to that plan. In mild terms, she despised Susan, and Zoe didn't blame her at all.

"Did Darkwing say how long she's been on campus? This really is a nasty development," George noted in his understated manner.

"No, he didn't. As usual, he didn't say much. He did say that Rowantree had more information. Just before I came over here, Mark texted me that he'd talked to Rowantree a little bit ago. I told Mark about Susan before I went to class." Zoe's hands started doing their stress-induced twisting routine again, and she forcibly pulled them apart and placed them, palms, down on her thighs.

"I think…um…that you…um…need to get involved, George. There's other things going on too." Zoe made herself look her mentor in the eye as she told him what he should do.

George raised one eyebrow. "You're right. I do need to pay more attention. And I apologize for not taking your earlier concerns as seriously as I should have." He gave Zoe an apologetic smile.

Relief coursed through Zoe. She knew she likely had more power in absolute terms than George, but he was her mentor in the academic world and, since the fall, the magical world.

He had far more experience in both worlds than she did. She needed him to be involved and around to answer questions.

"Is Mark in his office? If he's spoken with Rowantree, we should speak with Mark," George stated.

"I think he is…let me text him…" Zoe stabbed at her phone.

I'm here. R u coming over? Mark's response to her question was brief.

Yes. w/ George, Zoe sent back.

"He's there and I just told him we were coming over." Zoe looked back up at George.

"Wonderful. Sarah, you should come too. We can close up the office for a bit." George glanced at Sarah.

"I was going to anyway," Sarah growled. "If that bitch…sorry, witch, is back on campus I want the details."

Zoe raised an eyebrow, but George just smiled. "I figured as much."

Morgan Ammon, president of Summerfield, appeared in the hallway as the three of them left George's office and walked toward the stairs.

"Oh, hello George, Zoe," she said, pointedly ignoring Sarah. "Where are you off to?"

"Good afternoon, Morgan. We're on our way to a meeting and Sarah has graciously offered to be the note-taker for us. Nothing for you to worry about." George returned Morgan's stare with a slight smile that didn't quite reach his eyes.

The president's eyes narrowed. "What meeting?" she demanded.

"Just a history department meeting. I have not been to many this semester but there are some curricular issues within the department that need to be discussed and so I will be attending." George never took his eyes off Morgan.

"Oh. Of course. I hope it goes well." Morgan broke away from George's gaze and continued down the hall.

"Ladies, after you." George gestured to Zoe and Sarah and followed them down the hall to the stairs.

Once outside, Sarah took a deep breath. "That woman. Every time I look at her, I get pissed. And she always looks at me like she'd squash me like a bug if she could."

"It's okay, Sarah. She won't do anything to you." George put a hand on Sarah's arm.

"I know. But that doesn't stop her from *wanting* to squash me," Sarah retorted.

Zoe laughed. "She wouldn't dare do anything to you, Sarah. She knows you're friends with me and Mark as well as George. I think that worries her more."

"It's good to have magical friends," Sarah commented.

The three of them entered Davis Hall and started up the stairs. Reaching the second floor, Zoe spotted Kieran coming down the hall towards them. He waved and waited for them at the entrance to Mark's office. Approaching Mark's office, Zoe realized that others were there before them. She glanced in the door and saw Robyn Harper and Jessica Sanders standing in the office. Zoe, Kieran, George, and Sarah crowded in as best they could. Zoe knew from past experience that although the office looked small, it could hold a number of people in a pinch.

Mark gestured for Kieran to close the door. His face was grave. "Well, in the clichéd manner of things, there's good news and bad news," he grimaced. "And, it's the same piece of news."

Eyebrows went up around the room. "Well? What is it?" Kieran broke the short silence.

"There are two ley lines that cross under campus," Mark announced.

"What?"

"Are you sure?"

"Who told you that?"

"What's a ley line?"

The babble of voices threatened to drown out Mark's answer.

"I'm sure. Rowantree. A ley line is a source of almost pure magic that can be drawn on by somebody who knows how to tap into it," he managed.

The last statement was in answer to Sarah and Zoe, the non-mage and the learning-on-the-fly mage. Zoe grimaced. Maybe there were some books or articles she could read to catch up on background information. This was just like in grad school where it seemed like everybody in class knew what was going on except her.

George suddenly looked tired. He dropped into the guest chair that was, for some reason, empty. "What exactly did Rowantree tell you? Why is this the first we're learning of it?" He stared at Mark.

Zoe tried to hide her shock at George's questions. How did he not know? A magical power source right under campus, and he didn't know about it?

Mark held up his hands. "I don't know. Rowantree assured me that they had not felt anything previously. He thinks that maybe the work of the coven last semester pulled the lines closer to the surface and now they're much more accessible. He's informed the crows and they will carry the message to other Watchers."

He glanced at Zoe. "You will probably hear more from your cats tonight."

Zoe nodded. "I'll make sure to ask." *Assuming I know what to ask.* She looked at Kieran. "Did you tell them what happened the other night?"

"No, I didn't have a chance before now," he replied.

"What now?" Robyn asked.

"Carolyn, at least we're pretty sure it was Carolyn, set fire to my house the other night," Kieran said bluntly. "I think she threw a fireball into the front window. Zoe told me she can use balefire, but she definitely didn't use that."

"Carolyn who?" George asked reminding Zoe of why it was so important that he pay attention to more than the administrative stuff. He did not know that she was the source of the dark magic Rowantree had felt moving around campus.

"Carolyn Detweiler, assistant teaching professor in Psychology," Zoe answered. She filled him in on the tree branch falling on the students, the meeting where she and Jessica had witnessed her trying to run things, the attack on Simon and Declan and her response to Zoe's shield, and finally what Zoe had seen at Kieran's house.

"She's actually tried to attack me twice before that," Kieran added and told George the details of the coffee at the conference and the broken stair in his former apartment.

George turned to Zoe. "Okay. Yes, you did mention her, Zoe. Again, you are right. I should have been paying more attention. I apologize for my inattention."

Jessica waved a dismissive hand. "Don't worry about it. Happens to all of us. You're here now and that's what matters. We have to figure out a way to protect the ley lines and keep Carolyn and anybody working with her, away from them. God knows we don't need another demon showing up on campus and giving the students an excuse to skip classes!" Her joke lightened the mood in the room and George nodded.

"You're right. Okay, so what else do we have?"

Zoe and Mark filled everybody in on the details of the attack on Simon and Declan by Carolyn. After the shock of that story, it was clear to all that Carolyn was not going to stop at anything to get what she wanted, whatever that was. Zoe worried that they would always be chasing Carolyn if they didn't figure out her goals.

"Oh, and she's also working with Morgan and Meredith. They're up to their necks in this. Again," Zoe added.

"Great. I've been looking for an excuse to go after that skank," Robin snarled referring to Meredith. Meredith had used two of Robyn's students in her coven plans last semester and Robyn had not forgiven her for that.

"Okay. So, we have newly discovered ley lines, a psych prof who's a Night Mage attacking students and faculty, and a president and sociology professor in league with said Night Mage. Am I missing anything?" George gazed around Mark's small office.

Zoe and Sarah stared at George.

"Oh, yes. Of course. You should tell them," George nodded to Zoe.

Zoe cleared her throat. "There's one more piece of news...um...and it's not good." She swallowed. "Susan Barker has been seen on campus. Darkwing told me earlier."

Chapter Nine

THIS TIME the babble of voices was louder.

"Are you *kidding* me?"

"I thought she went down with the demon!"

"What the hell is she doing now?"

George waved his hands in the air. "Okay, okay. Everybody. Calm down. I think we can safely say that Susan's appearance and the ley lines on campus are connected. With the clarity of hindsight, I'm going to assume that her ultimate goal last semester was not merely raising the demon but also accessing the ley lines." His eyes swept the room. "We need to move *now* not later."

"Um…how did Susan know the…um…ley lines were on campus?" Zoe asked hesitantly. "I mean…um…*you* didn't know…"

George gazed at her thoughtfully and Zoe tried not to twist her hands together. It was a perfectly valid question.

"I have to admit…I'm not sure." George sighed and gave Zoe a rueful smile. "I have not investigated the history of this area as closely as I should have it seems. But, I will worry about that later. Right now we have to prevent Carolyn and Susan from accessing the lines, or worse, *preventing* any of us from accessing them."

It was Sarah, the only non-mage and, more importantly, non-faculty member in the room, who got them all pointed in the right direction and managed to create a list of priorities. "First of all, you need to make sure that all the faculty mages and all the student mages know what's going on. Morgan and Meredith used students last semester and I'm sure they're not above doing that again. Zoe mentioned that students have already been attacked. If they know what's going on, they can protect themselves. Also, you need to make sure that Simon LeGrande is in the loop. I know he can get … um … pompous … sorry, but he can, but he's also really good," she looked directly at George as she finished her comments.

"Yes, of course. Simon is one of the best Fire mages around. I will speak to him." George seemed chastened at Sarah's words.

Zoe knew that George didn't really get along with Simon and Sarah was on target when she said that Simon was pompous. Mark had regaled her and David with stories of his department chair over dinner. But Sarah was exactly right. They really needed to have Simon on board. He was the one who had done the most research into mage powers to the point of experimenting with his own to see how far he could take them. Zoe had a sneaking suspicion that Simon's knowledge of how Carolyn had acquired the ability to use balefire came frighteningly close to personal experience. She added Simon and ley lines to her list of things to ask Mark about.

Mark glanced at George. "Simon isn't on campus today, but he should be here tomorrow. Can we wait until then, or should we try to reach him at home?"

George sighed. "No, we can't really wait. I'll call him tonight. I don't want to do it from campus even on my own phone, but I will do so as soon as I get home."

Kieran gazed around the room. "Um, I think everybody

needs to check the warding on your house and even your neighbors. Carolyn almost took out the other two people in my building and she did destroy their apartments. I don't think she was really worried about innocents getting caught in her fire. Zoe and her neighbor have warded their entire block and I'm thinking that's the best thing for all of us." He sounded tired.

"Can I ask…um…can somebody do something for my apartment?" Sarah spoke up. "I mean, if Susan Barker is back, I think she might come after me just because I pissed her off." She grimaced.

"Oh, God. Of course. I'll do it as soon as we get home tonight," Zoe answered hurriedly, feeling guilty. Duh. She'd completely forgotten that Sarah couldn't ward her own apartment.

"Thanks." Sarah gave Zoe a relieved smile.

"So, what do we do now?" Robyn Harper asked. "I mean, do we go after Carolyn? Do we wait until she does something? Do we wait until Susan does something? And more importantly, how do we all ward against balefire? Or do we just do what we can and hope it doesn't come to that?" It was her turn to send her gaze around the room. "It doesn't seem very smart to wait. If we're always reacting instead of acting, we could be too late. While that battle with the demon was…um…exciting, I'd rather not repeat anything like that."

"No, you're correct. We need to act and act now," George answered. "But we do need to be coordinated about it. As far as warding against balefire goes, I think Zoe's method of weaving Elements together is the best. We can all work together to ward our offices and with the students to protect the dorms."

"But, at the same time, let's not telegraph what we're doing or trying to do," Jessica put in. "I'd like to try for some element of surprise here."

The group went back and forth on plans, tactics, and finding more information until Zoe felt a headache starting. She just wanted to find Carolyn and throw power at her until she disintegrated.

She glanced over at George and caught his thoughtful gaze as if he knew the direction of her thoughts. Zoe sighed. *Finesse. Right. And don't drain my power and end up killing myself.* She gave George a small smile and a shrug. He nodded and returned his attention to the wandering conversation.

Finally, Kieran raised his voice. "Guys. Guys! Look, we know who to be on the lookout for and we have an idea of *what* to look out for. Prepare yourselves as best you can against balefire. And just like we told the students...try not to go anywhere alone, even if that means going out of our way to walk together. If you go alone, text someone to let them know where you're going. Especially don't go anywhere alone like one of the back parking lots. Remember, Simon and Declan got ambushed by Carolyn in the lot behind Shelby. I agree with George about warding our offices...that's all I can think of. I'm tired and I'm heading home. Zoe, if you'll wait a minute for me to get my stuff, I'll walk back to your office with you and then we can go to our cars. I ended up parking next to you this morning."

"Okay, that sounds like a good idea, thanks," Zoe answered and then hesitated. She was still leery of taking charge, but she reminded herself that as the only Elemental mage in the group, there was a certain amount of responsibility lying on her shoulders.

"Okay. This time we have to include the students in everything. They are in as much danger as we are. I know our first instinct is to protect them, but we cannot leave them out of the loop in hopes that Carolyn and Susan will leave them alone. They've already been attacked once and Carolyn *knows* Declan is a student and she still attacked him when he was with Simon. I'll recreate the group texting that we had last semester and include the students. Please let everybody know when anything happens, even if it seems really small."

George stood up. "I will talk with Simon tonight. And, right now I will speak with Morgan Ammon. It appears that she is also involved in this and I wish to remind her of one or two issues that are left over from last semester." His voice was grim. He left Mark's office followed by Sarah who gave Zoe a quick hug on her way out the door.

Zoe and Kieran looked at each other. "Let's go get your stuff and then we can get out of here," Zoe said. Kieran nodded.

Mark regarded them both. "Call me when you get home," he ordered.

"Will do," Kieran responded. Zoe gave Mark a quick hug and waved at the others as she and Kieran left the office. It really did feel like everybody was gearing up for a battle. Zoe suppressed a shudder.

Kieran's office was just down the hall from Mark's and once they got inside, Kieran closed the door and turned to give Zoe a long hug.

"Are you okay?" he asked locking his hands around her back and leaning back to see her face.

"I'm good, just tired." She gave him a quick kiss. "Let's get your stuff and get out of here. I'll feel safer when I'm home."

"Yeah, me too." He sighed and grabbed his laptop and assorted books and articles.

* * *

The next morning Zoe and Kieran carpooled to campus. They had decided the night before that aside from enjoying time in each other's company, carpooling was probably the safer option for both of them getting to and from campus since

Carolyn likely knew where Zoe lived. Kieran was having all his personal mail directed to campus. He had no intention of giving the school his new address yet, since it was clear Carolyn was coming after them at home.

As they pulled into the parking lot that was almost equally distant from both their offices, they saw Declan and Geoff walking toward the middle of campus. Zoe waved at the students and then glanced at her phone.

"I've got fifteen minutes before my meeting. I guess I'll go over to my office and drop my stuff off and then come back here," she commented.

"No. Let's both go to my office. You can leave your stuff there," Kieran responded.

Zoe drew a deep breath to argue. She was perfectly capable of getting to her office and back by herself.

Kieran smiled. "I know what you're going to say…but we all decided to do our best to avoid going anywhere alone just yesterday. Remember?"

Zoe deflated. Damn. He was right. She sighed. "Fine. You're right. I'll go to your office." She climbed out of the car.

They started across the parking lot following Declan and Geoff, who were in front of them, obviously on their way to class. The day was on the cold side, but promised to become a bright, early spring day in the afternoon. Zoe enjoyed the contrast of the warm sun on her face with the cold air around her.

The sudden cawing of numerous crows and the acrid smell of smoke broke into her short reverie.

"What's that?" Kieran asked, pointing upwards.

Zoe followed his gesture and saw dozens of crows pouring upwards out of the trees surrounding the parking lot. Two dipped lower and circled near her and Kieran. Zoe thought she recognized Darkwing as one of the two.

"I don't know, but it's not good. Shield yoursel…" she

broke off as a stream of fire shot towards them from the back corner of the parking lot to their right.

"Shit!" Kieran yelled.

Zoe threw up a wall made from all four Elements between herself and Kieran covering them from the direction of the fire. She couldn't tell at first if it was ordinary Fire or balefire. It hit the ground and dissipated. Ordinary Fire then. Another rope of Fire snaked its way toward them moving faster than she had seen before. Acting before she could even think about it, Zoe extended her wall to cover her and Kieran's heads. She just had time to notice that the telltale black ring that marked balefire was *not* present.

Up ahead, Geoff spun around. He stared at the fire flying toward Zoe and Kieran and grabbed Declan's arm. The two students ran back towards the professors. Geoff was creating balls of Fire in his hands and somehow stacking them up. Declan frowned and stared past Zoe and Kieran looking for the source of the ropes of Fire. He stopped suddenly and closed his eyes. Two heartbeats later he sprinted to his left.

"Declan! Don't!" Zoe yelled, unsure of what he was doing, but certain that he was heading directly into danger. Zoe was convinced Carolyn was the one attacking them, and she'd already gone after Declan once. He shouldn't be giving her a second opportunity.

Geoff reached Kieran and Zoe. "What's going on?" he panted, a stack of fireballs in each hand.

"I'm sure it's Carolyn, Professor Detweiler, but I don't know where she is," Kieran answered.

"Declan was just telling me he's learned how to locate the source of magic, so if he concentrates he can find somebody using magic," Geoff informed them. "I think he's using that to find Detweiler."

"How can he do that?" Zoe asked.

"I don't know. Some djinn thing. He was just starting to

tell me about it when I felt somebody using Fire in a big way. It's not balefire...at least I'm pretty sure it's not. It feels the same as when I use Fire." Geoff stared in the direction Declan had sprinted toward.

"Wait. Nothing's happening anymore." Kieran held up a hand.

Zoe held her breath not sure what she was waiting for. Declan appeared walking slowly between the cars. Zoe dropped her wall and the three of them ran toward him.

"Are you okay?" Zoe asked.

"Dude. What did you do?" Geoff exclaimed.

Declan dropped onto the curb at the edge of the parking lot. "I sent her away again. But this time, I'm not sure where. I just didn't want her on campus. I don't think I killed her...um...I didn't want to...but...um...I don't know where she went." He glanced up at Zoe apologetically. "I'm sorry. I'm still figuring this all out."

"Don't apologize. You saved our butts," Kieran stated emphatically. "I really don't care what happens to her anymore."

"I think you need some food," Geoff put in, gazing at Declan. "You look exhausted and you didn't before this happened." He closed his hands and his fireballs disappeared.

"Yeah...um...I guess...I feel kinda like I ran a race or something," Declan answered his friend.

"Yes, let's get you some food. You still have a few minutes before the next class period. Somehow we managed to deal with this without anybody noticing. Well...except for the crows, but I don't think they'll post it on social media." Zoe thought fast. "There's a coffee place on the first floor of Davis. We'll all walk over there. I'll keep a shield around us for now." This leadership thing was getting a little easier every time she did it. Hopefully she didn't screw up too much. She did need to figure out how Geoff stacked up those fireballs. That was pretty cool."

"Good idea. Let's go." Kieran gave Declan a hand up from where he had collapsed onto the curb.

The four of them turned back towards the middle of campus and made it to Davis Hall without any further excitement.

The rest of the morning passed much more quietly. Zoe was glad for the small window of normalcy in another crazy, mind-bending semester. She managed to have a mostly productive day that was only occasionally interrupted by musings on ley lines and their power. Zoe disliked being ignorant on a topic that everybody else found extremely important and at the same time assumed she knew as much as they did. It was extremely frustrating and at times embarrassing.

She took a short break to eat some lunch and let her mind wander. And then the perfect solution to her ignorance hit her. David had mentioned he had a library of sorts of books on mages, magic, and magical phenomenon. Zoe decided to go over to Mark's office and see if he or David had anything she could borrow that would help fill in some of the gaps. There were still a couple of hours before Kieran was ready to leave and this way she could get a walk in as well.

Mark was in his office and it appeared that he, or David, had anticipated her question. He turned around and picked up two books from the floor next to his desk. "David sent these with me this morning. He thought you might want more information and knowing academics like he does, he pulled these for me to bring in today."

"Thanks. And tell David thanks." Zoe smiled.

She glanced at the books. One was a history of the discovery of ley lines and the other was some kind of analysis of power available through the use of ley lines.

Zoe looked back up at Mark. "Well, I know what I'm going

to read tonight. Forget grading or class prep!"

Mark laughed. "I thought you might find those interesting. That one on power should have good info for you when it comes to using the ley lines to enhance your own power. You need to figure out how to tap that power so you can use it for every Element at the same time."

"Yeah, true. Okay. I'm going to go to my office and start reading these. I'll have to put some kind of cover on them, so if Meredith does one of her surprise drop-ins on me, she won't know. Lucky I'm an historian and always reading old books." Zoe tucked the books into her bag and moved to the door.

"Let me know when you leave, okay?" Mark gave her another hug.

"I will. I'll probably be back over here anyway. I drove today." Zoe returned the hug.

When she reached the second floor of Cooper Hall, she glanced down the hallway to check on Meredith. Meredith's office door was closed and there was no light visible in the interior window. Good. She wasn't in. At least not right now.

Zoe slipped into her own office and pushed the door almost all the way closed. She never liked the isolated feeling she got when she closed the door all the way. This way she could still hear comings and goings in the hallway, and her students knew that if they needed her they could find her.

Settling down at her desk, she pulled David's books out of her bag. *Ley Lines: Discovery and Location* by Reginald Savage was a history of ley lines. *An Analysis of Power Acquisition from Ley Lines* by Victor McClain looked to be exactly what its title suggested. Zoe had to laugh. Leave it to academics to make magic sound boring. Still smiling to herself, she opened the McClain book and dove in.

Two surprisingly uninterrupted hours later, Zoe pulled herself out of the intricacies of acquiring and using power from ley lines to increase the reach and capacity of her own abilities. She was still shaking her head in wonder at the ability of academics to make even something as fun and exciting as magic seem overly scholarly and boring. She stuck a sticky note to mark her place and put the legal pad with her notes into her bag along with both books.

The *ping* of an incoming text pulled her thoughts away from ley lines and knowledge gaps. Kieran was ready to leave whenever she was. Zoe finished packing up and started across campus.

Chapter Ten

"These ley lines under campus…I got partway through one of the books that Mark loaned me. But it helps if I can talk it out too. How do you access them? And why didn't anybody know there were ley lines running under campus?" Zoe asked the room in general.

She, Kieran, Rob Armstrong, and Joe Chapman were sitting in Kim's living room that evening. When Zoe and Kieran had gotten home, Kim was outside working in the small garden plot in front of her house. After they told her what had happened that morning, she announced that they were having dinner with her and she was calling in Rob and Joe. Rob and Joe were Earth and Air mages respectively and had been part of the wider group of mages that had battled the demon at the winter solstice. They both lived on the block to the north of Zoe's street. While she was greatly appreciative of the help, Zoe was really tired of meetings, especially meetings about who was going to attack her next. She just wanted to crash for a day or so.

Over Chinese take-out, Kieran and Zoe had told the neighborhood mages everything that had happened on campus that day including the reappearance of Susan Barker (nobody was happy to hear that), the attack in the parking lot, and Declan's removal of Carolyn. Joe was fascinated by Declan's half-djinn powers. It turned out he'd done some research on djinn in North America and djinn powers in general having run across one while traveling in Asia.

Zoe had already texted Declan with Joe's phone number so the two of them could connect. Given Simon's new reluctance to continue working with Declan, Zoe wanted to be sure Declan had somebody who could help him figure out what he was capable of. Plus, she thought the easy-going Joe would be a good antidote to Simon's fussiness and Declan's nerves.

"Well, they're a power source, as you know, and if a mage knows they are near a ley line, he or she can tap into them for a power boost," Rob answered. "Earth mages usually have an easier time finding and using ley lines because we're attuned to the Earth. While ley lines aren't really underground exactly, that's the best way to describe them. I'm guessing that mages on your campus were drawing from the ley lines without really knowing it. The power was probably diffused enough that unless you were actually hunting, you wouldn't notice a specific source or location."

"What do you mean not exactly underground? George said that he thought the attempt by the coven to raise the demon last semester had caused the ley lines to move closer to the surface. I assumed they were something like…I dunno…buried sprinkler lines…or something." Zoe was puzzled.

"That's not a bad analogy actually." Rob smiled. "But they exist in a slightly different dimension than ours. I guess the best way to say it is that they parallel our dimension but are visible and accessible to those of us who can find them. Does that make sense?"

"Yeah, it does. Okay. So how do we access them, and can

we keep Carolyn and Susan Barker from accessing them?" Zoe massaged her temples to stave off the headache that was starting to creep in.

Joe swallowed a bite of food and took up where Rob left off. "I don't want to sound all hokey or woo-woo." He waved his hands in the air, "but to access ley lines you need to reach out with your magic and search for pure power. Remember the power in the fountain last time? Sort of like that but flowing. The fountain is stationary, I know that sounds wrong, but it's coming through in one place. The ley lines cross an area, and the power is moving through them. Just like the fountain, but instead of ending in one place, the fountain, it's moving through the ley lines. I don't know if that makes any more sense." He shrugged and took another bite of his kung pao chicken.

"It does…" Kieran said slowly. "In the fountain the power is coming from…wherever it comes from, and out through the fountain…or whatever spot it comes out in. With the ley lines, the power is moving from one point to another…like a river, only on campus, one river crosses another, so we have a…what?…power nexus?" He glanced over at Joe.

"Exactly." It was Kim who answered. "And when you get a nexus, you get a stronger power source than if you just had one ley line passing through the area. A nexus would explain why Summerfield campus has attracted Rowantree and his people and the crows. Watchers go to where they sense stronger magic. But that diffusion that Joe mentioned also explains why the Watchers weren't aware of the ley lines. It probably also accounts for why you have more mages in your faculty and student population than in general. Mages are also attracted to areas with power sources."

She turned to Zoe and Kieran. "Zoe, didn't you tell me that you and Mark were hired at the same time? And weren't you hired a year earlier, Kieran?"

"Yeah, but what does that have to do with anything? I didn't even know I had power until last semester…and I've been here for going on five years," Zoe replied.

"Something in the back of your brain drew you here," Kim responded confidently. "And your cats found you…they knew something about you."

Zoe shook her head. The headache was threatening to blow up to epic proportions.

"Okay. Fine." She didn't want to think about all that right now. The idea of her power drawing her to Summerfield bothered her for some reason.

"That still doesn't answer the question of how we can find and use the power…I know…reach out. I just don't know how to do that." Zoe was growing frustrated with the non-answers of the others. Even Kieran seemed to be deliberately obtuse in his answers.

Sensing her frustration, Kieran laid his hand over hers. "We're not trying to be all cute and secret society-y," he said quietly. "It's just that trying to explain something you grasp almost intuitively is hard to do. It's not your fault. I'll help you figure this all out."

"I'll help, too," Kim added. "You're our strongest mage, both because you're an Elemental, and just because you are very powerful. I think that's why this Carolyn bitch keeps trying to come after you. You're her biggest stumbling block."

"Oh, great. Just what I need!" Zoe threw her hands up.

"Oh, you know you love the excitement," Kim laughed.

Zoe had to admit that it was more fun than class prep. Oh, hell. She had to do some of that tonight. She glanced at her phone.

"I gotta get going. I have work to do tonight before class tomorrow. After classes, I'll try to see what I can 'feel'," she made air quotes with her fingers, "with the ley lines." She stood up and grabbed her jacket.

"I'll walk you home," Kieran said.

"No, I don't think you should," Kim said seriously. "You look drained and that's not good with a Night Mage possibly stalking you and her. Rob and Joe can walk with Zoe, you stay here where we're warded...even against Carolyn."

Kieran opened his mouth to object then shut it and sighed. "Yeah, you're right Kim. I'm in no shape to do anything right now."

He gave Zoe a quick kiss. "I can at least walk with you to the back gate. I'll text you in the morning...your turn to drive," he smiled.

"Good idea," Zoe replied.

The five of them walked into the small back yard and out to the gate. Joe sent out a small tendril of Air into the evening.

"There's nobody around, let's go," he said quietly.

Zoe gave Kieran and Kim a small wave of her fingers and slipped out the gate with Rob and Joe. The three of them didn't talk on the short walk to Zoe's front door. The two men kept alert and she noticed they were scanning the area. She started to do the same, sending out a small stream of Air to find anybody who might be lurking. She had never given much thought to her surroundings before, aside from looking for cars when crossing the street. It was an odd feeling, yet she understood on some gut level that she should have been doing it long before now. Rob and Joe left only after she had entered her house and closed and locked the front door behind her. She felt them cross out of her shields as she dropped onto her sofa and closed her eyes.

Okay. So things are getting interesting.

Two soft thumps on the sofa announced the arrival of Moose and Flash. She opened her eyes and gave simultaneous ear scritches to each cat.

"What's going on?" Flash turned to clean the base of his tail.

"Oh, nothing much. One Night Mage, one half-djinn, multiple attacks…oh, and a nexus of two ley lines on campus. Like I said, quiet," Zoe commented.

The cats paused their always-active cleaning routines and stared at her.

"So, nothing new?" Moose returned to chewing the toes of one front paw.

Zoe stared at him. "You're taking this all awfully calmly. Did you figure it all out already? Or is there something you need to tell me?" She was getting tired of the cats bringing out information at the last minute.

Flash lifted his head. "No need to get all sarcastic. You've been telling us about things on campus and we know about the fire at Kieran's. And, yes, the squirrels do pass on messages. Have they found Detweiler yet?"

"I'm sorry," Zoe sighed. They were cats after all, she reminded herself, and they looked at the world differently. "I have a monstrous headache, I'm worried about everybody on campus getting attacked, and no, we still don't know where Declan sent Carolyn. *He* doesn't know. Just somewhere with trees."

"We'll talk to the crows and squirrels about Detweiler. They, and we, really don't like the idea of a Night Mage, especially an angry Night Mage, wandering around this area. Things could get ugly," Moose commented between swipes at the long hair on his stomach.

"What do you mean *could* get ugly? Aren't things bad enough already? I mean the bitch burned down Kieran's house and tried to kill Simon and Declan." The cats were amazing at times. See the bottom of their food bowl? The world was ending. One destroyed house and two murder attempts? Eh. Things could be worse.

Flash stopped his grooming and sat up. He stared directly into Zoe's eyes.

"A Night Mage has no boundaries. You should have seen that by now. Remember when the witches raised the demon? We told you they promised a part of themselves, their souls, for power? Well, a Night Mage does something similar. A Night Mage is a mage who has used their power to harm the innocent, or to accrue more power to themselves. They harm others for the sake of harming them. Done often enough, this brings the mage to the attention of...creatures...demons...who are best left undisturbed. Once that happens, there is no going back if you change your mind. A witch, if she or he survives long enough, can atone to a degree for the evil they have committed. A Night Mage is all in from the very beginning. That's why it can, and will, get worse."

That had to be the longest speech Flash had ever given her. Zoe gaped at the orange cat. "So in religious terms – I'm trying to put this in some sort of context I can understand here – Carolyn has sold her soul, doomed herself to eternal damnation, and did it all for power...power in the regular and magical worlds...power she thinks she will wield forever? But...she's still human, right? She'll die eventually, right?"

"If a Night Mage finds a source, like the nexus of the ley lines, that source can be tapped to extend the life of the mage beyond normal human range. So, yeah, she probably thinks she can figure out a way to live forever and have unstoppable power. They're all kinda like that," Moose answered. He stepped into her lap and curled up, purring loudly.

Zoe dropped her head into her hands. The religious implications of all of this were almost as difficult to come to terms with as the magical power thing had been to deal with last semester. And, if she was honest, the whole idea of magic was still a bit difficult to deal with. And, now, it seemed that things like eternal damnation were a very real possibility. On top of all of this, she still had to do *something* for class tomorrow. Maybe she could just find a video, or reading, for them to discuss and analyze, or some sort of group work. She was not feeling up to anything more complex right now.

Earlier than she liked the next morning, Zoe nursed her second cup of coffee while she calculated how late she could leave the house and still make it to campus on time for her first class. She knew that Kieran's first class was later than hers, so she wasn't going to cause him any problems. The feeling of somebody coming through her wards and a knock at the door interrupted her thoughts.

She peered through the peephole to see Kieran on the porch. Even though she had set the wards to allow certain people through, she still sent a small tendril of Air out to make sure that it really was Kieran. The cats, and now her mother, had drilled that simple piece of security into her head.

Sensing nothing odd, she opened the door.

"Hey," Kieran smiled. "How are you doing this morning?" He walked in and Zoe closed the door behind him.

"I'm good. How about you?" Zoe gave him a hug and a kiss. "Do you want a cup of coffee?"

"Yes, please, that would be fantastic. I ran out already," he admitted sheepishly. "I've been staying up late doing prep and research and insurance paperwork and I powered through all my coffee."

"I told you, you should have gotten the bigger bag. Here, I have an extra travel mug. You can keep it." She poured the coffee for him and put some in her own travel mug. "We should probably head out so that I'm not racing to class."

"Okay. Besides classes, do you have anything else today?" Kieran asked as they walked outside.

"No. I was going to spend some time this afternoon after classes and see if I can find those ley lines. It's supposed to be a nice day today so I was thinking I'd take a walk around campus, see if I could find Rowantree or Alder and search for the lines."

"That sounds like a good idea. I'll come find you after my last class," Kieran said.

The drive to campus was quiet and Zoe was able to find a spot in one of the more open parking lots. She was wary of using the lot behind Shelby where Declan and Simon had been attacked. It was sort of hidden behind the building and she really didn't like the idea of getting ambushed.

They reached Davis Hall and Zoe turned to continue on to her office in Cooper. Kieran looked like he was going to object, but she just kept moving. Her concession to his worry was to put a shield against magical attack around herself. As she approached the door of Cooper Hall, she noticed two squirrels sitting just to the left of the door. Alder and Rowantree both waved to her and ran up the tree closest to the building. Zoe hurried inside and upstairs.

The squirrels were waiting on her window ledge as she walked into her office. She quickly closed the door behind her, dropped her bags and stepped over to the window to open it. The squirrels hopped over to her desk and sat down facing her expectantly.

"Good morning, Zoe. We spoke with the Air mage. Were you able to speak with him yesterday?" Rowantree greeted her in his formal manner using his own title for Mark.

"Yes, thank you, I was. I was going to try to find you later today, after I have finished with my teaching obligations." Rowantree's formal manner always rubbed off on her. "I am going to attempt to locate and tap into the ley lines."

Rowantree clasped his paws in front of him and Alder shifted. "Is that wise? The Night Mage will likely feel the attempt as we believe she has been doing the same thing," Alder asked.

"If she's either tapping into them already, or about to, I should too. For once I'd like to be ahead of things instead of running to catch up." Zoe surprised herself with her own statement. A few months ago she would have dithered around before taking such a step or even saying she was going to do something like that.

Both squirrels eyed her thoughtfully. Finally, Rowantree gave her a short nod. "Very well. We shall inform the crows and they and we will do our best to ensure you are not disturbed."

"Thank you. I think the Water mage will be able to help me and I plan on asking both the Air mage and George Wardmaster for help." Zoe shook her head at the formal tone she had adopted. Rowantree had really rubbed off on her!

"Where is the Night Mage? We do not feel her presence on campus," Alder asked.

Zoe grinned. "You'll have to ask Declan…the half-djinn as you call him. She attacked Mark and I in the parking lot the other morning and Declan and Geoff came to help us. Declan said he, uh, removed her. He wasn't sure where she went, he says it's woods. He wished her gone and she went. I believe he's looking."

Rowantree's eyebrows went up. "Much as I enjoy her absence, it is best if we know her whereabouts until we are able to neutralize her."

"I understand and I will make sure you are told as soon as I know anything," Zoe laughed.

"Very good. And we will do the same," Rowantree nodded. Alder bobbed his head and the two squirrels leapt back to the window and ran down the roof.

Zoe slowly closed the window thinking about what the squirrels had said. If Carolyn already succeeded in tapping into the ley lines that could explain why she had been able to launch two strong attacks, and set fire to Kieran's house, in the space of just a couple of days. Most of the energy she expended was renewed when she tapped the ley lines.

She glanced at the clock. Shit. Class started in fifteen

minutes. She hadn't managed to completely prep for any of them for today. Fortunately, she had taught all three classes before, so winging it wouldn't be too difficult. *Group discussions it is!*

* * *

After her classes, Zoe grabbed a quick lunch at one of the on-campus fast food joints. She usually tried to avoid eating at them as they were both overpriced and often less than appetizing. Although, she had to admit that burger had been pretty good. She walked back to her office affecting a casual stroll on a nice afternoon. As she moseyed her way through the quad, she sent out what she called her magical feelers. She still wasn't quite clear how it worked, but she was able to send out a sort of mental probe and test for any magic in the area. Zoe wasn't sure why she assumed that the nexus of the ley lines would be in the center of the quad, but it seemed like a logical place since the quad was at least the figurative center of campus.

There. What was that? Zoe stopped part way down the path that cut diagonally across the quad. There was a feeling similar to what she'd experienced at the fountain in Logan Square. A flow of magic moved under the quad. No. Two flows. Mark had said something about two ley lines crossing. She tried to follow one of the lines but didn't find any other lines. She reversed directions and after a minute got the impression of another flow of magic. The two lines did cross approximately in the center of the quad. But the feeling was faint and distant. If these lines were so powerful as the others had said why wasn't she getting a bigger hit from the nexus?

She glanced around again to make sure she was still alone or at least unnoticed. Cautiously she created a small bit of flame in the palm of her hand. She reached out to feed some of the nexus power into the flame. Nothing happened. She tried again, slowly reaching with just her Fire magic. She could feel the nexus, and tell that it was strong, but she couldn't get any of that power into the fire in her palm. Something was blocking her. It felt like a cover on top of the nexus. *It feels like trying to push through plastic wrap or something. Weird.*

She didn't want to draw any attention to herself, so she gave up on trying to pull power from the nexus and continued on to her office. She looked around for Rowantree or Alder feeling that she should let somebody know about this development as soon as possible.

Zoe entered Cooper Hall and trudged up the stairs to her second-floor office. As she passed through the small lounge at the top of the stairs, Declan Jin stood up from one of the comfortable chairs scattered around the space.

"Um...Dr. O'Brien?"

"Oh, hi, Declan. What's up?" Zoe smiled.

"Can I talk to you?" Declan's hands started to twist together, a sure sign of nerves in the kid.

"Of course. Come on in." Zoe led the way to her office.

Declan followed her in and turned to close the door. Zoe sat down and waved her hand towards one of her guest chairs. Declan sat down and Zoe noticed his hands twisting together in his lap.

"So, what's up?" she asked quietly.

"Um...I think like...um...that I like found Detweiler...I mean Professor Detweiler," Declan replied nervously.

"Well for one thing, I think we can drop the 'professor' title. There's no reason to be polite to somebody who tried to kill you," Zoe smiled. "And as for finding her, great. Where was she?"

"Well...um...she was like way out in the middle of Valley Forge. I-I don't know how I did that...or...um...why that spot...um...but I think she's like *really* angry now." Declan calmed down a little. "I left her there, though."

"Valley Forge? Wow. Um, okay. What were you thinking when you sent her there?" Zoe was surprised. Valley Forge was several miles away. She had to smile at the thought of the always meticulously dressed Carolyn stuck out in the middle of the woods wearing those heels and no car nearby.

"I just wanted her to go away...like far away. I guess I was thinking like in the middle of the woods or something..." he trailed off. "I guess if I can picture some place, I can send people there. Those woods must have been the closest thing to what I was picturing."

"That makes sense. I mean, you sent her back to her office that time she attacked you and Simon," Zoe responded. "But how did you find her, and does she know you found her?"

"I don't think so. I followed that sense of dark magic...um...remember when the squir...I mean Rowantree said he could feel dark magic moving around? Well, I felt it too so I followed that...um...I can send myself pretty much any place too...so I just sort of put myself near her to make sure, but then left again." Declan sounded more confident when he was describing his powers.

"Okay. Let's not get overconfident, but since she's still trying to figure out how to get back from Valley Forge, I'm not going to worry about her for now. We have another problem." Zoe grimaced.

Chapter Eleven

Declan gave Zoe a puzzled look. "What's happening now?"

Zoe took a deep breath. "You've heard that there is a nexus of ley lines on campus?" Declan nodded. "Well, I found it, or at least got close to the location, and I tried to access the lines…but I couldn't."

"D-do you…um…think that's because…um…you're new to mage stuff? I-I mean, not that you can't do it…b-but that maybe there's…um…some trick to it?" Declan's hands twisted slightly.

"No, you're right. I am new to this stuff. I don't know if there's a trick to it or not. I hope that's it and not that it's somehow blocked." Zoe shook her head.

"Maybe you can talk to Dr. LeGrande? I think he's still in his office right now," Declan responded.

"That's a good idea. Thanks, Declan," Zoe smiled.

"No problem. I'll walk over there with you. I have to talk to him about one of my required classes," Declan said with a shy smile.

Zoe closed her laptop and shoved it along with a couple of books and a small stack of papers into her bag. She had parked in the lot closer to Davis Hall, so she could find Kieran and they could go home after she talked to Simon.

She walked swiftly out of the building with Declan on her heels. Professor and student moved quickly across campus. They reached the halfway point when Declan suddenly grabbed Zoe's arm.

"Dr. O'Brien! What's that?" he pointed across the quad to a small black cloud of birds rising above Shelby Hall.

"It...looks like crows. What's going on?" Zoe squinted into the late afternoon sun trying to see what had disturbed the crows. The black cloud wheeled and flew across the quad toward Zoe and Declan. One bird detached itself from the flock and flew lower almost brushing Zoe's head.

"The Night Mage is nearby. She hunts *you*!" Darkwing screeched as he raced past.

"Shit!" Zoe exclaimed. She unslung her bags and thrust them at Declan. "You're faster than me...get to Dr. Davis or Dr. Ross or Dr. LeGrande, now. All three if you can. Get them out here A-S-A-P! And anybody else you can find!" She took two seconds to appreciate the fact that the faculty member in her thought to protect the laptop. *Figures. Personal danger looming but save the grading!*

"But..." Declan hesitated.

"Just go! We need help and you're fastest! I can hold on until you or somebody gets back." Zoe forcefully damped down her rising panic. Carolyn likely would be using balefire and Zoe only knew that she could block it temporarily. Hopefully, that would be long enough for reinforcements to arrive.

Declan took off at a dead run, Zoe's bags clutched in his hands. She glanced around the quad and was surprised to find it empty except for her and Declan's retreating figure. That was good. She really wanted to avoid any collateral damage or give Carolyn the opportunity to do something awful like take hostages or anything.

Zoe took a deep breath and attempted to slow her heart rate. As she did that, she carefully step by step built the strongest wall around herself that she could envision, bearing in mind Simon's warning to exclude Fire from the wall. She even remembered to put a shield over her head. In the middle of that process she caught a movement out of the corner of her eye. The trees were filled with squirrels. Rowantree and Alder dropped to the ground and ran over to her.

"I believe you should move closer to the edge of the quad." Rowantree was still formal even in the face of an emergency. "You are quite exposed out here. The Night Mage is moving in from behind Shelby Hall."

He was right. Zoe moved so that she had the library at her back. She faced Shelby Hall and the anticipated attack. It would have been nice if Darkwing could have been a bit more specific on the timing of Carolyn's arrival. But, she reminded herself, at least she got a warning.

She glanced around the quad again, wary of any passing students who might think it was a good idea to video the professor talking to squirrels on the quad. Thankfully, except for her, the quad remained empty.

"I saw the half-djinn run toward Davis Hall," Alder commented. "I assume he is bringing assistance rather than hiding."

"Yes. I sent him to get all the mages he could find," Zoe replied.

"That is good. Were you able to access the ley line nexus?" Rowantree asked.

Zoe shook her head at the surreal nature of the conversation. Standing in the middle of campus, waiting for an attack from a colleague who could throw a form of Fire that was unstoppable, having a discussion with two squirrels about whether she had accessed a source of magical power. Once again, she found herself in a situation that was absolutely not covered in the faculty handbook.

"I found it, but I couldn't access it. I can feel it, but when I try to pull power I run into some kind of barrier. It felt like trying to get through plastic wrap. I guess I'm doing something wrong. That's why Declan and I were out here now. We were walking over to talk to Simon to see if he had any ideas," Zoe replied.

Rowantree cocked his head to one side. "That is…unusual." His tone was worried. "You should be able to access the power if you can locate it."

Alder glanced back at them from his continuous survey of the quad area. "Perhaps the Night Mage is blocking access. I am not sure how that might be done, but we have not encountered a Night Mage directly before." He turned back to watch the quad.

Zoe stared between the two squirrels. "You mean Carolyn could stop the rest of us from accessing the nexus, but use all that power for herself? No wonder she is trying to take us all out!"

"Indeed…and I believe I see the half-djinn returning and he is followed by the other mages," Rowantree commented.

Zoe looked toward Davis Hall and saw Declan racing back followed closely by Kieran, Mark, Geoff, Josh, and Annmarie. They must have been in class in the building. Simon was at the rear of the group, phone in hand, moving at what could be best described as a rapid walk. Zoe was extremely happy to see them all.

Kieran ran right up to Zoe and stopped just short of grabbing her in a hug. "Are you okay? Declan says that Carolyn is here?"

"I'm fine. Nothing's happened yet." Zoe felt a tug at her pant leg. She looked down at Rowantree who was standing on his hind legs leaning on her.

"May I?" he asked politely.

"Uh, sure." Zoe wasn't quite certain what he wanted to do but figured it wouldn't hurt. She was surprised when he grabbed the material in her pants and scampered up to her shoulder.

"It is easier if I am at eye level with you all," the squirrel explained.

Simon puffed up to the group. "I've texted George. Hopefully he'll join us quickly."

Zoe nodded. She turned her head slightly to address Rowantree. "Do you have any more information? Darkwing was in a bit of a hurry when he went by."

Rowantree made a *tsk* sound. "He could have, no should have told you. But be that as it may, I will give you what information I have. When the half-djinn," he nodded to Declan, "sent the Night Mage to the woods at Valley Forge…"

"You sent her to Valley Forge? Cool!" Geoff interrupted, gaping at Declan.

Rowantree *tsk*-ed again and Geoff ducked his head. "Sorry."

"When the half-djinn discovered the Night Mage in Valley Forge, we alerted the crows and they in turn alerted the crows and squirrels in Valley Forge. The Night Mage believes that this is Zoe's doing as she does not believe that students have the ability or strength to stand against her. She is unaware of the powers of the half-djinn and believes him to be an ordinary mage," Rowantree continued in his formal tone.

"Well, I'm not going to try to change her mind on that one," Declan muttered. Mark gave him a wink and Geoff laughed.

"Wait," Zoe said. "How did you find all this out? Are you psychic or something?"

Rowantree glanced over with a slightly offended expression. "Of course not. The Night Mage has a habit of talking out loud to herself. The squirrels in Valley Forge simply followed her as she walked through the woods."

Zoe's mouth fell open and then she laughed. "Okay. That works."

"As we just heard, she, the Night Mage, has managed to extricate herself from Valley Forge and return to campus. As I said, she is looking for Zoe. Also, I do not think that she will expect the rest of you to stand with Zoe. Night Mages are jealous of sharing power and glory and so do not ally themselves with others except as they see others as useful. They do not have friends." Rowantree finished his short talk with a quick nod of his head.

CRACK! CRAAAACK!

Two whips of Fire exploded over the top of Shelby Hall and hit in the middle of the quad. The mages jumped and Zoe could see everybody creating the strongest shields they could. She expanded and shifted her own shield so that it acted as the outer layer of defense around all of them. When she and Mark had interrupted Carolyn's attack against Simon and Declan, Zoe noticed that while it didn't put out the balefire, her multi-Element barrier was able to stop it. Balefire slid off of Zoe's all-Element shields for some reason. She'd have to figure that out later.

Carolyn appeared around the corner of Shelby Hall. Carrying a fireball in each hand, she stalked directly toward Zoe. The fireballs didn't have the black edge to them that Zoe knew indicated balefire and she breathed a little easier. At first, Carolyn didn't appear to notice the others standing with Zoe, her eyes were locked on Zoe. Kieran shifted and moved closer to Zoe and Carolyn's head came up. She stopped and stared at the small group of mages. After a couple of seconds she laughed and continued forward.

"It really doesn't matter how many supposed friends you have, I have unlimited access to the nexus for power and you do not," she called across the quad and laughed again.

Damn. She just cackled.

"Is that true?" Kieran muttered to Zoe.

"Yeah. We have to figure that out," Zoe answered.

Rowantree jumped from Zoe's shoulder to the tree behind her and Alder quickly followed him up into the branches.

Catching sight of the squirrels, Carolyn lobbed a ball of normal Fire at the tree, but Zoe created a mobile barrier, like a knight's shield and swung it to meet the fireball. She could feel some heat as the fireball dissipated across her shield. Zoe quickly sent out a tendril of Air to check her barrier around the group.

Simon narrowed his eyes and stared at Carolyn. "She is not using balefire yet. When you see a black edge to her fire, *that* is balefire," he announced to the group. "I suggest we keep our response defensive for the time being so that she does not use the balefire. She is confident right now that she can succeed with regular Fire."

Carolyn launched several fireballs in a row, aiming each one at a different person in the group. Zoe noticed that at least three headed toward the students, while the rest were aimed straight at Zoe's head. Her barrier deflected the fireballs and Zoe launched her own in turn. Carolyn managed to dodge quickly, but Mark's well-timed blast of Air knocked her off her feet.

Snarling, Carolyn jumped back up and threw four fireballs in quick succession at Mark's head. Kieran created a firehose level of water that again knocked Carolyn down, in addition to soaking her expensive-looking pantsuit. Carolyn did not appear to be shielding herself and Zoe wondered if she was so arrogant she didn't think she needed the protection. Zoe suspected that would change quickly.

"Remember, we don't want her to think she *must* use the balefire. That will not end well for us!" Simon urged.

Mark turned and studied his department chair. "And how will this end for *us*, Simon, if we let her go? She'll just come back. Balefire or not, we cannot allow her to roam around campus taking out students and other faculty!"

Simon had the grace to look embarrassed. "No, no, my boy. I didn't mean to leave her free to continue her depredations. Not at all. I simply meant that we need to lull her into a false sense of security so that she does not decide to use balefire."

Mark stared at him for a long breath and then gave a curt nod. He turned back to face Carolyn, but Zoe saw him exchange a grim look with Kieran. What was going on? Why was Mark so angry at Simon?

She decided she couldn't worry about that right now. They needed to have a plan to deal with Carolyn and make it permanent.

"Guys? Let's focus on Carolyn. We need to stop her and stop her now," Zoe said tersely, keeping one eye on Carolyn as the Night Mage slowly came across the quad. "I agree with Simon that we don't want her to feel like she has to use balefire. But she'll probably use it anyway just to show that she can. Why isn't she shielding herself? Anybody got any good ideas?"

Simon threw Zoe a grateful look and cleared his throat. "Zoe, I believe that your ability to engage with all four Elements will work to our advantage. I noted that her balefire was reflected back at her when you…ah…assisted myself and young Declan in the parking lot several days ago."

"Yeah, I remembered that too. What are you thinking?" Zoe kept her eyes on Carolyn who was having some trouble walking across the quad in her heels. Zoe reflected that the most mundane of things could be what gave them the edge. Carolyn had given up trying to walk across the grass and planted herself so she was directly facing Zoe about a hundred yards away. Four more fireballs were in her hands.

"How much effort would it take you to enclose this group in a dome shield that will also allow us to return her attacks?" Simon asked.

"I'm already sort of doing that. I have a wall in front of us, and you've seen me, Mark and Kieran work through it." Zoe glanced back at Simon.

"Of course, of course. I'm sorry. I'm feeling a bit frazzled at the moment," Simon apologized. Zoe noticed he wasn't bouncing on the balls of his feet as he usually did. But then, being under attack by a Night Mage, for the second time she reminded herself, did tend to take the bounce out of one's steps.

"I can make it a dome. Any other ideas?" she waved off Simon's apology.

"Well, one…but I'm afraid it might be ugly…" Simon's voice trailed off.

"What do you mean 'ugly'?" Mark cut in. Kieran was standing sideways so he could keep Carolyn in view, but he had an alarmed look on his face.

"Well my dear boy, I mean…ah…the results may be permanent." Simon looked abashed.

"Um…professors? We need to do something *now!*" Josh cut into their discussion.

Zoe spun back to face Carolyn in time to see her launch all the fireballs in her hands, and then Fire tinged with black, balefire, appeared around her hands.

"Simon?" Zoe heard her voice go up a notch.

"Ah…you, me, and young Geoff need to combine our Fire and throw one fireball of the combined Fire at her. Well, many, but each one needs to be a combination," Simon answered hurriedly.

"Geoff! Get over here!" Mark said sharply.

Geoff rushed over and looked expectantly at Zoe.

"What're we doing?" his tone was excited.

"Combining Fire. You, me, Dr. LeGrande. Now." Zoe said shortly.

"Okay. How do we do that?" Geoff was grinning widely, and Zoe realized he was enjoying himself. *Men! Dangerous situation and they're all over it and having fun.*

"Simon?"

"If you both would create a fireball and hold them toward me," Simon began.

Zoe and Geoff immediately pulled Fire into their hands and pushed them toward Simon. He had created his own fireball and somehow enlarged it until it encompassed Zoe's and Geoff's.

"Now, please withdraw your hands," Simon requested.

After they complied, he had a large fireball sitting in both of his hands. The "feel" she got from the magic emanating from the fireball told Zoe it wasn't an ordinary one. Simon turned and stepped in front of Zoe and Geoff. He launched the combined fireball directly at Carolyn. She dodged rapidly to her left but the combined fireball turned slightly and followed her. Carolyn screamed and hopped awkwardly to her right. Her high heels were causing her a great deal of difficulty when it came to avoiding Simon's missile. The combined fireball didn't make the second turn and fell into the grass.

Carolyn managed to stay on her feet and threw four ordinary fireballs one after the other at Simon. For some reason she wasn't using the balefire she had called up. Simon's fireball had ignited the grass on the quad and was spreading. Groundskeeping was going to be really pissed.

From the corner of her eye, Zoe could see that Josh, Annmarie, and Declan had their heads together and were speaking in low tones. She really hoped they weren't trying to come up with something on their own.

"Again!" Simon turned around to Zoe and Geoff. They

immediately proffered fireballs and once again he absorbed them into his own. *I'm going to have to learn how to do that.*

Simon launched the second combined fireball and managed to catch Carolyn on her leg. She screamed and sent five more fireballs of her own in their direction. Simon gestured to Geoff and Zoe and they set him up for a third time.

"Yeah, that'll keep her from using the balefire," Kieran muttered.

Mark scowled in Simon's direction and sent a hurricane toward Carolyn while Kieran fired his water cannon.

Carolyn, unbalanced on her high heels, hit an uneven spot in the lawn and stumbled again.

"She is tapping the nexus! She will have the energy to use the balefire without limit!" Rowantree called from his perch in the tree over Zoe.

"Got it!" Zoe answered. She reinforced her three-Element wall with another layer.

Why wasn't Carolyn constantly shielding herself? It seemed like she was putting her shields up and then down again. For some reason Zoe kept worrying about it. Carolyn appeared scattered and not thinking clearly. She was a mage, she should know how to protect herself, so why wasn't she doing that?

Zoe glanced back over to where Josh, Annmarie, and Declan were standing. Declan was staring at Carolyn with a look of concentration. Annmarie and Josh were standing on either side of him, half-turned so they could see both Declan and Carolyn. Declan gave a short nod and Josh and Annmarie simultaneously hit Carolyn with a tornado of Air and a blast of Water. Carolyn staggered as she tried to stand up.

"Declan! What are you guys doing?" Zoe called.

He gave her a quick sheepish look and hurried over to stand next to her.

"I just now figured out how to take down her shields so

when I did that, Josh and Annmarie hit her...um...I probably should have said something, but that's the first time I did it...I'm sorry." He looked both excited and nervous.

"Just give us a heads-up next time. That explains things a bit." Zoe turned to Simon. "Simon, Declan can shred her shields! That's how Josh and Annmarie just hit her. If he does that and we hit her with one of those combo fireballs and the others hit her at the same time, can we take her out?"

She realized she was likely talking about killing Carolyn, but Carolyn was intent on killing them, or at least Zoe, so it seemed like a fair trade.

Simon raised an eyebrow. "Yes. That will work."

Mark and Kieran looked at Zoe. "Are you sure?" Mark asked.

Zoe took a deep breath. "Yes. We have to stop her and she won't just quit. Besides, you all said it the other day...she's made a pact with something evil. I don't see that we can just let her promise to be a good girl and walk away."

Simon turned to Zoe and Geoff once again. They gave him more fireballs. He looked at the others. "Be ready to hit her at the same time." His face was grim.

Mark and Kieran arranged themselves next to Josh and Annmarie so that the two Water and two Air mages were next to each other. Geoff and Zoe stood slightly behind Simon, with fireballs in each hand. Declan stood slightly apart to Zoe's right.

Zoe took another deep breath and nodded at Declan. "Go!"

Declan's eyes narrowed and he stared fixedly across the quad at Carolyn. She had made it back onto her feet looking damp and scraggly. But her face was twisted and she pulled more balefire into her hands until they disappeared behind black-rimmed Fire. She raised her arms and drew them both back in a move that signaled she was going to throw the balefire at the small group of mages facing her.

"Now!" Declan half-yelled.

Simon launched the combination fireball he held and immediately turned to Zoe and Geoff for more of their Fire. Mark and Josh built a combined hurricane and directed it toward Carolyn while Kieran and Annmarie created a wall of water and pushed it across the quad.

Carolyn screamed and drew her hands sharply forward flinging the balefire off them and into Zoe's wall. As it had in the parking lot, the multi-Element wall somehow reflected the balefire back toward Carolyn. This time, however, she was too preoccupied with the hurricanes, the wall of water, and Simon's second fireball, to notice what had happened.

The balefire cut through the attacks of the other mages and flew back directly at the Night Mage who had called it up. Zoe closed her eyes and plugged her ears, but she could still hear the horrible screaming as the balefire hit Carolyn.

The screaming suddenly cut off. Zoe opened her eyes and saw Carolyn lying on the ground, seemingly untouched, but not moving. There was no sign of the balefire.

She looked to her right and saw Declan gaping at Carolyn while his hands twisted themselves into knots. Josh was hugging Annmarie as she buried her face in his shoulder and Geoff had his arms draped over his head, staring into space.

"Hell," Mark muttered.

Kieran shook his head. "You know she's there," he said, his voice tinged with sorrow.

Simon glanced over at Zoe. "I believe you can remove your shield." He crossed himself, which surprised Zoe, and started walking toward the prone figure in the middle of the quad.

Kieran sent water toward the still-burning patch of grass.

Zoe removed her defensive walls and turned toward Kieran and Mark.

"Um…what do we do now?" She felt drained.

"We get the students out of here and tell Simon to find George. I believe Professor Detweiler had an aneurysm or heart attack while walking across campus. The provost will be the one to take care of everything," Mark said with a last look at Carolyn. Simon was bending over her, but carefully not touching her.

"Yes, students. Um…okay." Zoe's brain scrambled to take it all in.

"I'll let Simon know what we're doing. Will you guys be in Mark's office?" Kieran asked.

"Yes, we will," Mark answered. He gestured to students. "C'mon guys. Let's go." The four of them plus Zoe numbly followed Mark towards the dorms.

Mark walked with Josh and Geoff, their heads together talking in low voices. Zoe saw Mark pull out his wallet and hand money to Josh.

Zoe turned to Annmarie. "Are you going to be okay?"

Annmarie nodded. "I'm going to call my dad and all of us will talk to him. He's dealt with a Night Mage before. When I told my parents about last semester, they told me to call them immediately if anything else happened." She rubbed her face with one hand. "I don't think this is what they were thinking but I know they'll help."

Zoe glanced at Declan. "What about you?" He had stopped twisting his hands together at least, but he still looked nervous.

"I-I g-guess I'll figure something out. I don't really want to call my mom…" he trailed off.

"Talk to my dad, Declan," Annmarie said. "He's pretty cool, and he won't judge or anything."

Declan shot her a relieved look. "Um…okay…if you're sure. That'd be good."

"I'm sure," Annmarie answered firmly. "This will be a

group call. All of us with my dad."

Zoe felt better knowing she and Mark weren't simply dumping the students off to deal with the aftermath of the fight themselves. Annmarie seemed convinced that her father could provide a good sounding board for all of them.

Zoe and Mark got the students to their dorm and then headed back to his office. Kieran joined them there a couple of minutes later.

"Simon's gone to George's office…I don't know how George didn't hear everything, but Simon will fill him in. Rowantree and Alder will let the rest of the squirrels and the crows know what happened as well. They asked me to tell you to please tell your cats, Zoe." Kieran looked tired.

Zoe put her head in her hands. She didn't want to think about what had just happened yet.

She raised her head. "We are SO lucky nobody came through the quad just now."

"Yeah, we are," Mark responded. "That doesn't seem like a normal coincidence."

"No, it doesn't. But I'm too tired to think about it right now," Kieran commented.

Mark looked at the two of them. "David's making dinner tonight. You guys should come over. Just follow me home. We need to decompress and talk." He pulled out his phone to text his husband.

Zoe nodded.

"Thanks, yeah. Good idea," Kieran sighed.

Chapter Twelve

Zoe was silent as she drove, following Mark to his house. Kieran stared out the window with his elbow propped on the door and his chin in his hand.

After about ten minutes, Kieran turned to Zoe. "Are you okay?" His voice was soft.

"Yeah, I'm…well…not fine, but yeah, okay. I guess. What about you?" Zoe glanced at him.

"I know she did it to herself, but I still hate to see anybody so far gone…a Night Mage…she's in hell, literally, right now." Kieran sighed and turned back to stare out the window.

"Kieran? Um…until last semester…um…I…like I didn't really think about hell and demons and all that. Um…I mean I know what I research, but…um…is that for real?" Zoe had a difficult time putting her unease into words. She felt supremely ignorant.

"Yeah, it is. Remember, you told me that that woman's body, the coven member who was killed by the demon, disappeared at the fountain? While I was still knocked out? Well, she disappeared because the demon was right there and just took her when he went back. Carolyn…she was killed by magic, power that she traded for with her soul or whatever makes you human. She just kept going down a path of personal power. So, her soul was already gone. She just didn't realize it before. But she does now."

"Mark said…aneurysm or heart attack? What did he mean?" Zoe desperately wanted to make sense of the last few hours.

"When the medical examiner does their thing, her death will probably look like it was caused by one of those two events. As a Night Mage, and tapping the ley line nexus, she had a great deal of power." He rubbed his eyes. "We got lucky. She didn't shield at first and when she did, Declan's unique power combo was able to remove her shields. If it wasn't for that we'd still be out there…and maybe losing. And we had a lot of combined power…especially you."

"But why didn't she shield at the beginning of the fight?" Zoe asked tiredly.

"Have you *met* Carolyn?" Kieran snarked.

Zoe snorted. "Yeah, she's a bit arrogant, isn't she…wasn't she?"

She pulled up to Mark and David's house and parked behind Mark in the driveway. As they climbed out of the car the front door opened and David waved them in.

The three of them walked in the door and were greeted with bear hugs from David.

"Are you guys okay? Zoe you look exhausted." David handed her a glass of wine and gave Kieran and Mark each a beer.

"Thanks," Zoe replied. "I'm tired, but okay."

Kieran gave David a salute with his beer bottle.

David went back into the kitchen to finish dinner and the other three sat down in the living room.

Mark gave Zoe a hard look. "Are you really okay? This is the first time you've really dealt with this kind of thing…the death of another mage, I mean."

"Believe it or not, I am okay. Yeah, I'm a little shell-shocked at everything, but she attacked us, and it was her own balefire that killed her, so yeah, I'm okay…I think," Zoe answered.

Mark glanced over at Kieran. "Is she okay?"

Kieran turned to look at Zoe and put an arm around her shoulders. "Yeah, I think she really is. We talked a bit on the way over here about…everything. She didn't grow up in our world…mages and magic, so she's still figuring things out but I think she's getting a pretty good handle on things."

"I'll take your word for it," Mark sighed.

"Hey! I'm right here and I just told you both that I'm okay," Zoe protested.

Mark laughed. "You're like my own little sister. I'm always going to double-check what you tell me when it's about how you're doing."

Zoe stuck her tongue out at him, then her expression softened. "I really am okay, you guys. Really. I promise. I'm a big girl and I'll figure this all out. No, I haven't really had to think about it before, but that doesn't mean I'm not *capable* of thinking about it. Okay? Kieran and I talked about…um…hell, and Carolyn going there, and that's a little weird for me. But on one level I understand it. In my mind it's all connected, I think. I just learned about magic last semester, but I also fought a demon. Kind of a steep learning curve there. So, learning about the mage world and at the same time learning that hell exists, and the people really can sell their souls, makes a weird kind of sense. I mean if one of those things exists, why shouldn't the other?" She took a sip of wine.

Kieran shrugged and raised an eyebrow at Mark. "It *is* her research area after all," he commented.

"Yes. Yes, it is," Zoe retorted.

David stuck his head out of the kitchen. "Okay guys, dinner's ready."

They sat down to beef stew, mashed potatoes, and salad. Zoe silently admitted to herself that she would consider a mage fight on a regular basis if it meant that she could eat David's cooking more often.

After a few minutes of nothing but the sounds of four people eating, David turned to Zoe. "Mark told me what happened today, and he's told me about the other attacks. Have you talked to your neighbor, um, Kim, yet?"

Zoe raised her eyebrows. "Not about today obviously. She knows about the other stuff. She was there when Kieran's house burned down." She glanced at Kieran. "I figured we'd tell her when we got back tonight…or you could."

Kieran nodded. "Yeah, we need to. And we should tell Rob and Joe, too. They're the other mages in the immediate neighborhood," he added for Mark and David's benefit.

"I remember them, isn't one of them an Earth mage?" David asked.

"Yeah, Rob is," Zoe answered.

Zoe gazed at the three men. "So…there is something else I didn't get a chance to tell you guys yet," she started. She took another sip of wine and glanced up to find three pairs of eyes staring intently at her. She swallowed hard.

"Earlier today, before all the excitement, I tried to access the ley line nexus. It's in the middle of the quad, or at least right near there. I could feel it, but when I tried to…I dunno, tap into it? draw some power? whatever you do, I couldn't do it. It felt like I was trying to get at it through plastic wrap or something. Is there a trick to getting power from a ley line? Carolyn said she was drawing from it, so I assume it's possible…" she still got nervous talking about magic and using magic. It just seemed so weird to be talking about it so casually, or normally, or something. *But it is real and so you CAN talk about it with other people who are mages…deal.*

"That's what you were talking about earlier?" Kieran

asked.

Zoe nodded.

David frowned. "No, if you can feel it, you should be able to draw from it. There's no trick, other than making sure you don't drown yourself in power."

"Wait. Drown myself in power? What do you mean?" Zoe's anxiety returned.

"Well, you don't want to take so much power that you overwhelm your ability to focus and control it," Kieran replied.

"Yeah. Remember at the fountain when George told you that you needed to learn finesse?" Mark asked.

"Yeah…he said I could drain myself and die if I didn't learn to control it. But, if the ley lines are a power source, how can I drain myself?" Zoe gnawed her lower lip. She told herself she did need to learn control, but a small voice in her head kept asking what was the use of all this power if she couldn't just smash the people who tried to hurt her and her friends? *Because then you're using your power just to get your own way. And that's what Carolyn did. Is that really what you want to do?*

"Well, you wouldn't drain yourself, but taking in power from a strong source, like ley lines, and especially like a nexus of ley lines…or even better, something like the fountain in Logan Square, can overwhelm your system. And then it becomes very similar to throwing power around to smash things. There's a sort of burst of power when you first tap into the ley lines. You have to control the inflow same as you have to with the outflow. 'Zoe SMASH!' is not a long-term solution to things," David smiled.

"Well, it would feel good…at least for a little while." Zoe grinned before sighing and staring down at her twisting hands. "You're right, though. I can't and I shouldn't go around just throwing power out. George gave me some ideas, but then being provost took over his life. I really don't know much more about all of this than I did last semester."

"We should practice. Kim has the space in her back yard, and she can help too. Let's figure something out this weekend." Kieran put his hand on top of hers where they lay twisting together in her lap.

"Great idea. Now, who wants dessert?" David stood up and started clearing plates.

A little over an hour later, having updated Kim on their way home, Zoe and Kieran walked up to the gate leading into Kim's back yard and the door to his apartment. He'd taken Kim's warnings to heart and didn't use the door that opened directly onto the sidewalk.

"Let's get Kim, and we can maybe work on some stuff in the back yard. It's not that late so we can spend an hour or so. Do you think you should get the cats?" Kieran commented as he unlocked the gate.

"Okay. But why do I need the cats?" Zoe replied, puzzled.

"Because we can sense other magics in the area and sense how strongly you're pulling magic in or using it up." Flash's voice came out of the shadows in the yard.

Zoe jumped. "Damn! You scared me! What are you doing here?"

Moose sauntered into the small pool of light by the back gate. "The squirrels told us what happened today. You should close the gate." The long-haired cat sat down and resumed what seemed like a never-ending grooming routine.

Kieran glared at the cats. "Maybe a little warning next time? I practically had a heart attack. For some reason I'm not doing well with surprises right now." His tone held more than a hint of sarcasm.

"Like what? Meet you on the sidewalk? Do you know how many people would find that strange?" Flash stared up at them both.

"Fine," Zoe sighed. "Let's go find Kim and see what we can do."

At that moment Kim walked out onto the small deck off her back door and came down the steps into the back yard.

"What's up? The cats showed up here about twenty minutes ago saying that you were on the way." She leaned down and gave both cats scratches behind the ears. She was rewarded with lout purrs and head-butting.

Zoe stared at the cats. "How did you know we were on our way home? Never mind. I can guess…the squirrels."

"No, the crows this time. The squirrels couldn't have gotten us a message that fast." Moose sat down and neatly curled his tail around his feet.

"Okay. The crows." Zoe sighed and looked up at Kim. "It has been a hell of a day. I have been forcefully reminded that I really need to practice finesse," she made air quotes with her fingers, "in the drawing and releasing of power. I was told that 'Zoe SMASH' is not considered the best way to go about using my mage powers."

Kim laughed. "Yeah, probably not. But that sounds like a really fun way to go about it!"

"That's what *I* said!" Zoe agreed.

"She *is* getting good at that method," Kieran added. "It just leaves a lot of broken stuff in her wake."

"Okay, okay! I get it. I need to fine tune some things," Zoe surrendered.

There was a knocking at the gate. "That'll be Rob," Kim said heading over to open the gate. "I figured that maybe an Earth mage would help too. Joe's busy, or he'd've come too."

Zoe felt a little overwhelmed. All these people were volunteering to teach her how to use her powers. And except for Kieran, she'd only known them for a few months.

Correctly interpreting her expression, Kieran leaned over to her. "Nobody wants an untrained Elemental mage running around," he whispered.

She glared at him, but he only grinned. "Fine," she muttered.

"Hey, Zoe. How are you?" Rob ambled over and gave her a brief hug.

"I'm good, Rob. Good to see you." Zoe returned the hug. Rob was a tall, gangly man with brown hair and brown eyes. To Zoe he was the perfect image of an Earth mage – like the way people and their dogs seemed to look like each other. Did mages start to resemble their power? And what did that mean for her as an Elemental mage?

Rob and Kieran shook hands. "How about you?" Rob asked.

"I'm okay," Kieran answered. "Been a bit stressful, but I think I'm managing."

"Good, good. Kim told me about the fire. I'm sorry to hear about that. I heard about the Night Mage. So what's the problem?" Rob was laid back as always.

"Well, Zoe needs practice with her powers, and according to anonymous sources," Kim grinned at the cats, "she also needs to learn finesse. Apparently, she's been going all Hulk every time she finds herself in a fight."

Zoe sighed. This wasn't going to stop, was it? At least with Carolyn gone, she had some time to learn more about her power.

Rob grinned at her. "Well, sometimes you need to go all Hulk."

After an hour and a half spent working on fine-tuning her use of all the Elements, and getting critiqued by Moose and Flash, Rob walked Zoe and the cats back to her house. Both she and Kieran had class stuff to work on tonight so he was going to come over for breakfast the next morning and then they would go to campus together.

Zoe said good night to Rob and followed the cats into the

house. She thought about everything that had happened that afternoon and evening. The fight with Carolyn had exposed some weaknesses she knew she had but had put off investigating too closely. Zoe shoved Carolyn's death into a back corner of her mind and focused on what she'd learned about her own powers. She hadn't realized that she could raise or lower the amount of power she used. During tonight's work with Kim, Rob, and Kieran she'd figured out that she could use power from three of the Elements to increase her capabilities in the fourth. That was news to all of them.

Now, however, there was one last important issue that that required her focus, and they were headbutting her shins.

Zoe looked at the cats. "I'm going to guess that you guys want more food?"

"Of course. We're starving." Moose made a beeline for the kitchen followed closely by Flash.

She walked into the kitchen behind the cats and gazed thoughtfully at the bottle of wine sitting on the counter. *Nah. I already had some at dinner. I just need some sleep.*

The *thump* of a surprisingly hard cat head into her shin reminded her of her priorities. Zoe grabbed the cat food, filled the dishes, made sure they had fresh water, and then headed upstairs to bed.

The next morning, far too bright and far too early, Kieran knocked on her door. Zoe cracked it open and waved him toward the kitchen and the coffee pot. He gave her a quick kiss on her forehead and wandered off to find the coffee. Zoe, clutching her own mug, sank into the sofa and waited for him to come back.

"At least we don't have to teach today," she announced as he returned.

"Yeah. Small favors. I do have a couple of meetings around lunch time." Kieran dropped onto the sofa next to her, cradling his cup of coffee. Zoe leaned against his shoulder. It felt good to just sit with him. Flash and Moose jumped up and crammed themselves next to her.

"Um...guys? Do you have to squash yourselves in like that?" she glared at the cats.

"What? We're comfortable." Flash twisted around pushing his front feet into Zoe's thigh while he tried to clean his back legs.

"Well, as long as *you're* comfortable, that's what really matters," Zoe commented.

"Of course." Unperturbed, Moose gazed at her with wide eyes. Kieran laughed.

"Don't encourage them!" Zoe turned her glare on him.

"I'm sorry. But you have to admit..." he grinned at her, pointing at the cats.

"No, I don't! At least not in *front* of them," she shot back.

"Okay! Okay!" Kieran raised the hand not holding the coffee cup in defeat.

"Are you going to try to access the nexus point again today?" Moose asked, stretching out across her lap.

"I was thinking about it, why?" Zoe absently petted the grey cat.

"You should have somebody with you for protection," Moose answered. "You'll be distracted and need somebody to watch your back."

Zoe glanced at Kieran. "What's your schedule look like today?"

"Like I said a couple meetings around lunch. I should be done by two-ish. Want to try later? Like when there are far fewer people wandering around the quad?" Kieran took a sip of coffee.

"Good idea." Zoe looked down at the cats sprawled across her lap. "Do you guys want to come in with us today? You can wander around campus if you promise not to get caught."

Moose and Flash exchanged glances and Flash looked up

at Zoe. "Yes. We will. We should speak with Rowantree and Darkwing directly anyway."

Zoe's stomach did a small flip-flop. If the cats wanted to speak with Rowantree and Darkwing in person, they must be worried.

Reading her mind once again, Moose stared up at Zoe. "No, we're not worried. It will just be easier to get information. Stop panicking."

"I'm not panicking…yet." She looked at Kieran. "Let's get some breakfast and then head in to campus? If I'm going to be poking around the ley lines this afternoon, I'd like to get some work done before that."

"Good idea. What's for breakfast?" Kieran smiled at her.

"Bagels and fixings. It's serve-yourself," Zoe smiled back.

* * *

The drive in to campus was quiet. Neither Zoe nor Kieran had much to say that they hadn't already said. The cats in their carriers in the back seat were quiet too, which worried Zoe more than she cared to admit. Since she had learned that they could talk, it felt like they hadn't shut up. Between unending demands for food and more food, and smart-ass remarks about magic, punctuated by alarm over something, they talked a *lot*. Quiet was not their norm.

They were early enough that the lot behind Davis Hall still had some available spots in it. While this lot was further from her office, it was closer to the quad and Zoe liked the idea of a shorter walk to the car after working with the ley lines. She and Kieran parted ways at the entrance to Davis. Zoe, trailed by the cats, continued on the path that took her away from Shelby Hall and around the far side of the quad. About halfway down she spotted a squirrel sitting in the middle of the path.

The cats paused and Flash looked up at her. "That's Rowantree. We'll meet you here when you come to deal with the ley lines." He and Moose strolled off to the side toward a small grouping of three trees in the far corner of the quad. Rowantree darted off in the same direction.

Zoe watched the animals until they all disappeared behind one of the trees. She walked on to Cooper Hall and her office marveling at her calm acceptance of the strange reality that now made up her world.

Approaching her office door Zoe automatically glanced further down the hall at Meredith Cruickshank's door. Long habit born of self-protection, and the experience of a couple of surprise visits this semester, meant that now Zoe always checked to see if Meredith was in her office.

Dammit. The light was on and the door was slightly ajar. Meredith had decided to come into the office today. Why today of all days? *Well, this sucks.*

Zoe tiptoed the last few feet to her own office and quietly let herself in. She debated closing the door all the way, but that wouldn't stop Meredith from interrupting if she felt it was in her interest. In the end, Zoe didn't close the door quite all the way. In faculty door-language this signaled a hard-working faculty member who was willing to be interrupted but only for the very strongest of reasons. Zoe felt that it also subtly showed that she didn't really care if Meredith was around or not. Faculty politics could get as complicated as a long-running soap opera.

Sure enough, Zoe had barely gotten her computer turned on and was emptying her bag onto her desk when the sharp *clack clack* of heels against linoleum announced Meredith's walk down the hall. The clacking stopped outside of Zoe's door and was followed by a preemptory knock on the door which simultaneously pushed it open.

"Oh, hi, Zoe!" Meredith's faux cheery voice swirled into

the office, followed by the wanna-be witch herself.

"Hi, Meredith. How are you?" Zoe barely glanced up from opening up her e-mail.

"Well, you seem to be in a mood today. I just wanted to say hi." The faux cheerfulness was replaced by faux offense. Meredith could blow hot and cold inside of five seconds.

Zoe frowned at her computer screen in a delaying tactic and then looked up at Meredith. "I'm sorry, I'm just really busy today. Since I don't have to teach today, I'm hoping to get a lot of prep done and even get in some research work." She mentally kicked herself for still feeling like she had to justify her actions to Meredith. This untenured fear thing would not go away until she got herself over that hurdle.

"Okay. Whatever. I was just on my way to meet with Morgan Ammon. We're going to discuss some research I'm working on and a project that I'll start when I get back in the fall," Meredith smirked.

Zoe quickly turned away from the computer to stare at Meredith. "A project with the president? What's it on?" She tried to sound interested rather than nervous.

"Oh well, wouldn't you like to know? I guess you'll just have to wait and see like everybody else." Meredith's grin was nasty.

Maintaining a calm demeanor, Zoe forced herself to shrug. "Okay. Whatever. Just trying to be interested," she said in the same tone Meredith had used earlier. "Enjoy your meeting." Zoe turned back to her computer.

Meredith stood in the doorway for another heartbeat before turning around with a muttered "Bitch" and stomping back down to her own office.

Despite her racing heart, Zoe forced herself to continue going through her emails until she was certain Meredith was back in her office. She texted Mark and Kieran, giving them a very brief description of her encounter with Meredith and signed off telling them she would fill in the details when she saw them later that afternoon.

The encounter with Meredith and her flaunting her meeting with the president made it difficult for Zoe to concentrate on either class prep or research work. *What the hell are they doing now? That's just a bad combination.*

Zoe closed her eyes and focused on her breathing. There was nothing she could do right now. Kieran had meetings, Mark was teaching, and she was supposed to be working on class prep and her own research. She opened her eyes and stared at her computer screen. One of the emails was from a journal editor and contained reviewer comments on an article she had submitted. That should keep her busy enough until she could try to tap the ley lines again. She clicked on the attachment.

Chapter Thirteen

Zoe stood up and stretched, tilting her head from side to side to work out the kinks in her neck. She glanced at her phone. It was almost two o'clock. Kieran and Mark should both be finished with teaching and meetings and they could all go and again try to access the ley line nexus. Hopefully, with Carolyn's death, the block on the nexus would be gone too.

Zoe walked down to the restroom, checking the status of Meredith's door as she did so. It was still mostly closed with the light on indicating that Meredith was still inside. Zoe kept her steps as quiet as possible going to and from the restroom. She knew that if Meredith thought she was leaving the office she would find some excuse to interrogate Zoe as to where she was going and why. A year ago, hell a semester ago, that would have caused Zoe nearly sky-high anxiety, but facing down a demon (and winning) had given Zoe a much-needed boost of self-confidence. Even if Meredith did try to ruin Zoe's chances at tenure, Zoe knew she had all the support she needed from the faculty mages across campus. It helped if she kept telling herself that.

Nevertheless, old habits die hard, and grad school had deeply ingrained the need to be cautious around so-called superiors. Zoe left the restroom and walked very quietly back to her office and very quietly closed the door all the way. She texted Mark and Kieran to let them know she was going to drop her stuff in her car before going back out to the quad.

A knock on her door followed by Meredith's voice announced that Zoe hadn't been as quiet as she would have liked. She did indulge herself in a small act of revenge and finished putting her laptop and articles into her bag before opening her door.

"Hey, Meredith. What's up?" Zoe pulled the door open before turning back, picking up her bag and purse, and making it clear she was on her way out.

"You're leaving? I thought you had work to do? Or aren't you worried about getting your research published?" Meredith was in top form today, managing to make five hours of work seem like nothing. Zoe shook her head in disbelief.

"I've been working on a revise and resubmit actually. And, it's been about five hours of work between that and reading some stuff for the next article. How did your day go?" Zoe injected just the right saccharine tone combined with a level of disinterest that she knew would drive Meredith crazy.

"Great. It was good. So, are you heading home?" Meredith kept the sneering tone but retreated a few steps in the face of Zoe's continued move out the door.

"Yep. Going home, have some wine, do some class prep. Later." Zoe gave a brief wave of her hand, closed the office door and walked down the hall.

Another muttered "Bitch" followed her down the stairs. Zoe grinned. Small victories, even if they were petty, were fun.

Zoe emerged from Cooper Hall into a lovely early spring day. She immediately felt better about working with the ley lines. She moseyed down the path that would take her back to Davis Hall and the parking lot enjoying the feeling of sun on her face. A hard *thump* against her shin startled her out of her musings. Zoe looked down and found Flash and Moose walking beside her. She had almost forgotten they'd come to campus with her today. On the other side of the cats, Rowantree and Alder scampered through the grass. There was a fluttering of wings and Darkwing landed on her shoulder. A sudden image of a warrior princess character from an old television show flashed through her mind and she started laughing.

"What's so funny?" Moose asked, stalking beside her.

"I feel like some fantasy character going into battle with my animal spirits beside me," Zoe giggled. Darkwing pushed off her shoulder as she continued to laugh. She stopped walking and took several deep breaths. She was on the verge of genuine hysterical laughter and didn't want to lose control.

Zoe looked down at the animals as Darkwing flew back down to land beside the squirrels on the path. Zoe noticed that the crow and the squirrels kept a respectful distance from Moose and Flash although she was sure that Darkwing, at least, could easily take on the cats.

"You are headed to the ley line nexus, are you not?" Rowantree's tone was as formal as always.

"Yes. I'm dropping my stuff off in my car and then coming back here. Why?" Zoe was a little puzzled at the attitude of the Watchers.

"We will accompany you, but discreetly," Rowantree replied.

"Okay. Is everything okay?" Now she was really puzzled. What was going on?

"We'll wait for you over there." Flash nodded his head at a spot to Zoe's left where a couple of trees and some bushes created a shady area near the corner of the quad. Before Zoe could ask any more questions, the squirrels, cats, and crow all headed toward the area Flash had indicated.

Zoe stared after them for a minute before continuing to

the parking lot. She shook her head and brought herself back to the task at hand. Reaching her car, she pulled her phone out of her bag and stuck it in her back pocket. Everything else went on the floor of the back seat. Locking the car she turned to go back to the quad.

"Hey, Zoe. Can I drop my stuff?" Kieran came around the corner of Davis Hall into the lot.

"Oh, sure." Zoe hit the unlock button and waited while Kieran dropped his bag on the passenger seat.

He caught up to her and gave her a quick kiss. She couldn't help quickly glancing around the parking lot to make sure they were alone. They normally avoided any displays of affection on campus as neither one of them was comfortable with any other faculty, besides Mark, knowing they were in a relationship.

"You okay?" Kieran looked down at her.

"I'm fine. At least right now I am," Zoe answered. "The cats, Rowantree, Alder, and Darkwing are on the quad, in that little clump of trees and bushes, waiting for me…us."

"Well, they are all Watchers…so I guess that's what they're going to do. Watch." Kieran smiled.

"Ha! Good point," Zoe laughed.

They walked the rest of the way to the quad in companionable silence. Zoe always felt better when Kieran was around. And right now, she really needed to feel like somebody had her back. She glanced around the quad as they approached the trees where the animals were sitting. She still didn't know what exactly they were going to do or if they could help her access the nexus, but they would probably get around to telling her at some point.

Mark came out of the front door of Davis Hall accompanied by Robyn and Jessica. Zoe was surprised to see the two English professors. Mark must have called them and told them what was happening. When she thought about it, it didn't make sense that she would be the only one accessing the ley lines. Other mages could and should be able to as well. They probably knew what they were doing too. Zoe knew she had more power than the others, but she was also painfully aware that she knew far less than they did about mage life in general. She was still a total newbie.

Zoe wanted very much to *not* be a newbie. That meant figuring out what exactly George meant when he started going on about 'finesse'. Was that the same thing as fine-tuning her abilities? Or did he mean that she needed to pay more attention to what was going on around her? Like trying to find ley lines? Or was he talking about the politics involved in the world of mages and magic. Really what she needed was some down time that wasn't filled with life-or-death emergencies. Maybe she's get some of that now. Those emergencies really got in the way of learning to control and fine-tune her powers. Zoe sighed. It felt a lot like grad school and the first few years of teaching – learn as you go and don't let on that you don't know.

The other three caught up with Zoe and Kieran at the trees. Moose and Flash sauntered out from under a bush and started head-butting all the available shins. Once again, any dignity they might have claimed was destroyed by the leaves and twigs clinging to their fur. Clearly, they had been lounging in the dirt under the bushes. Moose had a small forest stuck in his long fur.

Zoe sensed movement in the tree above her head and looked up. Rowantree, Alder, and Darkwing sat on a branch gazing down at the humans. Robyn followed Zoe's gaze.

"Oh hi, guys. How are you?" she asked politely.

"We are well, thank you," Rowantree responded. Alder nodded and Darkwing bobbed his head.

Mark turned to Zoe. "I've asked Simon to try to talk to George again. I don't think he got very far last time. He, Simon that is, is going to meet us over here after he finds George."

"Okay. Should we just try again to access the ley lines? I'm not sure I did it right the last time, but maybe if we all try at the same time?" This leadership thing was tricky but maybe she was getting the hang of it.

Jessica nodded. "Yeah, let's just give it a try. Mark and Kieran can keep an eye out for anybody trying to interrupt us."

"Are we that vulnerable? Or are we doing it this way because I had trouble accessing it the other day?" Zoe was nervous at the idea that they needed some sort of lookout when trying to access the ley lines. Was she going to go into a trance or blackout or something?

"Normally, no, you're not vulnerable. You just touch the ley lines and draw the power you need. But, yeah, you had trouble the other day, so I don't know how hard we are going to have to work to get to the nexus. Think of this as putting on safety goggles in the lab," Jessica answered.

"It's fine. We're, well, Jessica, is just being overly cautious," Robyn smiled at Zoe. Jessica stuck her tongue out at Robyn.

Mark laughed. "Okay, kids. Get to work. Kieran and I will do the manly thing and stand guard for you ladies." Now Zoe stuck her tongue out at Mark.

Zoe took a deep breath and closed her eyes. She reached out with her power, envisioning it as a small thread made up of all four Elements questing into the dirt of the quad. She could feel the power of the nexus and the river-like feel of the ley lines running and crossing under the quad. Tentatively she sent her thread of power into the nexus guided by the "feel"of power…and got the same feeling of plastic wrap over the nexus as she had before.

She opened her eyes and looked over at the other women. "Do you feel that? Like plastic wrap?"

Jessica and Robyn both nodded. "It's weird. I haven't felt

anything like that before," Robyn commented. She turned to Mark and Kieran. "You guys try it."

"Okay." Kieran closed his eyes and concentrated. Almost immediately he opened them again. "There's something blocking access...yeah, plastic wrap is a good way to describe it."

"So, how do we break it?" Zoe asked.

The other four stared at each other. "There's got to be an edge or something to it, right?" Mark said.

"Oh, good thought. Yeah, there should be. The nexus pools power just like water would pool, so there should be a sort of...well, lake of power. I tried to access it where I thought the middle might be and I'm guessing you guys did too?" Robyn responded.

Kieran nodded. "Yeah, I did."

"Can we poke a hole in it and rip it from there? Like you can with real plastic wrap?" Zoe asked.

"Well, maybe. I think. Let's see what it's like and then go from there," Jessica answered.

Mark was rubbing his hand on the side of his face. "Yeah. Okay. I'll see if I can find an edge and get a line of Air under it." His voice was tense. Zoe fought to keep her hands from twisting together.

Mark closed his eyes and Zoe used her magesight to watch a small thread of Air moving out from Mark and down into the ground. Her magesight allowed her to follow the Air into Earth and under the quad. It was like swimming underwater except she couldn't really see ahead, she could just see the tendril of Air. There was a shimmering somewhere over to her right and she saw a thread of Air, which she assumed was Mark's – it *felt* like him – move in that direction. Zoe gasped. She could *see* the nexus point. The shimmering was power. A hand touched her shoulder jerking her back to herself.

Kieran gave her a worried look. "Are you okay? You looked a little out of it for a minute there."

"I was sort of following Mark's Air and I could *see* the nexus. Last time I just did it by feel, I wasn't looking. That's wild!" Zoe heard her voice shake.

Robyn put an arm around Zoe's shoulder. "Yeah. If you look with magesight you can see all kinds of magic. You knew that…right? You saw the webs or whatever you want to call them, on the heads of the students you found in the basement last year. Remember? We," she indicated the others, "could only see them vaguely because we only control one Element. You control all four. You have a *lot* of power, girlfriend!"

Zoe's hands had started twisting together again and she pulled them apart. "Yeah…I know…but, um, I didn't realize that I can *see* power like that. It's kinda…um…freaky."

Mark let out an explosive breath. "Okay, I think I got it. At least I got under whatever is blocking the nexus and then I was able to access the power. I think I've pulled whatever it was off of the nexus. Somebody else see if you can access it."

Zoe exchanged a glance with Robyn. "You got this!" Robyn gave her shoulder a squeeze.

Zoe closed her eyes and pulled up another thread of combined Elements. She opened up her eyes and switched over to her magesight. Breathing evenly, Zoe sent her thread of Elements in the same direction she had watched Mark go.

She could feel Mark holding up the edges of whatever was blocking the nexus. And under that she could feel the surging power of the ley lines as they crossed over, under, and around each other. Zoe cautiously dipped her tendril of power into the nexus. She was hyper-aware of the control techniques she learned and practiced the other day at Mark and David's house and carefully opened herself up to the power. Even at her most cautious the influx of raw power nearly knocked her off her feet. Kieran and Robyn reached out and grabbed her before she hit the ground.

"Wow! That's a lot!" she gasped.

Mark looked around at her and the others. "Can you guys give me a hand here? I think there's a sort of tear along the far edge that we can use to break this cover thing apart."

Kieran, Zoe, and Robyn linked hands with each other and Robyn grabbed Mark's other hand.

"Zoe, you lead. You can see Mark's Air better than we can," Robyn was terse.

"Okay." Zoe closed her eyes so she could concentrate better. She always felt like her magesight was stronger if she wasn't simultaneously trying to use ordinary sight. She could "see" the others following her.

Once Zoe reached Mark's end point she squeezed Kieran and Robyn's hands to let them know.

Mark let out a sharp breath. "Okay, see the tear or rip? If we all pull together I think it will break the cover."

"Right," Kieran's voice was tight.

"On three…one…two…three!" Mark barked out the last word.

Zoe sent a rope of all four Elements into the spot Mark had pointed out. She could feel the others working alongside her. And, after what seemed like an eternity she finally felt the plastic wrap start to tear. She visualized her rope of Elements acting like a saw and cutting the plastic wrap in half. The others moved ahead of her weakening the bonds and allowing her to move easily through the cover.

She reached the opposite edge of the cover and Mark let out an explosive breath.

"That's it!" He dropped Robyn's hand and sat down on the grass.

Zoe felt her knees give and sat down next to Mark before she fell. Kieran and Robyn sank down on the other side of her. Jessica reached into her backpack and took out some granola bars.

"It's not much and we'll have to share, but this will help a bit." She handed out a half a bar to each of them.

"Thanks," Zoe breathed.

Moose and Flash came out from under the bush and climbed into Zoe's lap. She'd almost forgotten they were there. Rowantree and Alder also appeared and Darkwing returned from wherever he'd perched in the branches overhead.

"I do believe you have restored access to the nexus," Rowantree said quietly. Alder bobbed his head.

Flash lifted his head to stare at Zoe. "This means that anybody, including the Night Mage, can access the nexus."

"What do you mean, the Night Mage? She's dead." Zoe stared at the orange cat.

"We are not certain of that," Rowantree answered.

"She's still here somewhere." Darkwing cocked his head to the side.

"But…I thought Simon was going to get George to deal with her and call 9-1-1…" Zoe stared at the other mages.

Mark rubbed his hand on his chin. "Damn," he said softly. "We didn't actually verify that she was dead. Simon said she looked like it, but he didn't touch her and then he walked away to get George. We didn't leave anybody there."

"Classic villain mistake…only she's the villain and we're the good guys. We're not supposed to do things like that. What happened?" Robyn asked.

"I'm not sure," Mark was puzzled. "At the time it seemed perfectly logical to leave her there."

Jessica gave him a sideways look and raised her eyebrows but didn't say anything.

"Yeah, she's a Night Mage. It's possible that even though her own balefire hit her that it only knocked her out," Kieran added.

"What the hell??" Zoe squawked. "But you said…" she

broke off, staring at Kieran and Mark. "Why didn't any of you say something before? And why didn't anybody stay here?"

Kieran's face was filled with guilt. "I don't know...I guess we all just assumed she was dead. We should have known better. I'm sorry. I guess it's another one of those things you just know...I forgot you don't know..." he trailed off.

Mark looked guilty too. "I'm sorry, Zo. Like Kieran said...I forgot you don't know some of this stuff."

"But that still doesn't explain why nobody stuck around." Zoe stared at the others.

"No, it doesn't. I'm not sure what happened," Kieran frowned.

Robyn gazed thoughtfully at Zoe. "Wasn't George supposed to be mentoring you? Academically and magically?"

"Yeah. But then he just sort of stopped. I think the whole provost thing caught up with him," Zoe muttered, dropping her head in her hands. She flashed back to the first week of grad school when she had no idea what was going on or if she even belonged there.

Robyn frowned. "That's really no excuse for him. You're new to magic *and* you're a powerful Elemental. You need to have somebody helping you figure this all out." She turned to Mark and Kieran. "And what have you guys done to help?"

"Hey, we've been helping...but probably, obviously, not enough. I'm sorry, Zo," Mark apologized again and glanced at Kieran. "We'll get together this weekend and do...something. I dunno. We'll figure it out."

Kieran nodded. "And we'll talk to Kim and the others. There are a lot of people who can help." His hand moved as if to take hers, but he stopped. Jessica caught the involuntary motion and raised an eyebrow at Robyn who grinned in return.

Zoe scrubbed at her eyes before she raised her head. Her colleagues didn't need to see her acting like a weepy teenager.

Flash and Moose head-butted her arms and purred.

"It's not you guys's fault. But what do we do now? Besides making you two atone for your oversight?" she managed a small grin at Mark and Kieran.

"Well, first off, we all go to George and tell him about the ley line nexus, the blockage, us clearing it, and Carolyn maybe being not as dead as we'd like," Robyn announced.

"Good idea," Jessica chimed in. "Besides Simon and John Gardner, George is the most senior mage on campus."

Rowantree made a small sound like clearing a throat. All the humans turned to look at him.

"If I may suggest, we," he gestured to himself, Alder, and Darkwing, "will inform our respective cohorts and murders regarding what has just been discussed. It may be that we can discover the location of the Night Mage. I agree that she is likely still alive. Although, I would not venture to guess her physical or mental condition at this point."

"Oh, great. You mean she's probably crazy...er. Crazier," Zoe grumbled.

"I'm afraid so," Rowantree nodded. "One does not use the kind of magic she has been using without some degree of mental damage."

"You gotta be mentally damaged to even begin to use that kind of magic," Kieran muttered.

Chapter Fourteen

"You need to go home, and we need to bring Kim and the others up to speed on what just happened." Kieran stood up and pulled Zoe to her feet.

"Good idea," Mark chimed in. "And get some food. And some sleep. You can grade tomorrow."

Rowantree nodded to Zoe and the others and then he and Alder scampered up the tree. Darkwing cocked his head and opened his beak. He glanced at Moose who was staring at him and closed his beak with a snap.

"We'll take care of it," Moose stated, his eyes never leaving the crow.

Zoe looked up at Darkwing and then back down to Moose. "Um…what's going on?"

"Nothing to worry about." Flash bumped her shin.

"I will speak with you tomorrow." Darkwing bobbed his head at Zoe and took off across the quad.

Zoe frowned at the cats. "You guys…" she started. Flash once again head-butted her shin.

"We need food. Can we go home?" He finished with his signature whiny meow.

Jessica laughed. "If I didn't know better, I'd say they're

trying to distract you and also trying to get you to go home."

"You're right and I *will* find out what they're up to." Zoe glared at the cats.

"Why don't you trust us? And, we're starving." Moose started another round of his seemingly endless cleaning routine.

Robyn and Jessica both laughed now. "I think you should just go home, Zoe!" Robyn grinned.

"Okay, fine! Sheesh. Well? Are you guys coming?" She glanced back at the cats as she and Kieran started across the quad. Out of the corner of her eye she could see Kieran trying to hide a smile.

"What?"

"Nothing. Nothing. I'm just hungry too. We should probably get home. Mark, we'll call you later," Kieran responded.

Mark nodded, hiding his own grin. "Okay."

"Why is everybody laughing at me?" Zoe grumped.

"We're not. We're laughing with you…honest." Kieran smiled at her.

"Hmph."

"Well, everybody knows that cats rule the house, but it *is* funny to see it happen when they can actually talk."

"And they all know we're right," Moose joined the conversation.

"We *are* hungry. You just needed to be told," Flash agreed.

Zoe rolled her eyes grateful that the cats couldn't see her.

Kieran laughed. "C'mon everybody. Let's go home."

Half an hour later Zoe sent up a short prayer of gratitude to the parking gods as she maneuvered into a parking spot in front of her house. She appreciated the small favors. She climbed out of the car while Kieran pulled the carriers out of the back seat and released the cats. Zoe grabbed her bags and trudged up her front stairs followed by Kieran. The cats were already waiting impatiently at the front door.

Once inside, Zoe dropped her bags and followed the cats into the kitchen so she could provide the promised food. Kieran dropped onto the sofa in the living room.

"Can we have a drink before we go to my place and hash this all out with Kim and the others?" he called out. Zoe smiled. He sounded almost as plaintive as the cats.

"Good idea. And, when their majesties are finally finished scarfing down their food, they can let us in on whatever it was that Darkwing was going to tell me." Zoe raised her voice to be sure Moose and Flash heard her. She was rewarded with identical tail flicks from the cats who kept their heads buried in their food bowls.

Peering into the refrigerator she found two bottles of beer. She pulled them out and opened them. The cats had finished eating and led the way back into the living room. Zoe plopped herself down onto the couch next to Kieran and handed him a beer. She turned to the cats who were executing their cleaning routines in the center of the room.

"Okay, guys. Spill. What did you stop Darkwing from telling me? What's going on?" She took a drink of beer.

Moose took a few more swipes at his ear before sitting up and wrapping his tail neatly around his feet. Flash copied his sitting position. Both cats gazed at Zoe unblinking. Her stomach started to do flip-flops and she reached for Kieran's hand. He returned her grip and she could feel the tension in him.

"We, meaning the Summerfield College Watchers and us, believe that the Night Mage is not, in fact, dead. She was gravely wounded, yes. But members of Darkwing's murder have seen signs that indicate she is alive. We are certain she is working with Susan Barker and that the witch managed to remove the Night Mage from the quad after you fought her,"

Moose spoke more formally than Zoe had ever heard from him.

Flash picked up when Moose paused. "The Fire mage, the one named Simon, left to inform Wardmaster of the incident on the quad and also inform the authorities as he believed the Night Mage to be dead. However, by the time Wardmaster arrived on the quad, the Night Mage was gone, and the decision was made not to call the authorities. It is unclear why nobody stayed on the quad, but one possibility is that a compulsion spell was utilized to ensure that the mages all left the quad. Rowantree, Alder, and Darkwing are exploring this possibility." Both cats remained sitting upright, their eyes fixed on Zoe.

Kieran frowned. "A compulsion spell? Why didn't any of us feel it?"

"Rowantree believes it was attached as a sort of ward on the Night Mage. It would have simply encouraged anybody looking at the body to leave and go for more help. It takes advantage of human compassion, but causes people to leave a body, or whatever, alone. That's how the witch was able to remove the Night Mage without anyone seeing her," Moose answered.

"Okay. I guess that makes sense. When you were talking, I did wonder why nobody stayed with the body, but that explains it. It's always the smallest and simplest things that get overlooked," Kieran mused.

Zoe stared back and forth between Kieran and the cats. "Carolyn, the Night Mage, is most likely alive and you guys are worried about a compulsion spell? What the hell are we going to do about Carolyn and Susan? And why are they working together?" She hated how her voice sounded shrill. She pulled her hand back from Kieran's and without thinking, started twisting her hands together.

The cats broke their statue-like poses and jumped up on

the sofa beside her. Kieran reached over and gently disengaged her hands, wrapping her left hand up in both of his.

"I know. It seems ridiculous. But that had to be a powerful spell and that means Susan Barker is stronger now or has help. It's not easy pulling somebody back from a hit with their own balefire. At least, that's my understanding. That would take some sort of high-level power or power assist. *You* might be able to do it, but I think it would take a lot out of you," his voice was gentle.

Zoe rubbed her free hand across her face. This mage thing was getting overwhelming. Once again, she found herself wishing she could go back to her previous academic life. It might have its stresses, but at least they were familiar and not directly life-threatening or world-ending.

She leaned into Kieran and he put his arm around her shoulders. Zoe looked up at him. "Let's go talk to Kim. I want to pick her brain. Something tells me she knows way more than she's letting on right now."

He nodded. "I think you're probably right." Kieran gave her shoulders a squeeze and then put his hands on his thighs and levered himself off the sofa. He reached back and held out his hand. Zoe grabbed it and pulled herself up. She glanced down at the cats, still sitting on the sofa.

"Do you guys want to come along?"

"No, we'll stay here. We need more food. I hope you left some for us." Flash slid his eyes in her direction while still chewing his tail.

Zoe sighed. "Yes, there's food. We'll be back in a couple of hours."

Kieran just laughed.

Zoe and Kieran walked in comfortable silence down the block to his new apartment in Kim's basement. They entered the back gate and found Kim sitting on her back porch enjoying the late afternoon sun.

"Hi guys. You look tired. What's up?" she called down to them.

Kieran exchanged a glance with Zoe, and they walked up the stairs to the small deck.

"Hey. Well, it's been an afternoon," Zoe sighed. "And, we have some news. Not good news."

Kim's eyebrows went up. "Okay. That sounds ominous. What happened?"

"Well, we were able to access the nexus point of the ley lines. But the Watchers believe that Carolyn Detweiler, the Night Mage, is still alive. We thought she'd been killed when Zoe made her balefire rebound on her, but it seems we were optimistic," Kieran answered. He filled Kim in on what had happened earlier on campus and what the cats had just told them.

As he spoke, Kim's expression shifted from interested to sad to angry. Zoe watched the changes with fascination. What was going through Kim's head?

Kim answered Zoe's internal questions as soon as Kieran finished the story. "Dammit! I was afraid of that when you told me she'd become Night Mage. If she recovered from a hit from her own balefire, she has help and that help is magical. Your normal Night Mage," she made air quotes, "if there's any such thing as a normal Night Mage, will have compromised their soul, but won't have direct protection outside of their own abilities. This is bad. Very bad." Kim frowned and drummed her fingers on the arm of her chair.

She picked up her phone. "I'm going to get Rob and Joe over here. Rob has done some research into Night Mages in the past. I think he had to deal with one when he was in high school. I know he has picked up some information." As she spoke her fingers flew over her phone, typing out a message.

Once the text was sent, Kim put the phone on the table

and turned back to Kieran and Zoe.

"Okay. So, do you have any ideas of what you're going to do next? The Night Mage isn't going to wait around for you to make your next move. She's going to come after you as soon as she can. You need to move while you have even this small window of time," Kim's tone was serious.

"Well, you know how faculty are," Kieran began. "That's why we wanted to talk to you. Except for Mark and David, pretty much everybody else needs a meeting or two before they actually *do* anything. And, we still haven't heard from George Wardmaster. We're not sure what's going on with him. Besides administrative b.s. that is."

Kim gave a short laugh. "Yeah, you guys do like your meetings, I've learned."

Zoe snorted. "No kidding. But I really don't know that much about Night Mages and I'm hoping you can help. I don't even have anything in my so-called normal research since mages like us are not even mentioned in fairy tales or anything."

Kim's phone buzzed and she glanced at the screen. "Rob has your answers and he and Joe are almost here."

Kieran stood up and went down into the back yard. "I'll open the gate."

He returned almost immediately, followed by Rob and Joe.

"Hey everybody. What's going on?" Joe asked.

"You mentioned Night Mages?" Rob asked Kim with a raised eyebrow.

"I'm going to let them tell you," Kim responded, waving at Kieran and Zoe. "They're the ones having the adventures again."

The two men laughed, and Rob looked at Zoe. "Whatcha do now?"

"It wasn't my fault!" Zoe held up her hands in mock

surrender. "I swear!" She launched into the story of the attempt to access the ley line nexus and the resulting fight with Carolyn followed by the successful removal of the block on the ley lines that afternoon. When she was finished the two men stared at each other.

"Well, shit," Joe commented. Zoe thought that was a very clear and succinct summary.

Rob frowned. "Like Kim said, I've done some research into Night Mages. They tend to be narcissistic individuals. You know, smartest person in the room so everybody needs to pay attention to me all the time, sort of thing. That and powerful magic are a bad combo."

"No kidding. And, yeah, Carolyn fits that description. She's playing all kinds of faculty politics games in addition to the magical stuff, and she's only been at Summerfield for about a year," Zoe responded.

"How'd she get the job, do you know?" Joe asked.

Kieran rubbed a hand on the side of his face. "I assume by the usual path of a search committee, but I can't say for sure. Did you hear anything?" he turned to Zoe.

"No…um…but she's in a different department, psychology, so we wouldn't necessarily hear about any of their hires until they're actually hired. Why do you ask?" she looked at Joe.

"Well, I don't know how faculty hiring works but, I was thinking maybe she had an inside track or something. Something that would put her in a position to do the greatest amount of harm almost immediately," Joe replied.

"Yeah, she could have been hired that way. Now that I think about it, she is on the faculty governance committee…she took over for somebody who's on medical leave. So maybe she was just brought in through the "who do you know" type of hiring. She was pretty certain she could run the meeting the last time the committee met. And based on a phone call I overheard, she's buddies with the president," Zoe commented.

"Is that an important committee?" Rob asked.

"It puts together the...I guess you'd say rules and regulations for how faculty deal with each other, handle student matters, that sort of thing," Kieran explained.

"So, she had the opportun..." a flutter of black wings interrupted Joe.

Darkwing settled on the deck railing next to Zoe. "What are you doing here?" she asked.

Darkwing cocked his head at her and then bobbed it toward Kim.

"Oh, everyone here worked with us last semester," Zoe answered the unspoken question.

She introduced the crow to her neighbors. "This is Darkwing. His murder is part of the Watchers at Summerfield. Darkwing, this is Kim, she's Fire, Rob is Earth, and Joe is Air." Zoe indicated each mage in turn. The mages and the crow nodded to each other.

"Susan Barker and the Night Mage are together," he croaked. "They were seen by Watchers near where the Air mage called Mark lives with the Earth mage called David."

"Shit!" Zoe and Kieran exclaimed simultaneously.

"Susan Barker? Who's that?" Kim asked.

"She's the one who started the coven and raised the demon last year. She was the admin assistant to the provost. She got the president involved and she got away after the demon fight. We'd heard she was back but weren't sure if she was connected with all this shit if she and Carolyn were working together." Zoe's voice rose in fear and her hands twisted together.

Kieran reached for her hands and pulled them apart. "It's okay. I mean, this isn't good, but we can handle this. Breathe."

"Oh, yeah. I remember now," Joe said. "She ran away

before anybody could do anything." He looked at Darkwing. "So, is she influencing the Night Mage?"

"We believe so. We also believe she was the one to remove the Night Mage after the fight." The crow turned to Zoe. "Your Watchers should be told. I will go do that now."

"Wait. Is there anything else? I mean how did they get together? Or what were they doing?" Zoe desperately wanted more information from Darkwing. She had been so focused on Carolyn and her maneuvering that she'd almost forgotten Susan Barker also had a hand in things. For some reason, the witch's involvement was causing her to panic.

"I do not know. Perhaps the ones who saw them told the Earth mage called Mark." He cocked his head and fixed her with one dark eye.

"Yeah, okay. I'll text him. Um…you're going to my house? Um…the back window should be open for the cats." She took refuge in something she could sort of handle.

Darkwing bobbed his head again and took off. Zoe picked up her phone to text Mark and felt it vibrate with an incoming message.

"It's Mark." She looked up at the other mages.

"Okay. Read the text," Kim replied gently.

"Oh. Right." Zoe's brain felt like it was packed in wool. *Get a grip! It's not the end of the world and you have to deal.*

She hit the message icon. *Got message from crows. Susan Barker and Carolyn coming after us. Call me.* Without thinking Zoe tapped the small phone icon next to the message. Mark picked up on the first ring. Zoe put the phone on speaker.

"Where are you?" he was clearly on speaker as well.

"I'm at Kim's with Kieran, Joe, and Rob." Zoe's hands started to shake.

"Good. David and I are on our way. We'll meet you there. Give me her address for GPS," Mark's tone was terse.

Kim gave the address and David's voice replied "Got it. Thanks."

"We'll be there in about ten-fifteen minutes." Mark hung up.

"I wonder what they heard from the Watchers in their area. They certainly got moving quickly," Kieran mused.

Chapter Fifteen

Zoe stared at Kieran. "Do you think Carolyn figured out where they lived?"

"Well, Susan knows…she attacked them there, last semester, remember? She tore up David's ornamental cabbages." Kieran grimaced.

"Joe, what were you going to say before the crow arrived?" Kim returned to the interrupted conversation.

"Well, there's a connection between Carolyn, the Summerfield president, and this Susan Barker person. If she, Susan Barker, raised a demon once before, why wouldn't she do it again?" Joe responded.

"But she needed a whole coven to do it last year." Zoe kept her hands on the arms of her chair in an effort to stop herself from twisting them together.

Rob ran a hand through his hair. "Well, she did it once, and now she has a powerful Night Mage working with her. I don't know that it really matters right now, how they met up, but they obviously did. And, since Susan knows where you all live, I'm going to guess she's after revenge."

"Hell. If Carolyn is buddies with Morgan and Susan Barker, then that's how she knew where I lived. One of them gave her my address." Kieran clenched his fists.

Zoe stared at him wide-eyed. "Revenge? You think Susan's going for revenge?"

"It does make sense," he nodded.

Kim nodded as well and glanced at Rob and Joe. They returned her look. "Yeah. We need to shield the whole block again," Kim said.

Zoe felt her hands start to twist in her lap. Kieran looked grim.

"We need to do it now." His voice held an intensity Zoe hadn't heard before.

"Right." Kim stood and reached out to Joe and Rob. Kieran took Zoe's hand and grasped Joe's while she held Rob's.

"Zoe, you can pull everything together. We'll each give you as much of our own Element that we can, and you can weave a shield together combining your power and ours. That way it'll be extra strong. I think it should cover a block above and below us here and to the east and west as well," Kim's voice was calm and matter-of-fact.

Zoe nodded and closed her eyes. She knew that wasn't necessary, but it helped her concentrate. She saw the energies from the four Elements in front of her. Holding her breath, she reached out with her own power and gently pulled the Elements together. Adding their power to her own, Zoe wove them into a small blanket, exactly the same way she had when Kieran first showed her how to make a shield last semester.

Once she had the blanket completed, she gradually poured in additional power from each Element to stretch the blanket to cover the two-block radius Kim had suggested. Sweat beaded on her forehead as she worked. After what seemed like hours, but was really only ten minutes, she let out an explosive breath.

"That should work. It looks like what I made last year

right before Susan attacked the block. Can one of you check it and see if it needs any work anywhere?" She leaned against Kieran for a moment before sinking back down into her chair.

"Looks good. You do nice work," Rob's slow drawl made her smile. He was the walking definition of mellow.

Zoe's phone vibrated and she glanced at it. "Mark and David are at the gate."

"On it." Kieran jumped down the steps and trotted through the back yard. He returned moments later with Mark and David and trailed by Moose and Flash. Darkwing fluttered down to once again land on the deck railing.

Mark took the steps two at a time and stopped in front of Zoe. "You, okay?" he asked leaning down to give her a hug. David followed suit.

"I'm fine. We just put up a shield over these couple of blocks," she waved vaguely to indicate the general neighborhood.

"So, that's why you looked wiped out," David commented.

"Yeah, I guess. What happened with you guys? Why are you here?" Zoe shifted the attention from herself to the new arrivals.

"Bitch went after my gardens again," David growled.

"What do you mean?" Joe looked puzzled.

Mark gave a short laugh. "David's put a lot of work into our yard and is very protective of the gardens and landscaping around the house. Susan Barker and Carolyn just destroyed them for the second time. This time though, instead of lightning, Carolyn just set them on fire."

"How did you guys get out if she was attacking the house?" Kieran asked.

David grimaced. "The neighborhood Watchers told us this afternoon that the two of them were moving and the crows thought they were headed in our direction. Then when one of the crows showed up with a message from Darkwing and told us those two were definitely looking for us, we quietly packed up my car and left. We were about three blocks away when we saw the fireballs hit. I have no idea what the neighbors think, but we decided we had to get over here. The house is strongly shielded so I doubt they can take that out and I don't think Susan will let Carolyn use balefire. Carolyn might be a psycho, but Susan doesn't want the attention that unquenchable fire would bring." he sighed. "Well, now I have an excuse to completely rework the gardens."

Moose and Flash jumped up into Zoe's chair. A small shoving match immediately ensued as both cats scrambled for a hold and a spot on her lap.

"C'mon guys! Stop." Zoe unceremoniously grabbed Flash, shoved Moose so he sat along one of her legs and then dumped Flash on the other. Both cats managed to look offended and yet satisfied with the arrangement. The others laughed while Zoe glared at the cats.

"Comic relief," Joe grinned.

Without missing a beat, Moose addressed the mages. "As Watchers, we advise that you not only alert the other mages to what happened to those two," he nodded at Mark and David, "but that you also return to the campus immediately in order to intercept what will likely be an attempt to access the ley lines and again block you from doing so."

Zoe swallowed hard. "But...um...what are Susan and Carolyn trying to do? Susan already tried to raise a demon last year...what is she doing now? And is she using Carolyn or is Carolyn using Susan?"

Mark shoved both hands through his hair. "I don't know who's using who. They both want more power? But for what?"

Joe cleared his throat. "Power for power's sake is a pretty strong drug. Remember, Carolyn's a Night Mage. Power for its own sake is how she got there to begin with. Maybe she thinks she can control the power of the ley lines and keep that for herself? You said earlier she's working with the president of your college. Maybe she wants to control the college? Use it as a base for whatever? And she appealed to the witch's sense of revenge to get her to help?"

"That makes a lot of sense," Kieran stared at Joe. "Last semester Susan was using students and was going to make one of them a receptacle for a demon…although the demon clearly thought that was insulting." He stopped, frowning.

"Do you think she wants to use students again? Maybe as a power source or some sort of biddable mage army?" Kim interjected.

Zoe's heart rate sped up and her stomach lurched. They were talking like they were facing some sort of magical take over. Like Susan Barker was some kind of evil genius bent on taking over the world. That idea was just too much like a bad movie. That couldn't be what they were implying.

"Um…guys…um…I mean…this sounds kinda crazy…um…I mean…like you think Susan's going to…um…take over Summerfield…and um…use the students for a power source…like what? Those stories where vampires stalk college campuses because it's easy pickings? I mean…um…that's just a story…" Zoe's voice trailed off as the others turned to look at her.

Kieran reached over and took her hand. "Zoe, it's not that crazy. This is another one of those magic world arguments where the stakes really are that high and some people, like Susan and Carolyn, really are that crazy. I know it sounds like a bad cartoon or movie, but really large amounts of power are flowing under campus and if that is used by somebody with insane intentions…well, it's a bad combo. But it's very real," his voice was gentle, and he rubbed his thumb over the back of her hand.

Zoe scrubbed her other hand across her eyes. She was *not* going to break down like some angsty teenager who thought life was unfair. Stopping Susan was a priority. *I'll worry about the weird desire to control the world later.*

A hand holding a red bandanna appeared in her line of vision. She took it and looked up to see Joe smiling at her with sympathy in his eyes. He made a small "go on" gesture with his hand, indicating the bandanna. Zoe returned his smile and blew her nose.

"Go ahead and keep that for now," Joe smiled when she moved to hand it back to him. "I've got another one."

"Okay. So, we need to get back to campus," Zoe's voice was shaky, but she was grateful it actually functioned.

"No. First, we need to eat," Kim countered. "I already ordered pizza and it should be here in a few minutes. *Then* we head back to campus. We will not succeed if we are not fully prepared when we face those two bitches."

* * *

Sitting with David and Kieran in Mark's car on the way to back campus, with Joe, Kim, and Rob following in Joe's SUV, Zoe concentrated on texting Declan and the other students, as well as Sarah and all the faculty mages. She was trying hard to focus on organization rather than fighting an actual battle. Reminding herself that a demon had been fought and defeated didn't seem to help. Right now, all she could remember from last semester was the fear she felt as she ran into the fight at Swann Fountain. That didn't help in the current situation at all.

Zoe sent the texts and almost immediately began receiving return messages from people. Faculty mages were returning to campus and the students were gathering up other students to help as well. By the time they reached campus, the only people she hadn't heard from were Sarah Riley and George Wardmaster. That was odd but more incoming messages from others didn't allow her any time to dwell on it. She would give Sarah a call later. She felt awkward calling George directly. First she wanted to see what the others had to say once everybody arrived on campus.

Mark pulled into campus and Zoe found herself sitting up and staring around as if she'd never been there before. The campus at night looked different from campus during the day. It wasn't as if she'd never been on campus at night before, but tonight, perhaps because she was afraid of what might come next, it had taken on a decidedly unfriendly look and feel.

Mark parked in one of the lots closest to the center of campus. "We'll be able to get back to the car more quickly if I park here," he commented to no one in particular. Joe pulled into the spot next to them. As she got out of the car, Zoe spotted Josh, Annmarie, and Geoff walking rapidly toward them.

"Hey, guys. Are you okay?" she asked as the students reached her.

"Hi Dr. O'Brien. Yeah, we're fine, but…um…" Josh mumbled to a stop and looked at his shoes.

"What? What's wrong?" Zoe felt her heart speed up. Kieran, Mark and the others moved in behind her. They were all gazing intently at the students.

"Nothing's really wrong, Dr. O'Brien, just…um…like a new…like development, I guess," Geoff started.

"Oh, come on. It's not that bad." Annmarie rolled her eyes. She turned to Zoe. "Declan's father seems to have showed up. He's a little scary, but I'm pretty sure he's on our side. Declan's back there talking to him." The girl gestured back towards the side of the quad.

"Wait. Are you saying there's a djinn in the middle of campus?" Mark's voice came out a little higher pitched than normal.

The students eyed each other. Geoff looked back at Mark.

"Yeah. Declan's dad. He...like just sorta...I dunno...appeared...in the middle of the quad. We were walking back from the dining hall when we got your texts, Dr. O'Brien, and Declan like suddenly grabbed his head and said, 'something just arrived on campus.' He looked like he'd gotten an instant migraine or something. Then he like looked around and told us to go over to the quad. There was a man...at least it looked like a man...standing there looking around. He...the guy that is...walked over to us. He stared right at Declan and said, 'You are Declan Jin, son of Aseyai the djinn.' Declan just kinda nodded and then his dad said they had to talk and told us to leave. We saw you and came over." Geoff's eyes were wide, and he was shifting from foot to foot. Zoe sympathized. Meeting a djinn was really not something she wanted to do.

"Well. That sorta changes the equation, don't it?" Joe commented quietly.

Kim snorted. "No kidding."

Mark shook his head like he was coming out of a daydream. "Okay. Wow. Um, we need to find the others still. And we really don't know where Carolyn and Susan Barker are right now. Let's figure that out and then we can go introduce ourselves to the djinn...Declan's dad."

Everybody nodded and Zoe silently repeated her new personal mantra...deal with it, deal with it, deal with it. Once again, she found herself longing for the nice, stressful, yet magic-free, academic world she used to know.

A blue Toyota pulled into the lot, putting the little group on alert. The small car pulled into the spot next to Joe's car and Robyn and Jessica emerged.

"Hi guys. We got your text, Zoe. I think I saw John Gardner when we got to campus. He's such a creature of habit, he's parking in the same spot he does on a normal day," Jessica laughed.

Kieran looked at Zoe. "That means he's on the other side

of the quad. He'll likely run into Declan."

"Yeah, if Declan is on the quad, probably. What's the problem?" Robyn was puzzled.

Zoe took a deep breath and waved a hand at the students. "These guys just told us that Declan's dad showed up tonight."

Jessica's and Robyn's mouths fell open at the same time. "The djinn? It's…he's here?" Robyn gasped.

"Yeah. On the one hand, scary. On the other hand…maybe he'll stick around and help us deal with Carolyn and Susan. That would be a big help," Zoe answered.

A short silence fell over the group. It was interrupted by a *ping* from Geoff's phone.

"Declan says his dad wants to meet us." Geoff stared up at the group with wide eyes.

"Well, okay then," Kim took a deep breath. "Let's go meet a djinn." She started toward the quad and Zoe hurried to catch up. Declan needed to see that she was there. The others fell in behind Kim and Zoe.

As they approached the center of the quad and the nexus of the ley lines Zoe could see two figures standing together. They were about the same height, but the djinn was stockier than Declan. She was slightly surprised to see that the djinn was dressed in jeans, a button-down shirt, and a leather jacket. She wasn't sure what, exactly, she expected but modern clothes were not it. *C'mon. This isn't a movie or TV show.*

The small group of faculty and students approached Declan and his father. Zoe saw John Gardner approaching from the other side and gave him a small wave. She could see him pause when he caught sight of Declan and his father, but then he continued across the quad. They all reached the center at about the same time. The djinn turned to Declan with an unspoken question.

"Um … D-Dr. O'Brien … um … th-this is my father …

Aseyai ... um ... th-this is D-Dr. O'Brien." Declan's nerves were about to get the better of him.

The djinn turned his gaze to Zoe and gave a small nod. He seemed to radiate power. Surprised at the acknowledgement, she quickly returned the nod.

"I have seen you assisting my son and he tells me that you have been instrumental in his discovery of his powers. You have my thanks." Aseyai's voice boomed out in a disconcerting imitation of a cannon and Zoe glanced hurriedly around the quad. That had to have been heard on the entire campus. Aseyai caught the look and waved a dismissive hand.

"No-one can hear me if I do not desire them to," the djinn said.

Zoe tentatively held out her hand. "It's a pleasure to meet you, sir. And I am happy to help Declan."

The djinn stared at her hand for a moment and then reached out his own and gave a brief handshake. He gazed at the others around Zoe.

"Oh! Um ... these are other faculty mages and Declan's friends ... who ... um ... are also mages." Zoe quickly made introductions.

"My son informs me that there is what you call a Night Mage and possibly some other creature threatening you. I have seen some magic-workings, but since they did not directly involve my son, I was not interested. You have great power available here," he pointed down at the ground, "why are you not using it to dismiss the Night Mage and its friends?" Aseyai sounded genuinely curious.

Zoe was not thrilled that she seemed to have become the spokesperson for the mages. One of the others, like Mark or David, would be better at this. But when she looked around at the group, they simply looked at her in anticipation. *Hell. I guess I'm doing the talking. Great.*

"Well, um...the Night Mage managed to temporarily

prevent access to the ley lines, the power source, and…um…we just recently overcame that obstacle," Zoe started. She was starting to sound like Rowantree but the formal language felt right. "The other one working with the Night Mage is a witch who was the leader of a coven that tried to raise a demon on the winter solstice. We just found out that she has returned. We believe they will come here tonight to attempt to access the ley lines again. And destroy us."

Maybe saying *us* would get the djinn to help out. Based on the little she'd seen of Declan's power, a full djinn had to be a huge asset.

The djinn gazed around at the group. "You will fight your Night Mage with these…individuals?" He appeared amused.

"There are others coming," Zoe answered defensively. This was who they had, so this group would deal with Carolyn and Susan. She saw another group of students walking toward them from the dorms, and more faculty coming from the direction of the parking lot. She recognized Simon's bouncy walk, and Jennifer Bailey from the biology department. And even Andrew Smith from chemistry was coming over, walking with a man and a woman she didn't recognize. The two groups approached the center of the quad. Everybody was looking curiously at Aseyai. He appeared disinterested, gazing around the quad.

Andrew grinned at Zoe. "I heard something was up and brought my cousins. They're the ones with power." He gestured toward the two people with him.

Zoe stared at Jennifer Bailey who simply said, "It's not something I advertise…Earth." Zoe nodded.

The students grouped themselves alongside Annmarie, Josh, and Geoff. Mage or not, finding out that many of your professors were also mages was likely a little disconcerting for them. But where were George and Sarah?

Aseyai suddenly looked toward Shelby Hall. "What is in

that building over there?"

"Offices, why?" Mark followed the djinn's gaze.

"There is magic working there…and pain. If you have others of your mages in the building, I believe they are experiencing difficulties," Aseyai answered.

As if in response to Aseyai's statement, a huge wave of Earth moved across the quad.

"Brace yourselves!" David yelled. He, Rob, Jennifer, and John Gardner all held out their hands toward the wave. It broke apart and collapsed leaving a ditch about a foot deep running the length of the quad.

"What the hell is going on?" Kieran snapped.

"That felt sort of like George's work," John said quietly.

Simon eyed Aseyai. "You said you felt magic working and pain…what kind of pain?"

Aseyai returned the look calmly. "The pain felt by humans when they are injured."

Zoe stared at the others. "Where is George? And Sarah? I texted them, but I just realized I never got an answer…" she trailed off.

Before anybody could answer, a large wave of mud lurched out of the ditch that had been created by the wave.

"Shit!" the exclamation spilled from David as the Earth mages linked hands once again, joined by three students. Zoe, using her magesight, saw the waves of magic moving out from them toward the wall of mud bearing down on everyone.

"Ice!" Kieran nodded at Annmarie and the two Water mages grabbed hands. One of Andrew's cousins and two other students joined them. A coating of ice formed over the mud wall, freezing it in place. Well-placed blasts of Air from Mark and Joe shattered the now frozen mud.

Zoe felt a sense of helplessness as she watched the others work almost seamlessly together. It never occurred to her that the mud could be frozen and then blown apart. She had so much to learn still. Then she recalled what the djinn had said in answering Simon's question.

A renewed sense of urgency hit Zoe. "You guys! Where. Are. George and Sarah??"

Aseyai glanced at her. "In the building over there is one ordinary human, and three magic-working humans. I do not know if two of them are your George and Sarah, but one magic-worker is injured and the ordinary human is close to unconsciousness."

Chapter Sixteen

Zoe stared at Aseyai and then turned to Simon and Mark. "That has to be them! Carolyn did something! I'm sure of it!" her voice rose in panic.

Simon hesitated. "I do not believe that I should go into Shelby. Carolyn almost defeated me the last time we met, and I do not know how she will react this time. She is capable of overpowering a Fire mage, even someone with a great deal of experience." At least he had the grace to look embarrassed.

"Zoe, Kieran who else is Earth, Air, and Water?" Kim spoke up.

"I'm Earth, and Mark is Air," David answered immediately.

Andrew's cousins and the students raised their hands, calling out their Elements.

"Well, we've got the band back together and then some," Kim smiled grimly. "Mark, David, Kieran, and I will go into Shelby with Zoe and see what's going on in there. Rob and Joe can help the others out here, in case more attacks come this way."

"Wouldn't it be better if more of us went into Shelby?" Zoe was puzzled by Kim's organization.

"No. I have an idea of what we'll find, and I believe that we're going to want more people out here." Kim was matter-of-fact.

"Um...d-do you want me and m-my da...father to stay out here or c-come in with you?" Declan's stutter gave away his nerves, but his voice was stronger than usual.

Aseyai shifted to look at Declan. "This is not my fight."

"But it's mine. And I will help my friends." Declan held his father's eyes.

After a moment, Aseyai inclined his head in a short nod. "Yes."

Zoe wasn't sure if that meant Aseyai would help them out or if he was just agreeing with Declan's statement that this was his fight. Having a djinn on their side would certainly be a game-changer.

Kim stared thoughtfully at Declan. "If you could stay out here that would be a big help. I think that Carolyn and Susan are trying to coerce George into attacking us by threatening Sarah. You would be a big help in countering those attacks."

Declan nodded, glancing sideways at his father.

Kim glanced at Zoe. "Okay. Let's go see what's going on in Shelby Hall." Zoe looked at Declan and Aseyai. Declan nodded.

Zoe felt Kieran's hand slip into hers as the little group Kim had put together started across the quad. They reached the front entrance to Shelby and Kim stopped.

"Do you guys feel that?" she asked quietly.

"Yeah. That feels like that cloud that was around Shelby last semester when the coven was working," Mark answered.

"But it's not as strong as last time," Zoe added.

"What's the plan?" David squatted down to place his hands on the dirt under the bushes in front of the building. "There's something off about the Earth magic coming from here. I don't like it."

"What do you mean 'off'?" Zoe's stomach started doing a slow roll.

"I'm not sure exactly. But it just feels wrong." David dug his fingers into the dirt. "It feels wrong. That's all I can come up with." He sounded worried.

"Let's go." Mark pulled open the door.

Zoe looked at him. "Shouldn't it be locked at this time of night?"

"You're right," he paused, one foot over the threshold.

"Trap or arrogance. Either way, I don't like it. Everybody stay alert," Kim's voice was tense.

Mark gave a short nod and stepped into the entryway. The others followed quietly, with Kieran bringing up the rear. Zoe pointed up and Mark led the little group up the deeply carpeted staircase. He paused at the top, holding up one hand and staring down the hallway. Zoe peered around him and saw light coming from the door to George's office. She thought she heard voices too, but they were still too far down the hall to make out individual voices much less what they were saying. Mark continued silently down the hall and the others followed. Zoe sent up grateful thanks for the deep carpet muffling their steps. She would never again complain about administrators spending too much money on renovating their building.

As they approached George's office, Mark slowed down and once again held up his hand to signal a halt. Voices drifted out of the partially open door. At least two women and one man. Zoe's heart sped up as she recognized the voices of Carolyn, Susan, and George.

"You pathetic old man. Did you think I would let you get away with humiliating me like you did?" Susan snarled. "I *will* have access to the ley line nexus and this time you and the ridiculous faculty at this stupid school won't stop me."

"Ms. Barker, I'm not sure what you hope to accomp…" a

sharp sound, like a whip cracking rang out followed by a cry. "Stop! Don't hurt her!" George shouted.

Zoe stared at Mark. *Sarah*, he mouthed.

"She's just a stupid secretary. I don't know why you care what happens to her." Carolyn's voice was arrogant, confirming Zoe's fears about Sarah.

Zoe took a deep breath and reached for her power.

Kieran touched Zoe's shoulder and put his mouth against her ear. "Wait. We have to find out what's what before we charge in." His fingers tightened on her shoulder. She turned to stare at him. Her mentor and her friend were trapped in there with a crazy witch and an evil Night Mage. What the hell else was there to know?

Kim moved to her other side and locked eyes with her when Zoe turned. Kim tilted her head toward Kieran and nodded. Zoe released the breath she'd been holding. They were right. In fact, she could hear George's past admonitions about finesse in her head. They had to finesse this so that Sarah and George didn't get hurt…or worse. She nodded at Kim and put her hand over Kieran's. A small amount of tension went out of the group.

David slid silently around Mark and quickly moved past the open door, turning to look into the room as he passed. He turned around once he passed the door and raised two fingers. Then he turned to face the wall and patted his own back, then moved his hand out into the hallway. Zoe got it immediately. Carolyn and Susan were standing with their backs to the door. She glanced at Mark. He was better at plans for fighting than she was. Of course, she'd only been in one mage fight and that time she'd just gone in guns, or rather power, blazing.

Mark waved the others closer. He made a diamond shape with his fingers and pointed at the door. He pointed to himself and then the tip of the diamond indicating that he was going in first. Zoe was to go in last. This was a similar formation to what they had used when they rescued the students Susan had been holding in the basement of Davis Hall last semester. Zoe knew that she was the anchor.

"Send out another wave," Susan's voice came again. "I know they're all out there on the quad. You need to make a bigger wave!"

"Do it old man, or the secretary burns...forever," Carolyn growled.

Zoe started and caught herself. Carolyn was clearly threatening to use balefire on Sarah. She started to pull in power from the ley lines. The only thing that she knew of that worked against balefire was her shield of mixed Elements. And, even then, in her experience, it didn't put out balefire, but simply directed it back to Carolyn.

"Witch! I feel something!" Carolyn said sharply. "The shroud I put over the ley line nexus...it's been manipulated!"

"I thought you covered the ley lines. Were you lying or is your block so weak it was removed?" Susan's voice dripped with sarcasm.

Zoe allowed herself a small grin. No love lost there, that was for sure. That might make it easier to take the bitches out.

"No, you bitch. *I* blocked it. None of them are powerful enough to open it back up," Carolyn answered scornfully.

Mark looked back at the group of mages crouched in the hall. He brought his hand down sharply and strode into the office.

"Good evening, ladies," he said in an icy tone.

David was right. Carolyn and Susan were standing with their backs to the door. Zoe realized that her defeat at Swann Fountain had not diminished Susan Barker's arrogance even a bit. She was so certain that nobody would figure out what she was doing that she stood with her back to an open door.

Carolyn had whirled around at Mark's voice and drew her hand back in a throwing motion. Anticipating what was coming, Mark wrapped a small tornado of Air around her arm and pulled, knocking Carolyn off her feet.

Kim moved in and raised a ring of Fire around Susan while David and Kieran worked together using the dirt and water in the air to create a horizontal wall over Carolyn. Coming in behind the others, Zoe saw Sarah curled up on the floor against the far wall. There was a wall of balefire surrounding her. Sarah's eyes were closed, but she was breathing. Zoe looked for George. He was sitting in Sarah's guest chair and there were rings of balefire keeping him in place.

For a moment, Zoe panicked. There was too much going on at once. She knew that Carolyn could use her balefire to break the sort of ceiling that David and Kieran had created over her. But she also wanted to get Sarah and George out of their bindings.

A scream of outrage brought her back to her senses and she turned to face Carolyn. The Night Mage was pushing at David and Kieran's ceiling cover thingy with whips of balefire and Zoe could see that it was having an effect. She immediately created a shield like the one she made in the parking lot to defend Declan and Simon and threw it between Carolyn and the shield David and Kieran had made. Since she'd been able to reflect the balefire back on Carolyn in the parking lot, Zoe was hopeful the same thing would happen now.

She glanced over at Susan just in time to catch a snarling glare from the former administrative assistant. It did not look like the last few months had been kind to the witch. Her face was pale and drawn and there were dark circles under her eyes. Zoe had once described Susan as looking like a slightly demented grandmother. And that was still true, although Zoe mentally substituted the "slightly demented" with "demonic" as she noticed the evil stare directed her way. Susan obviously had some power as Zoe could see a shield hovering around her. But could the shield defend Susan against balefire? Looking at it with her magesight, Zoe didn't think so.

Zoe dismissed Susan as an immediate threat and turned back to George and Sarah while the others concentrated on holding Susan and Carolyn in place. She moved quickly over to the chair where George sat with the rings of balefire hovering around his torso. His shirt had burned through and she could see the beginnings of welts on the skin beneath. It was clear that Carolyn hadn't actually set the balefire *on* George or Sarah, as they'd be dead, and the building would be a smoking ruin. *Good one Obvious O'Brien. Focus. What did she do?*

George gave Zoe a grim smile as she peered at the rings of balefire around him. "I'm sorry to have caused such trouble," he said. "Obviously, I allowed myself to be surprised."

"Sure, whatever. Let me look at his for a minute," Zoe answered distractedly. It looked like she could insert one of her multi-Element shields between George and the balefire.

"I don't think there's anyth..." George started.

"Hush. I'm working," Zoe replied. George raised an eyebrow but didn't say anything more.

Zoe created what she was starting to call her Unique Patented Multi-Elemental Shield and carefully expanded it and slid it between the balefire ring and George's torso. Then, much as she had done in the parking lot fight, she rolled the shield over and around the balefire. Immediately the balefire jumped up and started to fill the shield ring. She slowly stretched her shield rings out in order to enlarge the inner circle and pull the balefire away from George.

The growing commotion behind her made her glance over her shoulder. Mark and the others were having an increasingly hard time keeping Carolyn under their control.

Zoe concentrated for a moment and sent out a tentative thread of power toward the ley line nexus. An immediate surge of power flowed back to her. Grabbing that power, she recreated her multi-Elemental wall and doubled it around Carolyn. The psychology professor must have felt something because she immediately stopped using balefire, obviously remembering that Zoe's shield was able to repel balefire. Zoe inwardly cringed at the hate-filled glare that Carolyn shot her way.

Covering up her nerves with a perfect mean-girls finger wave, Zoe turned back to George. He was staring down at his chest and the now-enclosed ring of balefire circling him.

"I admit, I'm not sure how to do this," he said to Zoe as she looked at him.

"I think if you slide out of the chair onto the floor, you can slide out of the ring," Zoe told him.

"Um...okay." George closed his eyes and pushed himself lower in the chair.

"Um...George? Um...I think you should open your eyes so you don't accidentally bump the fire ring there. I'm not exactly sure what my shield will do if you hit it," Zoe said tentatively. She didn't like experimenting with her mentor's life on the line, but she really didn't have much choice.

"Right." George opened his eyes to a slit, and pushed himself down in the chair. He came to rest on the floor. Scuttling sideways he moved away from the chair and stood up.

George stepped back to Zoe and gave her a quick hug. "I can't thank you enough," he said.

Zoe awkwardly returned the hug. "Um...you're welcome. But I think those guys could use some help...Rob, the tall one, is an Earth mage too." She indicated the group behind them struggling to hold Carolyn.

George gave Zoe a short nod. "Sarah?" he asked.

"I'm on it. Don't worry, she's my friend," Zoe answered.

And idea struck her and Zoe turned back and stared at the ring of balefire that had been around George. She tentatively reached out with her power and nudged her circular shield. The ring, including the balefire within it, moved sideways in response. Inspiration hit. She looked at the stalemate behind her. Pointing her hand in Carolyn's direction she shoved the ring closer to the Night mage. Carolyn glanced over and her eyes widened at the sight of the balefire ring moving toward her head. She made a slashing gesture with one hand and the fire inside Zoe's shield container disappeared.

Zoe grinned. Carolyn was afraid of her own balefire. Good to know. She dismissed her circular shield and gave her full attention to Sarah, who was curled up against the wall. She was unconscious, but Zoe could see her chest rising and falling regularly.

Zoe also noticed that because whatever happened had caused Sarah to lie *against* the far wall of the office, the rings of balefire trapping her could not go all the way around her. If they had, the wall and the building would have burned.

That gave Zoe an idea. She moved around so she was standing at Sarah's head. Yes. There was a small gap between the wall and the end of the ring of balefire. Zoe noted that it was a bigger gap than there had been between George's shirt and the balefire. The wall was not even slightly scorched. Carolyn must have been worried about setting the building on fire while she was in it.

Zoe took one more look at the others to make sure that they were still in control of the situation and turned back to Sarah. Moving carefully, she once again created a smaller version of the Unique Patented Multi-Elemental Shield and inserted it between the wall and the balefire. This time, she extended it in an arc, mirroring the arc of fire surrounding Sarah. As before, she wrapped the balefire in her shield and remembered to cap off the ends. It would not do to have balefire leaking out the ends of her cleverly contrived shielding.

Zoe breathed a sigh of relief as she pushed the balefire away from Sarah's inert form; she'd toss it at Carolyn in a second. Sliding behind the balefire ring, she created another layer of her shield and reached over to put a hand on Sarah's shoulder.

"Sarah! Sarah!" Zoe gave the shoulder a slight shake. Sarah groaned and her head rolled over a bit.

"Sarah!" Zoe shook her again, but there was no more response. She looked at Sarah with her magesight and saw that there was a web of red lines covering Sarah's head and down to her waist. The lines were very similar to the blood webs that Zoe had removed from the students that Susan had been controlling last semester.

"Look out!" Mark yelled from the other side of the room.

Zoe looked up in time to see Carolyn throw a whip of regular Fire at him as she leapt for the door. The Fire was immediately met with two streams of Water as both Kieran and Zoe acted.

Carolyn raced out of the office and, despite the carpeting, they could hear her running down the hall.

"Shit! She's probably headed for the quad and the power nexus!" Kim exclaimed.

"But she could access that from up here...why does she need to run down there?" Zoe was totally lost. She'd wondered why Carolyn hadn't fully accessed it. It'd been easy enough to do. And she'd obviously felt Zoe accessing it. No, wait. Zoe thought back to what she'd overheard. Carolyn had felt something happen to her *shield* over the ley lines.

The others turned to stare at her. "Well, babe, it's a lot easier if you're right on top of the power source," Kieran said.

"But...it's not that hard...I just did it...what?" Now they were all looking at her like she'd grown horns. Zoe stopped herself from putting her hands up to her head just to make sure.

"Um...no, it's not that easy. Even if she's a Night Mage. That just gives her access to...uh...a wider repertoire of actions, not necessarily stronger power. Also, being a Night Mage doesn't mean she's any smarter or more self-aware than she was before," Kim grinned.

"She's a psychologist," Zoe started, then stopped. Kim laughed.

"You bitch! I'm not going to..." Susan started screaming at Zoe.

"Oh, shut up," George said tiredly. "I underestimated your capacity for revenge, which was my mistake. But I won't do that again."

Susan stared at him in shock.

Rob had gone to the office window that overlooked the quad. "I think we need to get back down to the quad right now," he said displaying more urgency than Zoe had ever seen from him before.

George glanced at Mark. "Bring her," he lifted his chin towards Susan. "We'll meet you down on the quad."

"Don't you even think about it!" Susan screamed. "I still have all your information...I know where you all live!"

Mark nodded and created a vortex of Air around Susan. As it closed in on her, she was lifted up in the center of the small tornado. As her feet left the ground, Susan suddenly stopped screaming and stared horrified at the air under her feet. Mark gestured with his hands, and the vortex preceded him out of the office.

Zoe took one last glance at Sarah lying on the floor. The spells would have to be dealt with later. She grabbed a jacket that was hanging on the back of the door and put it under Sarah's head before following the group.

Chapter Seventeen

Zoe raced down the hallway after the others and leapt down the stairs two at a time. The group hurtled out of the front door of Shelby and across the quad.

Carolyn was standing with her back to Zoe and Shelby Hall, facing the remaining faculty and student mages on the quad. Zoe noticed that Declan and his father were standing a little bit apart from the others. Declan appeared to be lecturing Aseyai. At least Zoe could see Declan gesturing and Aseyai nodding occasionally. Whatever they were arguing over, she hoped they'd finish in time so Declan, at least, could help. She had no illusions about Aseyai. Djinn were notoriously self-interested and as Aseyai had pointed out, he had no stake in this battle.

Mark pushed Susan and her tornado over to one side but kept her behind Carolyn. Carolyn herself hadn't seemed to notice that the small group had emerged from Shelby. She was alternating throwing balefire with regular fire against the faculty and student mages. Zoe saw that those who remained on the quad had formed a combined shield similar to her multi-Elemental shield. But there was something off about it. It was keeping the Fire away from everybody however Zoe could see that a part of it eroded when it was hit with the balefire.

Seeing the failing shield, Zoe immediately created one of own and placed it between the eroding shield and Carolyn. The next burst of balefire immediately splattered against the shield and bits of balefire flew back towards Carolyn. The Night Mage spun around and glared at Zoe through narrowed eyes.

"Get me out of this!" Susan screamed, pulling Carolyn's attention away from Zoe. Carolyn's eyes widened at the sight of Susan suspended about two feet off the ground in the middle of a whirlwind.

"You're on your own, witch!" Carolyn laughed.

Zoe took advantage of the distraction to put up a shield in front of the small group that had come out of Shelby Hall.

On the other side of the quad, Simon had also taken advantage of Carolyn's momentary inattention to throw two large fireballs at Carolyn's back. Both hit, but slid off her, doing nothing more than singeing her shirt on the way down.

Zoe stared at the fireballs sliding off Carolyn.

"How the hell did that happen? I can't see any shields around her?" she asked George.

"I'm not certain, but it likely has to do with a combination of her being a Night Mage and use of the ley line nexus," George answered.

"You bitch! You can't leave me up here!" Susan was still yelling at Carolyn. For her part, Carolyn continued to laugh at the witch.

"Did you really think I was going to do whatever you wanted? I will have access to the power of the ley line nexus. I don't need a washed-up witch!" Carolyn was gleeful.

If looks could kill (and Zoe figured if anybody could kill with a look it would be Susan Barker), Carolyn would have dropped dead right there. But apparently, being held in a small portable tornado was blunting Susan's ability to use magic. Which was just as well, since Zoe preferred dealing with one problem at a time.

"Zoe!" She was pulled out of her reverie by Mark's urgent voice. "Zoe!"

"What?" Zoe shook her head.

"Can you access the ley lines? You're the strongest. Use the extra power to get us closer to Carolyn. That way we'll have a better chance against her," Mark was not quite yelling.

Zoe spared a glance at Carolyn, but she seemed to be enjoying watching Susan in her tornado and wasn't paying any attention to the faculty behind her.

"Yes, I can...but the shields...what should I do?" Zoe started to panic again. She was expected to be a leader here, but she didn't know what to do next or how to use all this power that was available to her. Mark was asking her to do several things at the same time. She didn't know if she could access power, hold a couple of shields, and go after Carolyn. How was she supposed to control all that?

"Um...okay...um...I need to hold the shields...and...can you do your own?" Zoe looked around at the others.

"Don't panic," Kim said. "You're the one that knows your power best. We can all do our own shields, and we can all create a group shield. Don't worry about that. I'd say, see what you can do to wrap that bitch up. Improvise. You got this." She gave Zoe a wicked grin.

Kim's attitude was infectious. Zoe found herself grinning back at her neighbor. She pushed out cautiously and felt the power of the ley line nexus. Once again, she was astounded at the amount of power that flowed into her when she opened the smallest of channels. The thought of how much more she could access was intoxicating. Zoe forcefully pulled her mind and attention back to the present.

The students and faculty who had stayed on the quad

were launching everything they had at Carolyn. The small group that had gone into Shelby Hall was doing the same. However, Carolyn was dealing with the two-pronged attack with ease. She was not using balefire at the moment, but Zoe figured it was only a matter of time until the Night Mage became annoyed, bored, or angry, and let loose. Now that everybody had access to the ley lines, they provided power but no overwhelming advantage.

Zoe forced her mind to function. *You did something like this just a few months ago. C'mon! Focus!* She took a deep breath and gazed around the quad. Carolyn was still easily handling the attacks from the two groups of mages. Zoe watched for a minute. There had to be something. Something she could use or exploit to their advantage.

A movement out of the corner of her eye caught her attention. Declan was walking away from his father and back to the group of his friends. Aseyai was still standing a little to the side of the faculty and student mages. The djinn made a slight movement as if to walk away but stilled. It was clear he was watching Declan. *Well, he said it's not his fight. I don't think we're going to convince him now.* Zoe sighed. She was pretty sure this whole thing could be over in less than a minute if the djinn decided to step in.

She turned back to the attack-parry fight going on between the faculty and student mages and Carolyn. That was it. The mages, in an effort to avoid hurting each other, were timing their attacks so both groups didn't attack at once. That actually made it easier on Carolyn as she only had to face one side at a time.

Watching the back and forth, Zoe had an idea. The attacks by her friends were not going beyond Carolyn because Carolyn was stopping those attacks. It obviously hadn't occurred to Carolyn that if she simply dodged, rather than stopping or returning an attack, she should get the mages to hit each other. The mages' worry about harming each other was unfounded. If they could make their attacks more random, more frequent, and from different directions, maybe they could throw Carolyn off balance. That might just work. But how was she going to tell the others?

Something poked her ankle and she looked down. Alder was standing next to her. The squirrel tapped her pant leg and Zoe nodded. Alder scrambled up her leg and onto her shoulder.

"Rowantree says we need to move quickly. The Night Mage is increasing her power using the ley lines and he believes she will unleash a great deal of destruction very soon," he said in her ear.

"I have an idea, but I need your help," Zoe responded. She quickly gave Alder the outlines of her idea for unbalancing Carolyn.

"That might work. I will inform Rowantree and the others." Alder jumped off her shoulder and disappeared into the quad.

Zoe walked over to her small group of mages. "Guys! Spread out in a half circle around her. I'll shield. Alder's telling the others. We'll hit her in a sort of rotation, so she'll have to deal with continuous attacks. If you go for precise, you shouldn't have to worry about hitting the others."

George glanced at her. "That's a pretty good idea," he smiled.

"So, go!" Zoe waved her hands at everybody.

"I knew you'd think of something." Kim laughed as she moved to her left, followed by Rob and Joe.

Across the quad Zoe could see Robyn Harper gesturing to the others as they spread out in a half-circle. The two half-circles almost met, placing Carolyn in the center. Kim ended up standing a few feet from Josh Selford on one side of the circle and Zoe ended up with Robyn on her right on the other side. Carolyn stared around the circle, but continued to smile. She obviously believed she still held an advantage.

"Good idea," Robyn grinned. "Keep her spinning!"

"I hope so," Zoe muttered.

Kieran stood on Zoe's left. She shifted a little closer to him. "Can you access the ley lines now?"

He gave her a thumbs up and let loose with another fire hose of water at Carolyn. The Night Mage laughed and used a wall of fire to push it back toward him. Kieran gave a small nod and cut off the fire hose. At the same time, Josh created a small tornado like Mark's, and it landed on Carolyn. As she fought off the tornado, George shifted the ground under her feet causing her to stagger, at that point Simon sent a lance of fire right at her feet. Carolyn was off balance and forced to divide her attention between the multiple attacks from different directions. Once again, it didn't look like she was shielding, and Zoe couldn't figure out why. Was Carolyn really that arrogant?

Zoe tried to keep her shield up around the ring of mages, but her concentration kept slipping as she shifted her attention to fighting. A bolt of normal fire from Carolyn got through at one of those moments of inattention and laced Annmarie's leg.

The girl screamed and fell but retained enough presence of mind to pour water onto herself. Josh ran over and helped Annmarie back to her feet. Limping, Annmarie moved back into the circle of mages.

Zoe was starting to feel frazzled between keeping the shield up between Carolyn and the faculty and student mages and sending her own attacks at Carolyn. Despite that, the whole thing felt like it was at a stalemate. Every time somebody got a hit in on Carolyn, she simply pulled more power from the ley lines. Zoe corrected her earlier conclusion about Carolyn's shields, or lack thereof. Carolyn *did* have a shield. She was using it like a knight used an actual shield and moving it around as she was attacked instead of creating a wall as Zoe had.

Carolyn started moving toward the side of the circle where the students were. She didn't quite cackle, but her laugh was frightening.

"So, students...have you learned anything yet? Like don't attack your professors? Or even better, don't listen to professors who tell you to control your power? Where's that djinn kid? Oh, there you are..." she sent a lance of fire directly at Declan.

Zoe saw him leap to one side and avoid it. But he caught his foot on a tuft of grass and fell backwards. Carolyn laughed again and launched a fire ball directly at his chest. Declan seemed to have forgotten his magic in his panic over being attacked. He did nothing more than roll away.

Finally Declan managed to get his hands in front of him and he made a pushing gesture. Carolyn staggered back several steps but came back up with an ugly look on her face. Zoe looked around for Aseyai, surely he would help Declan? But she couldn't see him.

"You're the asshole that sent me to Valley Forge, aren't you? I owe you for that, you little shit!" Carolyn raged at Declan.

Declan shoved again and Carolyn staggered back once more. Carolyn screamed in fury and threw a beach-ball sized ball of balefire toward Declan. Zoe yelled and tried to throw her wall of mixed Elements in front of Declan. Behind him she could see Simon reaching out to grab him. But Simon cringed away from the balefire before he reached Declan. Zoe cursed. If Simon had more backbone he could have pulled Declan sideways and away from the balefire.

Mark and Kieran shouted simultaneously and tried to send a waterspout down on top of Carolyn, but she pushed up with her left hand, sending a ball of balefire toward the water spout while continuing to guide the balefire flame toward Declan. Declan managed to roll away again from a direct hit, but the balefire hit the grass and created a line of fire that divided the mages on that side of the quad. Now they were in three separate groups, unable to effectively work together, and panic was setting in.

Zoe looked frantically around for George. He was her mentor and had much more experience with fighting with magic than she did. He had to have some ideas. She spotted George on the far side of the circle next to Rob and Kim and started toward him just as he collapsed to the grass.

"George!" Zoe screamed and ran over to his side. He was breathing, but clearly unconscious.

"He drained himself. He was drained so badly earlier, that even the boost from the ley lines couldn't fully overcome the exhaustion. Those bitches were pushing him and forcing him to use his powers. He didn't have as much left as he thought he did." Kim knelt down beside Zoe. "You go back and deal with the Night Mage bitch and I'll get Rob to help me carry George out of here."

"Is he going to be okay? I mean…" Zoe couldn't finish the sentence.

"He'll be fine with about twelve hours of sleep and no magic," Kim said. She glanced over her shoulder. "Rob! A little help here!" Kim turned back to Zoe. "Go. You have to figure out a way to stop the Night Mage before she takes us all out."

Zoe slowly stood up as Rob jogged over. "He'll be okay," Rob said giving her shoulder a squeeze.

Zoe nodded once and then turned back toward Carolyn. While she'd been distracted with George, the mages on the other side of the quad had managed to put a wall around the balefire that had hit the grass, although that shield was already eroding where the balefire touched it. Declan was up on his feet and facing Carolyn once more. Behind him, arrayed in a sort of arrowhead formation were Annmarie, Josh, Geoff, David, and Robyn Harper. Simon and Joe were concentrating on containing the balefire.

Zoe felt helpless. All she'd done so far was run around like a headless chicken. Okay, so she'd put up a wall, but it obviously hadn't stopped Carolyn, so what good was it? How the hell was she supposed to stop somebody with balefire when balefire couldn't be stopped?

She ran around to the other side, away from George and Kim and Rob. She didn't want to draw any attention to George when he couldn't defend himself. Carolyn was putting together another ball of balefire and taunting Declan and the others.

"Do you really think a bunch of students can stop me? You guys are pathetic! And what kind of faculty takes the side of students against other faculty?" Her face twisted into a nasty snarl.

The last comment was obviously directed at Robyn who simply growled and threw a small tornado at Carolyn who contemptuously batted it away. Zoe stared in fear. An ordinary mage would not succeed against Carolyn. They were going to lose this fight.

Zoe's mind spun on a treadmill of doubt and worry. What was she going to do? How were they supposed to stop Carolyn? She was just a history professor! How did she get out of this mess and go back to just being a faculty member? Her throat started to close up and panic set in.

"Zoe! Zoe!" Kieran's voice cut through the fog that was descending on her head. "Are you okay?" His voice held a barely concealed note of fear.

Zoe shook her head, trying to clear out the dread and force herself to think. "What are we going to do? How are we going to stop her? I don't know what to do!" Her voice rose as the panic reasserted itself.

Kieran put his hands on her shoulders and gave her a gentle shake. "Stop! We'll figure it out. Please don't panic."

She was panting like she'd just finished the fifty-yard dash. Kieran's hands were still on her shoulders and she clutched at his arms to ground herself.

"O-okay. You're r-right…but how? How d-do we stop her?" Zoe stomped down on the terror.

"Put up your wall…whatever you did before to make the balefire slide off. I'm going to go talk to Mark. There has to be something…some sort of combination of power that we can do that can at least knock her out. Then maybe we can get Declan to send her to Mars." He gave her a smile.

"Yeah. Okay. Yeah. Good idea. Mark. Okay. Go to Mars. Yeah. Okay. I'll shield." Zoe knew she'd only understood about every third word, but it sounded like a good idea. She turned back to Carolyn and quickly put together her multi-Element shield. Remembering what she'd done when she and Mark had found Carolyn attacking Simon and Declan in the parking lot, she created a cylinder and dropped it over Carolyn.

Duh. She was standing over the ley lines. Zoe poured energy from the nexus into her shield around Carolyn. That seemed to contain her ability to throw fireballs.

Feeling a slight sense of relief at having stopped the chaos for the moment, Zoe started across the lawn to meet the other group.

FOOMP.

A huge fireball of balefire was launched upward from Carolyn's raised hands. It went up and up until it finally arced over and started back down. Zoe gasped. She hadn't put a shield *above* Carolyn. The Night Mage had launched her fireball over the shield. Shitshitshit!!

The balefire came hurtling down from a height of about forty feet.

"Run!" Zoe shouted at the others. She waved her hands and ran toward them. After a moment of startled silence and standing around, the small group scattered.

Declan ran right into the path of the fireball.

"No! Back up!" Zoe yelled again.

Declan stopped and stared at her in confusion.

The fireball hit him directly on the head. His screams echoed around the quad.

"Declan!" Zoe screamed.

Two streams of water from Kieran and Annmarie immediately hit Declan, to no avail. Balefire couldn't be put out with ordinary water.

Zoe grabbed for power from the ley lines and tried to smother the flames with Water and Earth. That didn't work either. Exhaustion started to creep in despite the power boost from the ley lines. Her own power reserves were diminishing. Was this what George had been talking about? Literal burn out? Zoe shook her head and drew more power from the nexus. She'd worry about burnout later, after she made sure there *was* a later.

She ran toward Declan, who was writhing on the ground.

Suddenly Aseyai was standing next to Declan. He put his hand on his son's head and the flames went out.

Zoe skidded to a stop next to Declan. "H-how...?" she panted.

"I am a djinn," Aseyai answered. "And he is my son."

Declan was curled into a ball on the ground, arms wrapped around his head. He was whimpering slightly. Annmarie, Josh and Geoff ran over to him, followed by the others.

"Declan! Buddy!" Geoff gently grabbed Declan's shoulders. "You're alive!"

The three of them helped Declan up. Aseyai looked at Declan.

"Why did that one throw balefire at you?" He pointed to Carolyn still standing in the middle of the quad inside Zoe's shield wall and screaming curses at Zoe. She had balefire in her hands but seemed to have forgotten it in the midst of her ranting.

"B-because sh-she doesn't like m-me and b-because sh-she's t-trying to control...the ley lines...the p-power here." Declan pointed down to the ground.

Aseyai frowned. "Why should she not?"

"B-because she will use it against all of us...especially m-me." Declan stared at his father.

Zoe looked back and forth between father and son. Aseyai returned Declan's gaze.

"I will not allow that," Aseyai stated. "She will not hurt my son again."

Carolyn chose that moment to launch another ball of balefire at Declan. Aseyai waved a hand and the fireball disappeared. Carolyn screamed and immediately threw another. Aseyai made that one vanish as well. The djinn gazed steadily at Carolyn.

"You shall not attempt to harm my son or those under his protection," his voice reverberated across the quad as it had before. Susan Barker's eyes grew wide and she stood motionless and silent inside her cyclone.

"You can't tell me what to do, old man!" Carolyn screamed. She drew back her arm to throw yet another fireball.

Aseyai stared at her calmly. "You were warned," he boomed.

Carolyn snarled and launched her fireball. Aseyai shrugged and waved his hand. Carolyn and the fireball disappeared.

"Wha...?" Robyn gasped.

"Wh-where did she go?" Zoe gulped.

"To the realm of the djinn. She is not djinn. She will not be able to return here," Aseyai's tone was final.

"Th-thanks…um…Dad…Father," Declan stammered.

"You are my son. You fought well and have honor. I am not ashamed of you," Aseyai stated.

He put one hand on Declan's shoulder and the burn marks on Declan's head and clothing disappeared. Aseyai then walked over to where the balefire was still scorching the grass and earth of the quad and waved a hand over it. The balefire went out and the grass was restored. The djinn nodded once and vanished.

After the chaos of the last several minutes – Zoe was surprised to realize they'd only been outside for about fifteen minutes – the quad was almost eerily quiet. The mages stared around in shock. If you ignored Susan huddled in her personal tornado, it looked like nothing had happened.

"Zoe! You guys! Get over here!" Kim's voice rang across the now silent quad.

Zoe and the others sprinted over to Kim as she knelt on the grass next to George. He was stretched out on his back. Zoe's stomach did flip flops. He was just exhausted, right? That was all. She sank down next to Kim.

"George? George?" she gently shook his shoulder. His eyes blinked open but didn't focus.

"Wha…ha-happened?" George blinked a few more times before Zoe saw his eyes focus on her. "Zoe? What's going on?" his voice was tentative.

"You wore yourself out. I think you collapsed. But Carolyn's gone…Aseyai, Declan's father, sent her to the world of djinn he said. Are you okay?" Even though his eyes were focusing now, Zoe thought George still looked very confused.

Kim slid an arm behind George's shoulder and with Rob's help, maneuvered George into a sitting position.

"No, I mean…what am I feeling? It's like…uh…a force

beyond the ley lines. I've never felt anything like that before. I can tell who's accessing them...you are connected to them right now, Zoe." George stared at her.

John Gardner, Rob, and David all shared a look.

John cleared his throat. "George? Ley lines...sometimes they have a guardian...someone who can sort of monitor them...a warder..." his voice trailed off.

David gave a short laugh. "Well, George. I guess you really are a Wardmaster now!"

Chapter Eighteen

George shook his head. "I had not anticipated this," he said ruefully. He looked up at John Gardner. "Did you know about this?"

"Well, I had an idea…we've discussed it years ago…but I didn't put it together until just now. I mean, the fountain doesn't need a guardian, Calder took care of that. And the city, although the mayor doesn't realize it. But I've never been this close to a nexus before, so I guess yes and no is my answer." John smiled.

"You could have said that up front you know," George grinned at him.

"I thought you could use some background and context," John retorted. "You're the historian after all."

Zoe was relieved that George seemed to be back to his old self. But she had the nagging feeling she was missing something. George gave her the answer when he glanced around the quad and saw Susan still trapped in Mark's mini-tornado.

"What are we going to do with her? And, where's Sarah? She was in my office when those two showed up," his voice held a worried note.

"Sarah!" Zoe exclaimed. She raced back into Shelby Hall followed closely by Kieran, Mark and David.

She took the stairs two at a time and tore down the hallway to George's office. Mark, by virtue of his long stride, was the first in the door of the office. He came to an abrupt halt and the other three just missed plowing into his back. Zoe steadied herself against the door jamb and peered around Mark. Sarah was still curled up on the floor, but the balefire that had surrounded her was gone. More surprising was seeing Aseyai crouched over Sarah with one hand on her forehead. As Zoe watched, Sarah's eyes fluttered open and she stared uncomprehendingly up at Aseyai.

Zoe switched to magesight. Aseyai appeared as a glowing, vaguely human-shaped blur. But more importantly, the web of red lines over Sarah's head was gone.

The djinn gave a short nod and stood up facing Zoe and the others. "She will recover. At least physically. I believe you should help her mind," he said brusquely.

"Um...thank you. I appreciate your help," Zoe managed.

"My son says you helped him, and I owe you for that assistance. I have now repaid that debt, Elemental." Aseyai gave another nod and vanished.

"Close your mouth, Zoe." Sarah's laugh was weak but very Sarah.

Zoe ran over to her friend and helped her sit up. "Are you okay?"

Sarah rubbed her face. "Yeah, I guess. What happened? Those two bitches walked in...where's George? Is he okay?" She tried to stand.

"Here." Kieran brought her desk chair over and helped Sarah into it.

"George is okay. He...well, it's a long story..." Zoe said.

"Of course it is. It's George. The bitches...where are they?" Sarah leaned back in the chair. Whatever Aseyai had done seemed to be helping her recover faster than Zoe would have expected.

"Well, Carolyn is gone. Aseyai, the guy who helped you a minute ago, sent her to the plane where djinn live. I don't think that will be pleasant for her," David's voice was a sarcastic drawl.

"Djinn? What?" Sarah frowned at David.

"Declan's dad. He showed up to talk Declan tonight…and ended up helping us," Kieran put in.

"Okay. Sure. That makes sense…not." Sarah was still frowning.

"Maybe we should just go down to the quad and I'll fill you in on the details you missed and then you can talk to George and the others," Zoe suggested.

"Good idea. Because you guys are just confusing me," Sarah muttered.

"We're not *trying* to confuse you, but it's been a really weird night," Zoe apologized.

Mark and David got on either side of Sarah and helped her up. Her first couple of steps were shaky but then she regained her balance and moved more easily. She still held on to Mark and David, but she didn't look like she'd fall over if they let go. Zoe let out a sigh of relief. Her friend was going to be okay. And, besides being confused about what had happened, it seemed like Sarah was coping mentally as well. Of course, Zoe was still confused by everything and she'd been there. Still, given Aseyai's warning, Zoe kept an eye on Sarah's reactions as Zoe explained what had happened in the last half an hour or so.

By the time they'd reached the group on the quad, Zoe had given Sarah the basic outline of the night's events.

"So, Declan's dad really is a djinn? And he showed up here? Why?" Sarah asked as they neared the small group.

"I'm not sure. Right after he helped you, he told me that

since Declan had said I'd helped him, he, Aseyai – that's his name – had now repaid that debt. But he didn't get involved in the fight with Carolyn until Carolyn hit Declan with that balefire. I think he was pissed off," Zoe shrugged.

"Well, dads do tha...what's that?" Sarah broke off and pointed at Susan in her tornado. The witch stood trapped in the vortex, glaring at everyone around her.

"That's how Mark got Susan to shut up and leave us alone," David laughed.

Sarah looked over at Mark. "Can you keep her there? I mean, like, forever?"

Mark chuckled. "Tempting as that is, I don't think so. We do have to figure out what to do with her. I don't think turning her over to the police will work. I mean what would they charge her with?"

Zoe frowned. "But we do need to do something. We can't just let her go. I mean, she can create another coven and start up all over again."

Sarah let go of Mark and David and slowly made her way over to George. He gave her a hug. "Are you okay? I'm so sorry about all of this," he apologized.

"I'm fine, boss, but I think I'd like a couple vacation days," Sarah grinned at him.

"Of course! Of course!" George answered.

"Zoe told me most of what happened, but she said there was something you should tell me. So, what are you supposed to tell me?" Sarah prodded her boss.

"Well...ah...it appears that I really am a wardmaster. I...ah...collapsed and when I came to I could feel the ley lines...ah...I mean feel them. It's a bit hard to explain, but along with Summerfield's Watchers – Rowantree, Darkwing, and the others – I am the guardian of the ley line nexus." George managed to look sheepish when relaying this information.

Zoe watched George struggle to explain his "new job" to Sarah. In a sudden flash of insight she recognized the problem. George had always been very certain of his skills both as a professor and as a mage. Now, after a fight with a Night Mage, a fight he nearly lost, he finds out he's the guardian of a ley line nexus running through campus. A nexus he didn't realize was there until a week or so earlier. Zoe thought that had shaken George's confidence a bit. She hid a small smile. There was actually something he didn't know about.

George's discomfiture made Zoe feel better about her doubts about her own powers and leadership skills. If George was uncomfortable in a new role, then that gave her license to positively wallow in doubt.

As if he read her mind, Kieran came up behind her, put his hands on her shoulders and leaned down. "You still have to figure out your powers, love," he whispered in her ear.

Zoe dug an elbow into his stomach and shook her head. "Fine. Whatever," she whispered back.

"Um...Dr. O'Brien?" The hesitant voice came from behind her, and she turned around. Josh Shelford and Geoff Bradley were holding Declan between them trailed by the other students who had come out to help. Annmarie approached the faculty group.

"Oh, Annmarie. I'm sorry! Are you guys okay? How's Declan?" Zoe felt a stab of guilt realizing that she'd forgotten about the students.

"He's okay, but we were going to take him back to the dorms. Dr. Harper thought we should tell you so you wouldn't worry about where we were," Annmarie told her.

"Oh, okay. That's a good idea." Zoe glanced over at Robyn who gave her a small wave. "If you need anything, just send me a text." Zoe gave Annmarie a quick hug, and the group of dazed looking students turned back across the quad and headed for the dorms.

Once they were out of earshot, Robyn came over to Zoe. "I ordered pizza for them. They just need to eat and decompress. Annmarie said something about calling her dad again. I also wanted them away from Susan Barker and whatever's going to happen with her. They don't need that on top of everything else," she commented to Zoe.

"No, you're right. Do you have any ideas about what to do with her?"

"You mean besides leaving her in that tornado? Sadly, no. And besides, I don't think Mark can maintain that indefinitely," Robyn grimaced.

"No, unfortunately he can't. He already told us that," Zoe replied.

Movement out of the corner of her eye caught Zoe's attention. There were a couple groups of students walking down the path at the far side of the quad.

"You guys? Do you think they saw or heard what happened?" Zoe turned anxiously to the others, indicating the groups of students with a small wave of her hand.

Mark watched the students for a few seconds. "I don't know. But, they're walking by as if they're not interested in us. I'm pretty sure if they noticed anything, they'd have their phones out videoing us."

"Susan's in a tornado right there. How did they not notice? I mean, last year, people didn't see the demon, but they thought there were fireworks at the fountain." Zoe was confused.

"A compulsion spell might keep them from looking too closely," David mused.

"Yeah. But that would mean that Susan put one on the entire quad. And did it ahead of time," Kieran said.

"Maybe George has some ideas. After all, he's the true Wardmaster here now," Zoe replied. They drifted over toward the small group around George.

"Um, George?" Zoe began, staring at Susan Barker in her vortex, "We've been wondering how come nobody on campus heard what happened just now?"

George raised an eyebrow and looked at Susan.

She glared back. "I don't have to tell you anything," she snarled.

"Well, we might be inclined to release you from that tornado if you cooperate." George gave her a small smile.

Susan stared at him and the rest of the group tensed. Zoe's heart rate went up. Would George really release Susan? Apparently, Susan was willing to believe that. Zoe hoped that George knew of some way to keep Susan from using magic again.

Susan gave what Zoe figured was supposed to be a real smile. Instead Susan just appeared more feral than usual.

"Fine. Yes. I put a general compulsion spell around the quad. It encourages everybody to ignore it. It should have worked on you all as well. I'm not sure why it didn't. I'll have to work on that. Now let me out of here." Susan eyed George closely.

"Well, there are of course some conditions," George began.

Zoe held her breath. What kind of conditions could George impose that would be effective? She knew that given half a chance, Susan would continue to go after any and all power sources, including the ley lines.

Susan stood still, eyeing George.

"What kind of conditions, old man?" she growled. "I told you what you needed to know, now let me out of this damn tornado!"

"She also is responsible for bringing harm to my son, Elemental. I claim right of restitution." Aseyai's voice came from behind Zoe. She jumped around to face the djinn.

"Uh, with all due respect, what does that mean? What are you going to do with her?" Zoe carefully kept her tone neutral.

"That is not necessary for you to know," Aseyai replied.

"I know you have unlimited power, um, can you remove her ability to do magic? So she's just an ordinary human being? I mean..." Zoe hesitated. She was pretty certain she knew what Aseyai meant when he talked about restitution and she was also certain she was very uncomfortable with that idea.

Susan and the mini-tornado vanished.

"What the hell?" Zoe exclaimed.

Aseyai gazed unblinking at Zoe. "She will not return to this plane."

"Um...okay. Are you...did you...um...send her to the plane of the djinn also?" Zoe wanted to tread very carefully around Aseyai. Right now it seemed like he might actually like her. Or at least want to avoid harming her. But she was under no illusions that if she did something that he perceived as harmful to Declan, he would not hesitate to take whatever actions he felt were appropriate and necessary.

"That is not necessary for you to know. I have decided." Aseyai nodded once to Zoe and the group in general and vanished again.

Kim let out an exaggerated sigh. "Okay. Note to self, don't get on Zoe's bad side. She has djinn disappearing people for her."

Zoe gaped at Kim before giving a short laugh. "Yeah, right. I don't think he takes special orders, though." Hopefully, whatever Aseyai had done meant Susan wouldn't be coming back to bother them.

George cleared his throat. "I believe that Sarah should go home, she needs rest. For that matter, we all do." He cleared his throat again. "I...uh...I owe you all an apology and a great debt. I allowed myself to get caught up in the mundane tasks of the provost's office. I have no excuse for that except overconfidence and even arrogance. In hindsight, I believe Morgan piled on the work on purpose. My only explanation is that I am an academic at heart and I let my immediate concerns for faculty override the greater threat posed by Carolyn. I thought I could take care of Carolyn when it became necessary. I am deeply sorry for my negligence."

Zoe moved over next to George and gave him a hug. "Apology accepted and I promise that if something like this ever comes up again, I will annoy you until you pay attention!"

"Me, too!" Mark said while Kieran and the other faculty members nodded vigorously.

Zoe saw Simon moving closer from the fringes of the group. The little man looked exhausted and, strangely, ashamed. She caught his eye and he looked down at the ground. Simon continued to sidle over toward George and Zoe wondered if he'd had a bit of a comeuppance. She glanced over at Mark and noticed that he too was watching Simon as he made his way over to George.

George looked around as Simon approached. The two men exchanged an unreadable look and Zoe saw Simon flush.

"My apologies, George. I feel partially responsible. In my work with the young man, Declan, I overlooked numerous concerns he voiced." Simon was unnaturally subdued as he spoke to George.

George gazed at the little man with sympathy in his eyes. "All's well that ends well, Simon. We can discuss particulars later," he said softly.

"Yes, indeed." Simon managed one bounce on his toes and then slowly walked back to the edge of the group.

Chapter Nineteen

THE SUN SHONE IN around the edges of the bedroom curtains. Zoe muttered imprecations against the light and turned over to bury her head in Kieran's shoulder. They had gotten in late last night after cleaning up on campus and making sure that George did indeed go home to get some much-needed rest himself.

Kim, Rob, Joe, Zoe, Kieran, and Sarah had all crammed into Joe's SUV and headed back into the city. Zoe and Kieran had walked Sarah back to her apartment and made sure she was okay. Before leaving, Zoe reinforced the wards on Sarah's place yet again. It felt a bit like closing the barn door after the horse left, but Zoe didn't want to take any chances with Sarah's safety when it came to magical attacks.

Zoe and Kieran had walked back to her place and crashed. Now, Zoe tried to remember what day it was and if she had to teach. Or if she did have classes, what was she going to give them in place of class because she was certain that there was no way in hell she was up to lecturing today. She sat up in bed. *I'm wide awake. Might as well make some coffee and see if I can figure out what's going on.*

Kieran muttered and rolled over. Zoe smiled down at

him. She felt so comfortable around him. It felt like they'd been together for years. Comfortable, fun, and mutually supportive years. She thought he felt the same, but she wasn't about to jeopardize anything by saying that out loud. Not yet.

Zoe stood up and stretched. She grabbed a sweatshirt, sweatpants, slippers and snuck out of the bedroom. She stepped quietly into the bathroom only to have something hard and furry knock against her leg as she was pushing the door closed. Moose and Flash barged into the bathroom behind her.

"What the hell, guys? Why do you have to watch me pee?" Zoe kept her voice down.

"We're starving! And we missed all the fun last night," Moose whined.

"Yeah. You never let us do anything," Flash chimed in.

"Oh, for..." Zoe resigned herself to taking care of her morning business with an audience.

As she negotiated the stairs with the cats winding around her ankles as was their habit, Zoe gave them more details of the previous night's adventures. She asked them what they'd heard from the squirrels about Rowantree and Darkwing. She had not seen either Watcher in the aftermath of the fight and was concerned.

"They're okay. I think Alder got his tail singed, but he'll be fine," Flash said as he leapt down the last two steps.

"Okay, good." Zoe headed into the kitchen and made a beeline for her coffee and coffee maker. Then she fed the cats. Coffee took priority even over the cats.

She heard movement and running water in the bathroom overhead just as the coffee maker beeped to tell her it was done brewing. She pulled two mugs out of the cabinet and got the cream out of the fridge for Kieran.

Zoe looked up from pouring coffee as Kieran shambled into the kitchen. He gave her a quick kiss and grabbed his mug of coffee.

"Oh, you're wonderful," he sighed, and Zoe laughed.

"Which? Me or the coffee?" she teased.

"Both. You're both wonderful. You're wonderful for making it and coffee's wonderful for existing," Kieran grinned.

"Oh, good save!" Zoe laughed again. She picked up her own cup and went back out into the living room to flop down on the sofa. Kieran followed and sat down next to her. The cats, having gobbled down their breakfast shoved their way up onto the couch beside Zoe.

Kieran looked over at them. "Hey, guys. Did you know about the ley lines on campus? Or about George's new job?"

"No. The Night Mage was the one who forced the ley lines closer to the surface, and that's when Rowantree detected them." Moose had already started yet another cleaning routine and was carefully chewing the toes on his back foot.

Flash glanced up from licking his lower back. "Sometimes things happen or appear when needed," he commented cryptically.

"What does that mean?" Zoe took a sip of coffee.

"Well, think about your own powers. We got here two years before you figured out what you are." Flash licked his front paw and swiped it over his ears.

"Are you saying that I only figured out my powers because I needed to?" Zoe frowned.

"Well, would you have believed you had mage powers if you hadn't felt the cloud that was around Shelby?" Moose asked, referring to the noxious cloud created by the Summerfield coven around the administration building.

"Um, probably not," Zoe admitted.

"There, see?" Flash commented.

"But what does that have to do with ley lines?"

"Nothing. Why?"

"You said..." Zoe grew frustrated.

"No, I didn't," Flash was complacent, licking his paw.

Kieran put his hand over Zoe's. "Let it go. He's being a cat."

Flash simply flicked his tail in Kieran's direction.

"Okay, so George just figured out that he has a new job. He *was* planning on retiring in a few years, right? So where does that leave us with the ley line nexus? Does George have to stay employed by Summerfield if he's the wardmaster for the nexus?" Kieran managed to drag the conversation back to his original point.

"Well, he can tell if somebody is tapping into that power and who is tapping into it," Moose answered.

"And, no, he's doesn't have to be employed by Summerfield, but he won't be leaving the general area," Flash added.

"Okay. But so, what? That just means he knows. What can he do about it? What if there's another Night Mage? What if they try to access the ley lines?" Zoe went straight to what was really bothering her. How many people now had access to the immense, almost endless supply of power represented by the ley lines?

"He's got all you mages on campus. If he's paying attention he can act before anything really bad happens." Moose, as always, appeared completely unconcerned about the possibility of another fight to save the world. Zoe was morbidly convinced if she were to get killed by some evil witch or mage while she was sleeping, the cats would go down to Kim's house or Kieran's for food before they'd tell anybody that Zoe was dead upstairs.

Zoe and Kieran shared a look.

"Are you teaching today?" she asked Kieran.

"No. I know you have class. Are you going or canceling them?" he answered.

Zoe glanced at the clock sitting on her fireplace mantle.

"Well, my first class starts in an hour. And I have two sections of that back-to-back. That's not happening. I was already thinking I'd give them a reading and video assignment for discussion next week. My brain feels fried and I am not up to lecturing." She got up to find her laptop and send off the necessary emails.

"I was thinking I'd go in anyway," Kieran mused. "I think I want to see the quad in daylight. And, maybe talk with Mark."

"Hmmmm?" Zoe looked up from her email. "Yeah, I'm thinking I'll go in, just in case students want to talk. And, I really want to talk to Declan and the others. But especially Declan."

"That reminds me," Kieran said. "Can Declan access the ley lines? Does he even need to? I mean, he's half djinn, so his power is probably enormous."

"With an itty-bitty living space," Zoe quoted the movie.

"Ha! Well, he does live in the dorms right now," Kieran responded.

"Okay, emails all sent, online assignments up. I'm going to shower and change and then while you're doing the same, I'll make some breakfast and we can go in." Zoe closed the laptop and stood.

"Sounds like a good plan," Kieran leaned back into the sofa and cradled his coffee cup, cats draped across his lap. "Lemme know when you're out of the shower."

* * *

A couple hours later, they pulled into the parking lot closest to Cooper Hall. Kieran headed off to his own office in Davis Hall and Zoe climbed the stairs to her second-floor office. At the top of the stairs she saw Josh, Annmarie, Geoff, and Declan all sitting in the lounge. They all looked tired, but otherwise fine.

"Hi, guys. Are you all okay?" She walked over to the corner where they were seated.

"Hi Dr. O'Brien, we're good." Josh was acting as spokesman for the group. "But we did want to ask you about a couple of things."

"Sure. Come on in." Zoe headed down the hall to her office trailed by the four students. Once they were all in the office, Geoff closed the door. Zoe sat down in her chair and let them figure out the arrangements between four students and two guest chairs. Annmarie and Declan sat while Josh and Geoff stood to one side.

"Okay. So, what did you want to know?" Zoe asked.

"What happened to Professor Detweiler and Ms. Barker?" Annmarie spoke up.

"They were sent by Aseyai to the plane of the djinn from what I understand. At least, I know that's what happened with Detweiler. I'm not sure about Susan Barker because Aseyai wouldn't give me any details," Zoe said.

"What does that mean?"

"Are they dead?"

Geoff and Josh spoke at the same time.

"No," Declan whispered. His three friends stared at him while Declan sat hunched over in the chair, twisting his hands.

Zoe gazed at Declan for a few seconds. "No, they aren't dead, I don't think. But Aseyai, Declan's father, was angry that they had harmed Declan, so he made the decision. But I don't think we have to worry about them any longer," Zoe said quietly, still watching Declan.

"I-I'm s-sorry Dr. O'Brien. I didn't mean for him t-to d-do something like that," Declan's voice was just above a whisper.

"Declan, there's nothing you could have done, and nothing for you to apologize for. None of us, the faculty that were there, had any idea what to do with them. Your father solved a big problem for us. And I'm glad he did," Zoe said firmly.

"Told you so," Geoff's voice was kind. "You're not the boss of your dad."

"Nor are you responsible for his actions," Zoe added.

Annmarie reached across and squeezed Declan's hand. "Yeah, we told you it's not your fault."

"B-but what if he gets angry with one of you guys?" Declan sounded miserable.

"Is that what you're worried about?" Zoe asked. Declan nodded. Zoe gazed around at the others. "Any of you planning on trapping Declan in a spell, or setting him on fire?"

A chorus of no's and grins answered her. Zoe turned back to Declan.

"As long as you don't hang out with people who try to harm you, I don't think your father is going to interfere. And I think he knows they're your friends," she smiled gently.

Declan slowly raised his head and stared at his friends. "You're not worried about it? I mean…he can just show up…"

"Dude, how about we worry about that if one of us *does* set you on fire?" Josh punched Declan on the shoulder. There was an easing of tension in the office as the students grinned at each other and Zoe.

"Thanks, Dr. O'Brien. We told him the same thing, but he didn't believe us," Annmarie commented.

"No problem. I'm glad I could help." She looked at Geoff, Annmarie, and Josh. "Can you guys give us a minute? I need to ask Declan something."

"Sure." Geoff pushed himself off the wall and opened the door. The other two followed him out and Annmarie closed the door behind them. Zoe looked at Declan.

"Are you really okay?"

"Yeah, I am. Thanks for talking to me. Annmarie was

right, they did try to tell me, but they're my friends so I thought maybe they were just trying to make me feel better." Declan had a slightly sheepish expression on his face.

Zoe smiled. "I wanted to ask you...have you talked to your mother about all this?"

Declan's hands twisted together again. "No, not yet. Do you think I should? I don't know how she'll react."

"I think you should do what you feel is best for you and best for her, but remember, she has Sight, so she probably has an idea of what happened. At least let her know you're okay." Zoe grimaced as she remembered she hadn't told her own mother anything yet.

"Okay, Dr. O'Brien. I'll call her this afternoon." Declan stood up. "Thanks for everything. I'll see you in class next week." He opened the door and took a step out.

"Well, Declan! Back for another conference with Dr. O'Brien are you?" Meredith's snide tones rang down the hall.

Zoe jumped up and got to the door just as Meredith arrived. "Oh, give it a rest, Meredith. Your schtick is getting old."

Josh, Annmarie, and Geoff appeared at the end of the hall and started toward Zoe and Meredith. Declan inched around Zoe and moved toward his friends.

"Oh, I see you brought your minions with you," Meredith sneered.

"I said, give it a rest." Zoe was really tired of Meredith's bullying and attempted manipulation. She put up a wall of Fire between Meredith and herself and the students. A visible wall of Fire.

Meredith jumped back as the flames filled the hallway. "What the hell? Who do you think you are? You can't threaten me! You don't even have tenure!"

"I don't give a damn what you say any more and guess what? Your BFF Morgan is not going to be caring much either." Zoe had no idea what Morgan Ammon really thought of Meredith, but she was pretty sure the president would dump Meredith in a heartbeat if she thought Meredith was a liability.

Plus, George had said he would be talking with Morgan. Since Meredith and Morgan apparently had nothing to do with Carolyn's plans, Zoe figured the president was just using Meredith to gain some revenge for Zoe's role in destroying the coven and embarrassing Morgan. In other words, pure faculty politics.

"Bitch!" Tossing out her favorite insult, Meredith fled back to her office and slammed the door.

The students grinned at Zoe. "That was pretty cool, Dr. O'Brien!" Geoff laughed.

"What was? I didn't do anything," Zoe winked.

"See what? I just saw a conversation between two professors. Okay, so one was being kind of rude, but that was it," Annmarie said.

"Exactly. I'll see you guys next week," Zoe gave a quick wave and went back into her office.

Chapter Twenty

The next week brought some much needed (as far as Zoe was concerned) changes to the administration of Summerfield and to the Psychology Department. Morgan Ammon was still president, but George informed the faculty mages that he had had a long talk with her about her attempts to gain power in the magical world. It seemed she had indeed interfered in the hiring of Carolyn at the request of Susan Barker. But, it turned out she did it more because Susan had told her that Carolyn would be able to make George's life difficult.

Unfortunately for Morgan, she couldn't object to what George had called the "increased input from the provost's office with regard to college issues." Meaning that George was going to have a hand, one way or the other, in everything Morgan decided.

Luckily for Morgan, once Carolyn had been hired, Morgan had all but ignored the Night Mage's activities on campus and only used her to engage indirectly in petty faculty politics, such as trolling the Faculty Governance Committee, or messing with Meredith Cruickshank.

Zoe had been correct in her guesses regarding Morgan's objectives. George told Zoe that part of Morgan's game-playing with the Governance Committee was getting Meredith to report so-called violations of school policies. That was the reason for Meredith's continued harassment of Zoe for having male students in her office.

George had commented that Morgan admitted she found Meredith to be an annoying butt-kisser and had simply used her to do some of Morgan's spying on faculty.

But because Meredith was tenured, nothing could be done about her and Zoe couldn't move to a different office.

"So, I have to put up with her petty little insults and continued pathetic attempts at bullying me for at least the next three years," she lamented to Kieran one night over burgers and beers at the Faire Mount.

"Well, you've finally figured out she can't really hurt your tenure chances, right?" Kieran smiled.

"Oh, I know that…now," Zoe responded. "But she's so damn annoying and the thought of having to listen to her for another few years is just depressing."

"Well, you could always put up a permanent wall of fire in the hallway," he laughed.

Zoe snorted. "I wish! But I think the others would be a bit alarmed."

Kieran waggled his hand. "Maybe…maybe not. If you put it around her office, you might find some support. I know she's not popular, even in her own department."

"True, true."

A couple of days later, Zoe was walking across campus on her way to class when Declan caught up with her.

"Hi, Dr. O'Brien! How are you?" Declan called cheerfully.

"Hi, Declan. You're in a good mood today," Zoe smiled.

"Well, honestly, I like your class…I'm not trying to suck up or anything, I really do like going to your class. And I wanted to tell you that I did talk to my mom," he answered.

"You did? Good. How did she take it? Is she okay?" Zoe

knew that Declan's mom hadn't told him about his father, but she didn't know why. Although, her own mother hadn't told Zoe anything about Zoe's father until confronted by Zoe over the Christmas holidays. Zoe supposed when she was a parent she might understand these things a bit more clearly.

"Yeah...she's okay with everything. She said she hadn't told me because Aseyai said he wanted to see how I turned out. I guess djinn are super proud and he wanted to be sure I didn't embarrass him or anything," Declan paused, staring at the ground. "That kinda makes me angry, but he's not human so I have to remember that."

"Yeah, he's not going to see things like we do," Zoe smiled slightly. "Well, at least you know he's proud of you now."

"I guess. I don't know if he's going to come back or not, though. I kinda wish he would so he could teach me about these powers," Declan sounded wistful.

"What about your mom's power…Sight?" Zoe changed the subject. She didn't really want to discuss father issues while walking to class.

"Oh, she said she'd show me how to know when I'm getting a vision and stuff like that and we're going to see if I can do it on command, like she can. But she said that mixing Sight with djinn powers is something she's never seen before, so she doesn't know how it will work." Declan took the change of subject in stride.

They reached Davis Hall and the classroom. Declan went to sit in back with Geoff, Josh and Annmarie while Zoe went to the front.

After her two classes, Zoe walked over to Shelby Hall and George's office. Since the fight with Carolyn and the discovery that he really was the wardmaster for Summerfield College, he had renewed their magic tutoring sessions. Zoe knew George felt guilty about letting them slide before, but she also excused it as a reaction to the pressure Morgan had been putting on him. Of course, now that he knew that pressure was a diversionary tactic, he was more determined than ever to help Zoe. And, while she appreciated his help, she did find herself preferring the more hands-on approach favored by Mark, David, Kim, and Kieran. They tended to say, "try this" and wait to see what happened, where George, as was his habit with almost everything, wanted to fully explain the process and possible results before she tried to do anything.

"Hi Zoe!" Sarah smiled at her as she walked into the secretary's office. "How are you?"

"Hi Sarah. I'm good. How're you?" Zoe gave her friend a hug.

"Good. George will be here in a minute. He had a meeting that should be ending about now," Sarah said.

"Okay." Zoe sat down in one of the guest chairs, leaned back, closed her eyes, and stuck her legs out in front of her. "I could use a couple minutes of down time anyway."

"I get it. Hey. I have a question for you," Sarah sounded uncharacteristically hesitant.

Zoe opened her eyes and stared at her friend. "Okay. What? Is everything okay?"

"Yeah, yeah. Just...do you know Andrew Smith...in Chemistry?"

"Yeah. A bit. He seems nice and he knows about magic even though he's not a mage. Why?" Zoe answered. She thought she knew where Sarah might be going with the question.

"Well...um...after the fight, he started coming by here...and we started talking...and um...he asked me out." Sarah was blushing.

Zoe laughed. "You like him! I don't think I've ever seen you blush!"

"Oh shut up. Yes, I like him...I guess...what I'm asking is...is it okay for me to go out with him?" Sarah's tone was worried.

"Sure. Yes. Why? Because he's faculty? Nobody's going to stop either of you and it's not against any rules or anything like that. Go for it." Zoe sympathized with her friend.

Sarah gave her a relieved smile. "Okay. I just wanted to check. I didn't want to do anything that might hurt his chances for tenure. I know from what you said it can be tricky..." she trailed off.

"Well, it *was* tricky for me because Meredith was doing her best to make sure I was afraid of her. But, since George is back to paying attention to things, I'm not really worried about Meredith anymore. I don't think there's anyone one on campus who's worried about Meredith right now."

"Good. Oh, hi George." Sarah looked up as George walked into the office.

"Hello, Sarah. Zoe, how are you?" George's green eyes crinkled as he smiled.

"Hi George. I'm fine," Zoe returned the smile.

"All the recent excitement pushed it out of my mind, but I've been meaning to ask you about your plans for the summer. Are you still planning on traveling to the UK and Ireland to research the fairy tales? And, have you applied for grants to help with your expenses?" George asked.

"Yes, to the plans, and no to the grants. Isn't it too late to do that?" Zoe responded.

"No, there are still a couple available. There are also a couple of other ways to get the college to provide funding or in-kind funding. Come on in and let's talk about it." George stepped into his office and gestured for Zoe to follow.

Zoe grinned at Sarah. "Guess I'm getting money for research!"

Sarah grinned back and gave her a thumbs up.

ABOUT THE AUTHOR

Becky R. Jones started life as an Army brat, and then became a die-hard Southern Californian when her family ended up in San Diego. She currently lives in Philadelphia with her husband and one cat (there have been several at various points in time).

Becky is a recovering faculty member with a PhD in political science. After over twenty years teaching, she discovered that faculty politics had lost their allure. *Night Mage* is the second book in the *Academic Magic* series. You can follow her Amazon author page or for more fiction shorts and political ramblings, please visit her at: ornerydragon.com.

Made in the USA
Middletown, DE
14 May 2021